Production Notes for Hwang Sun-wŏn / TREES ON A SLOPE

Cover and interior designed by Barbara Pope Design
in Adobe Minion Condensed with display type in Gill Sans

Composition by Josie Herr

Printing and binding by The Maple-Vail Book Manufacturing Group

Printed on 55# Sebago Antique, 360 ppi

*Hwang Sun-wŏn* (1915–2000) was born near Pyongyang, the present-day capital of North Korea, and educated there and at Waseda University in Tokyo. By the mid-1930s he had published two volumes of poetry, and in 1940 his first volume of stories appeared. Thereafter he concentrated on fiction, producing seven novels and more than one hundred stories. In 1946 Hwang and his family moved from the Soviet-occupied northern sector of Korea to the American-occupied South, where he began teaching at Seoul High School. Like millions of other Koreans, the Hwang family was displaced by the civil war (1950–1953). From 1957 to 1993 Hwang taught creative writing at Kyung Hee University in Seoul.

*Bruce Fulton* is the inaugural holder of the Young-Bin Min Chair in Korean Literature and Literary Translation at the University of British Columbia. He has collaborated with *Ju-Chan Fulton* on several other translations of Korean fiction, including Hwang Sun-wŏn's The Moving Castle (1985) and the award-winning Korean women's fiction anthology Words of Farewell (1989). He is also the co-translator, with Kim Chong-un, of A Ready-Made Life (1998).

*Trees on a Slope*

## MODERN KOREAN FICTION

*Bruce Fulton, General Editor*

Hwang Sun-wŏn

# TREES
## ON A SLOPE

Translated by Bruce and Ju-Chan Fulton

University of Hawai'i Press

Honolulu

This book has been published with the assistance of the
Korea Literature Translation Institute, Seoul; and the Sunshik
Min Endowment for the Advancement of Korean Literature,
Korea Institute, Harvard University.

**Library of Congress Cataloging-in-Publication Data**

Hwang, Sun-wŏn.
    [Namudŭl pit'al e sŏda. English]
    Trees on a slope / Hwang Sun-wŏn ; translated by Bruce Fulton
and Ju-Chan Fulton.
        p. cm.—(Modern Korean fiction ; 1)
    ISBN 0-8248-2767-8 (hardcover : alk. paper)—
    ISBN 0-8248-2887-9 (pbk. : alk. paper)
    1. Fulton, Bruce. II. Fulton, Ju-Chan. III. Title. IV. Series.
PL991.29.S9N313 2005
895.7'33—dc22

                                        2004020158

Designed by Barbara Pope Design

Printed by The Maple-Vail Book Manufacturing Group

*In memory of Chang Wang-rok*

# *Contents*

TREES ON A SLOPE                                    3

AFTERWORD                                         191

Part One

# I

**LIKE WALKING** *through a big hunk of glass. Feet don't want to move.*

The afternoon sun beat down relentlessly as they neared the foot of the mountain. Unlimited visibility. Dwellings crouched beneath them, half a dozen or more, thatched roofs looking impossibly heavy. The structures seemed untouched by the war, but where were the occupants? You would think they had died off, so still were the surroundings. Not a single living thing was in evidence.

Why did this calm, clear, lucid space feel so resistant, so stifling? It really was like walking through dense, thick glass, Tong-ho told himself again. He had to force himself to move. With every measured step, rifle close to his side, muzzle forward, that massive hunk of glass blocked him, closing all over him, leaving only enough space for the outline of his body. He heard himself panting. Sweat streamed from his forehead.

Six feet ahead walked Hyŏn-t'ae, rifle at his side. Tong-ho felt the other man look back at him. Another wisecrack coming? Tong-ho ignored him. If he allowed his focus to wander, the dense glass barrier that begrudged his movements would harden fast, immobilizing him forever. It was no more than forty yards to the nearest dwelling, but those forty yards felt interminable.

The house search claimed Tong-ho's attention and his feeling of oppression eased. Hyŏn-t'ae beckoned Tong-ho and two others to keep watch while he and the remaining man prepared to enter the first dwelling. Normally slow to action and fond of clowning, Hyŏn-t'ae grew alert and determined—an altogether different man—when it came time to fight. In an instant he flattened himself against the side of the house and yanked open the door.

"Freeze!" he said in a voice that managed to be forceful but not loud.

The door's rice-paper panels, patched with cloth remnants, were mottled dark yellow from years of exposure to the sun. The open door revealed a dark interior.

"Come out with your hands up!"

The three men on watch sucked in their breath. There was no response from the dark room.

Hyŏn-t'ae poked the muzzle of his rifle inside, then quickly scanned the room. No one there. He checked the kitchen, and finally the outhouse. There were signs that the occupants had made a hasty departure with their meager possessions.

It was the same with the next few homes. Hyŏn-t'ae flattened himself against the side of the house, yanked open the door, and shouted, "Freeze! Come out with your hands up!"

Tong-ho began to feel less anxious. Somehow what Hyŏn-t'ae was doing seemed to be taking place in a world of unreality, a world that did not involve Tong-ho. When another soldier offered Tong-ho a potato left behind in the inner yard, he stuffed it quickly into his pocket. That potato seemed more real.

But then came a new source of tension. Yun-gu, one of the others on guard, discovered a shoe in a pile of ashes next to an outhouse. There were holes in the worn sole and the upper was frayed. Clearly not a shoe the people of this village would have worn.

The ash bins of other dwellings yielded chicken feathers, pig bristles, and dog hair. One of the houses had a larger yard strewn with the bones of those animals—a sure sign that a group had eaten there. A group of outsiders. The mess they had left suggested they had departed in a hurry—and not long before, judging from the fact that the bones swarming with blowflies were not yet dark and discolored.

The five men looked all about. Ahead were long, narrow patches of corn and sweet potato bordering a valley. Across the valley were hills. Behind them loomed the mountain they had recently crossed, its upper half strewn with light gray rocks and boulders. The summer sun continued to beat down. The surroundings felt too still. Was someone in this deserted place watching them? The mere thought brought a sense of unspeakable oppression. Once again Tong-ho was overpowered by the feeling that he was entering a glass monolith. *If that corner of it shatters, the whole thing will end up in pieces and there's nothing I can do to stop it. Those sharp fragments will stab me, every one of them.* Tong-ho's flesh crawled and he heaved a great shudder.

All he could do to relieve the unbearable sensation of pressure was move. The squad began to search the remaining houses. They arrived at the sixth house. Hyŏn-t'ae flattened himself against the side of the house, jerked open the door, and shouted "Freeze!" Someone stirred inside. The tension sharpened.

Hyŏn-t'ae's eyes flashed. With a jerk of his head he beckoned Tong-ho. Then, in a steely voice, "Come out with your hands up!"

The three guards advanced from left and right, the muzzles of their rifles leveled toward the dark cavity framed by the open door.

"Come out, and make it quick!"

A moment later the ashen face of a woman appeared in the gloom at the entrance, only to jerk back inside.

"Hurry up, you!" Hyŏn-t'ae barked.

The next instant the woman stepped barefoot down to the ground. Her lips trembled. She appeared to be in her early thirties.

"The rest of you, come out!"

The woman shook her head a couple of times. Her pointed chin quivered.

Hyŏn-t'ae quickly inspected the interior. Toward the back of the dark room, lying motionless beneath a soiled wrapping cloth, was a tiny little child.

"Who were they? Chinks? Or those People's Army sons of bitches?"

"Northerners."

"When?"

"They came last night . . . and they left this morning, before it was light."

"Which way did they go?"

The woman's quivering chin jerked toward the front of the hamlet.

"How many?"

"Fifty? . . . A hundred?" said the hill woman, who seemed unable to grasp the concept of numbers.

"Where's everybody else?"

"They took the young men . . . and the rest of us ran away, 'fraid they'd kill us. . . ."

"How come you stayed?"

Hyŏn-t'ae's tone softened but his gaze continued to bore into the woman's eyes.

The woman blinked several times, then turned her trembling head away from Hyŏn-t'ae and back toward the room. Inside, the child lay still, an emaciated arm outside the wrapping cloth. A dark cluster of flies had settled about its nose, mouth, and eyes.

"'Fraid if I set off with the little one on my back," the woman said in a strained voice, "it wouldn't last the trip."

After searching the last two dwellings and finding them empty, the men filled their canteens at the village well, then set off back up the mountain behind the hamlet. Five forms flickering against the base of the mountain in the broad light of day—dangerously exposed. After passing through woods higher up they found shade beneath some boulders on a ridge near the top.

The first order of business was to make contact with base. Some two years had passed since the start of the drawn-out cease-fire talks, and by now hostilities were reduced to sporadic skirmishes involving search parties—no large-scale fighting to speak of on any of the fronts. And even if the evacuation of the people in this hamlet was only an enemy ploy, it was unusual in the light of recent intelligence.

Yun-gu was the man who packed the radio, and Hyŏn-t'ae now

ordered him to radio base. Yun-gu picked up the mouthpiece, pressed the transmit button, and called out, "Toad . . . toad . . . toad," using the code word for base. As soon as he released the button there was a response.

"Tadpole . . . tadpole."

Yun-gu looked expectantly toward Hyŏn-t'ae.

"Tell them we're four miles to the northeast."

Yun-gu translated this into code and radioed: "Four squid and pollack."

"Eight thatched houses," said Hyŏn-t'ae.

"Four pairs of straw sandals."

Hyŏn-t'ae had Yun-gu report the evidence of two or three People's Army platoons passing through the village and moving west. Finally: "All the villagers have been evacuated—there's no one left."

Yun-gu, hand covering the mouthpiece except when transmitting, looked quizzically toward Hyŏn-t'ae, wondering about the woman.

Disregarding Yun-gu's gaze, Hyŏn-t'ae quietly repeated: "The villagers have evacuated—every last one of them."

Yun-gu radioed: "Straw all blown away."

Base responded with orders: The men were to hold their position till nightfall and watch for signs of enemy activity.

After Hyŏn-t'ae had positioned men on both sides of the path where it bent around the hillside, he lit a cigarette. He took several deep drags, then turned to Tong-ho, sitting beside him.

"Hey, Poet, what was going through your mind back there?"

*Now what,* Tong-ho thought as he fished hardtack out of his pack. He didn't respond.

"Poet, there's nothing like a smoke at a time like this. Lonesome mountains, clean air, makes a cigarette taste fantastic! Gives the brain a good jolt."

Some time ago their unit had arrived at the edge of a steep outcrop. As the others looked down and flexed their aching knees or complained of dizziness, Tong-ho had simply mentioned that he was cold. That one word had earned him his nickname, Poet.

Hyŏn-t'ae tried again. "You know, Poet, I felt *lousy* back there. I mean, here we are heading down to a deserted village and I feel like I'm walled in somehow. Now why should that be? You were looking awful serious yourself, you know, like you were trying to fight off something. What a weird feeling."

So Hyŏn-t'ae had felt it too? Hyŏn-t'ae, always resolute and self-possessed once he had readied himself for combat. So he too had experienced that peculiar feeling of oppression from the silent clarity? Tong-ho had wanted to tell Hyŏn-t'ae how he'd felt—the sensation of making his way through an endless glass shield. That inside this shield he somehow felt less burdened by the possibility of the enemy appearing. But he had kept quiet, wondering what would happen if the enemy actually were lying in wait for them and a firefight broke out. How many times had Hyŏn-t'ae seen him lose his composure in battle? He couldn't for the life of him talk to Hyŏn-t'ae about combat now.

There was that time they had come under enemy bombardment near Ch'up'a Pass. They were on level ground with no place to hide. Nothing to do but lie flat on the ground. Tong-ho, in spite of himself, had kept trying to worm his head beneath Hyŏn-t'ae's waist. Suddenly Hyŏn-t'ae had bolted to his feet. Tong-ho had jerked his head up to see Hyŏn-t'ae, bent low, running toward the pit where a shell had just exploded. Tong-ho realized he should follow. He knew that no two shells ever land in the same location, even if they're aimed there. It was a kind of law called the scatter effect. Tong-ho saw other soldiers scrambling one after another toward the pit, Yun-gu among them. But Tong-ho's legs wouldn't obey. Through the dust he could see Hyŏn-t'ae's eyes beneath his helmet and his beckoning hand. But Tong-ho's legs felt rubbery and he couldn't move. It didn't seem to be a matter of their different battle records—reflected in Hyŏn-t'ae's rank of sergeant first class and Tong-ho's rank of sergeant second class. Yun-gu was a sergeant second class too, and look how sharply he had moved. Finally Hyŏn-t'ae had run back to Tong-ho, slung him over his shoulders, and toted him to the crater. An incongruous realization had loomed large and clear in Tong-ho's shattered mind as he was carried along, his hearing numbed by explosions: the contrast

between Hyŏn-t'ae the unflappable warrior and himself who couldn't
have been more cowardly and stupid.

This was the longest bombardment the unit had sustained to date,
and there was considerable loss of life. Tong-ho felt certain that the
soldiers who had flattened themselves on the ground next to him had
been hit. When the shelling finally stopped, Hyŏn-t'ae, his copper-
colored face covered with dust, displayed a toothy grin. "How come
a skinny fuck like you has such a heavy ass? You ought to clean out
your pipes now and then—lighten your load and your body will do
what you tell it." This was how he kidded Tong-ho when they had
been transferred back to the rear. Though Hyŏn-t'ae and Yun-gu had
taken to visiting the women at the "comfort centers," Tong-ho had
never felt up to joining them. As soon as Hyŏn-t'ae returned from
one of these visits he would start in on Tong-ho: "Hey, Poet. Lose
that look of disgust—what do you think I am, a dirtball or something? I'm just being true to myself—remember that. Love, hate,
all that emotional crap—I'm free of it, free and easy. If there was
a pretty girl beside me right now, I'd just ignore her—that's how
peaceful and relaxed I feel. But you wouldn't understand." After
rambling along drunk like this he would sprawl out. Tong-ho had
never responded. Instead he would wait for Hyŏn-t'ae to fall asleep.
But now he said: "Good thing you're not free of all that emotional
crap today. Otherwise you wouldn't have thought of dragging me to
that hole, right?" "Yeah, all of that hero stuff is useless," Hyŏn-t'ae
had rejoined. "It's kind of ridiculous playing the brave fool—not
worth giving up my life for." Tong-ho had listened silently. "Yeah,
thanks to that, they could call me the bravest guy in the world, but
so what?" Hyŏn-t'ae had grinned, revealing his white teeth. "You're
quite a guy—a little while ago you were shaking in your boots, but
now your yap is working. To be honest, pulling you over here wasn't
a matter of us being old friends or war buddies. Maybe like you say it
was an outburst of courage. Maybe what it comes down to is being
rash, you know?"

And there was that battle near the Kŭmsŏng River. In the confusion of the fighting their unit had come under friendly fire. Too pan-

icked to find shelter, Tong-ho had allowed himself to be led to the
foot of a tree by Hyŏn-t'ae. Hyŏn-t'ae drew Tong-ho close against
the back of the tree while keeping an eye on a fighter plane coming at
them. Along with the roar of the engines came the staccato pop of the
fighter's machine guns, the bullets making a furrow in the ground
from left to right and thudding into the tree. The impact of the bullets
made Tong-ho feel as if the rounds had slammed into his chest. From
several directions he heard screams of agony. Tong-ho squatted,
trembling, behind the tree, too scared to stand; Hyŏn-t'ae, in back,
held him motionless. The strafing ended and the fighters circled back,
sunlight glinting from their silver wings. Again Hyŏn-t'ae moved so
that he faced the oncoming planes, and calmly he told Tong-ho to
drop his arms to his sides—it was dangerous to hug the tree. Suddenly Tong-ho experienced an oppressive feeling of constriction, the
stifling sensation he remembered when as a child he had been playing
in an alley near home and a big, strong neighbor boy had come up
behind him, put his hands over his eyes, held him tight, and refused
to release him no matter how he struggled. But along with the feeling
of confinement that came from being under Hyŏn-t'ae's sway was a
hint of a firm, unshakable friendship.

Tong-ho took water from his canteen to moisten his mouthful of
hardtack. "Say, how much of a burn does it take to kill someone?"
he asked no one in particular.

Yun-gu broke a cigarette in half and rolled a piece of paper into a
holder. "A third of your body would probably do it."

"What about broken glass?"

"Hard to say." Yun-gu used Hyŏn-t'ae's cigarette to light his own.
"Glass is awful. Get it in you and it keeps going deeper. I stepped on
a flytrap once when I was a kid and boy did that glass hurt—much
worse than a knife. And even if you manage to get the slivers out, it
still smarts like hell. Couldn't sleep at all that night and when they
took me to the doctor next day I still had a couple of pieces the size
of millet seeds in me. Darned if they weren't pretty deep inside. That
prickling and smarting I felt all night long were those things worming
their way inside me."

Once again Tong-ho felt as if the imaginary block of glass enveloping him had shattered and countless shards were stabbing him.

"What's this, a poem about glass?" Hyŏn-t'ae rose. "Poems are fine, but first let's get out of the sun."

It was early July and though the sunshine wasn't quite so strong at this time of day, it felt terribly hot striking their foreheads directly. They found shade beside a boulder.

"You can think about poetry all you want, but when we're talking let's talk about something more pleasant. Where'd you come up with this glass business, anyway?"

Tong-ho understood what Hyŏn-t'ae meant by "something more pleasant." He wanted to hear about Tong-ho's sweetheart. Tong-ho still hadn't told his two friends that there was a woman who loved him. But Hyŏn-t'ae and Yun-gu had guessed as much from the letters that arrived for Tong-ho. Tong-ho never read those letters on the spot. Instead he stuffed them deep in his pocket until he could find some privacy. Once Hyŏn-t'ae had tried to play a trick on him. It was lunchtime a couple of weeks earlier, and the front was quiet. Hyŏn-t'ae began rummaging through Tong-ho's pack. Tong-ho jumped at Hyŏn-t'ae and tried to snatch it away from him, but Hyŏn-t'ae, anticipating this, tossed the pack to Yun-gu and held Tong-ho fast. Hyŏn-t'ae was about to tell Yun-gu to find a love letter and read it out loud when suddenly he released his hold on Tong-ho's waist and jerked backward, a bite mark on the back of his hand. The next instant Tong-ho sprang like a tiger at Yun-gu, butted him in the temple, and knocked him backward. Hyŏn-t'ae had expected resistance, but never a reaction so strong. Tong-ho clutched the pack, panting, his eyes bloodshot like those of a drunk. Hyŏn-t'ae made the best of the situation, saying with a smirk, "That son of a gun, next time we're in battle we'll have to stick that pack out in front of us—that'll make him brave."

If Tong-ho hadn't yet admitted to having a sweetheart, he wasn't about to do so now. But Hyŏn-t'ae brought it up anyway just for the fun of it: "Since you're so sweet on this little cutie of yours, why the hell not tell us about her? Afraid she's going to disappear if you mention her? The thing is, it's not good for you to be so damned pure of heart."

Tong-ho ignored this and let his eyes wander to a pine grove below. Among the larger pines stood younger branchy ones. Tong-ho noticed that the tips of the branches were reddish and wondered if the trees were infested with caterpillars.

"I worry about you," Hyŏn-t'ae went on. "You think you own this lover girl of yours? You think you can make a girl yours as long as your heart is pure. Well, it doesn't work that way anymore. Unless you have a real memory of a woman's skin, you're wrong to think she's yours. You have any memories like that?"

"If you don't have anything more useful to talk about, why don't you go sack out for a while?"

"Listen, pal, I'm doing this for your own good. For God's sake, just tell me about one part of her you'll never forget. Lips, maybe? The palm of her hand? Or maybe you-know-where? . . . Uh-oh, he's spitting at me. You going to wash my mouth out with soap? You know, the nicest people can do some pretty strange things. Maybe you put a brand on her back for all I know. Now take our buddy here."

Yun-gu had smoked his cigarette down to the paper holder. "Hey, I'm just an innocent bystander," he said. Yun-gu was not one to be drawn into conversations about women.

"You telling me you don't have any tricks up your sleeve? I know how picky you are. And when it comes to the cuties you've got all the angles covered. You always pick the older ones. Get more loving that way, right? You're a step up on the rest of us."

Every three hours the sentries on the hillside changed. Tong-ho finished his watch and by the time he returned to Hyŏn-t'ae the sunlight was waning and the cool breeze of oncoming evening was stealing inside his fatigues. On the last day of March snow had blanketed this mountainous region midway up the east coast, forcing a suspension of operations. And even now in summer, once the sun started to set, the daytime heat gave way to chill.

Hyŏn-t'ae sat silently behind the rock, sheltered from the wind, arms folded over his chest. Tong-ho sat beside him and silently replayed the images of Sugi that had risen to the surface of his mind during his recent watch. Two years earlier, he and Sugi had spent a snowy night at a hotel at Haeundae Beach the day before he had left for the army. They had kissed until their mouths were numb. But an even sharper memory was the discovery the next morning, in the clear sunlight after the nightlong snowfall, that Sugi's double eyelid had developed a third fold. Seeing this, the two of them had laughed like children. Whenever he thought of Sugi, he recalled the sensation of their lips rubbing together all night, the feel of her cheeks, the back of her neck, part of her chest. But even more precious to him was the mood, like their own perfect secret, of their innocent laughter at the sight of the difference between her eyelids. In her first letter to him in the army she had written about her eyes. It had taken two days for the eyelid with the third fold to return to normal, and during that time she hadn't ventured from home. What was more, she had avoided her family's gaze, afraid the difference between her eyelids would reveal the secret she shared with him. How she looked forward, she had written, to the day when Tong-ho would return and make her eyelids unequal again. *Those eyelids. . . .* The thought always brought a smile to his lips in spite of himself.

"What are you grinning about, pal?" ventured Yun-gu. "Hey, it's getting chilly." He rose and stretched his arms out front and sideways to warm himself.

Evening had arrived in the mountains. Before the bright orange of sunset had disappeared over the mountains to the west, gray dusk filled in the lower reaches of the valleys and gradually thickened as it rose to the mountaintops. The process seemed slow but in fact was rapid.

Before they knew it stars had begun to appear in the violet heavens. The sentries returned from the hillsides. All awaited Hyŏn-t'ae's order to return to base.

"Somebody's got a fire going," muttered a soldier who was looking in the direction of the village. Beyond the shadows of the darkly outlined pines drifted a faint wisp of smoke. It came from a chimney.

"I've got a vision of a cloud of steam from a pot of rice," muttered a second soldier.

"Corn gruel's probably the best they can do. Didn't you see? There wasn't a single potato down there—they got cleaned out of anything fit to eat."

"A hot drink of water would suit me just fine."

"Hey, that woman," said the first soldier. "I hope she's not a spy."

Hyŏn-t'ae rose. "Radio base," he told Yun-gu. "Tell them we're on our way back." And with that he shouldered his rifle and strode off down the hill.

Tong-ho had a hunch that Hyŏn-t'ae would do away with the woman. Even if she wasn't an outright spy, there was a chance she'd tell the enemy about their movements. To prevent that they would have to take her back to base. But that would be a bother to Hyŏn-t'ae and he'd be inclined to get rid of her instead. *So that's why he radioed base earlier that no one was left here!*

Tong-ho gazed down at the gloom where Hyŏn-t'ae had disappeared, waiting any minute for the report of the rifle.

Yun-gu approached. "What are you looking so serious for? Don't get sidetracked. Just worry about getting back to base."

Presently Hyŏn-t'ae returned. He was wiping his hands.

*What happened?*

"All right, let's get out of here," said Hyŏn-t'ae. And then to Tong-ho, who was still gazing down the hill: "Why the idiotic look?"

Tong-ho made no reply.

The following day Hyŏn-t'ae noticed a strange look on Tong-ho's face.

"Don't give me that disgusted look—you're provoking me."

"What did you do with that woman?"

"Oh, so that's it. Okay, chump, I'll tell you. She wasn't scared like she was in the afternoon. She didn't put up much resistance either. But guess what—when I get up she grabs me by the hand. Well, I knew what that meant. She's scared, and she wants me to stay with her. Can't very well do that, can I? So I got rid of her. Simple as that."

# 2

SEVERAL DAYS LATER. July 13, 1953, precisely two weeks before the conclusion of the armistice agreement. Ten p.m. The enemy had launched a full-scale attack along a thirty-mile segment of the mideastern front, throwing a force of 150,000 strong into battle. They wanted every additional foot of territory they could occupy to the south and seemed intent on capturing the Kumalli power plant in Hwach'ŏn as well.

Tong-ho, Hyŏn-t'ae, and Yun-gu's unit occupied a position east of a landmark dubbed Sniper's Ridge.

The enemy had penetrated the Capital Division, which served under the American Sixth Army Corps, pushing it back until it gave way to the American Third Division. Next the enemy turned its main force eastward toward the ROK Second Army Corps and began laying siege to the Sixth and Eighth Divisions along the mideastern front.

On July 14 the unit was forced to evacuate to the south of the Kŭmsŏng River.

The day had broken with fair-weather clouds riding a stiff southeasterly wind high across the sky. But the enemy bombardment, as intense as anyone could remember, sent up columns of smoke that mixed with the clouds to produce a gradually lowering sky. Among the clouds and smoke ranged UN bombers, appearing suddenly to bomb the enemy prominences. The deafening explosions of shells and bombs shook the earth. Blast after blast swept the battlefield with smoky plumes of gritty dust. Through it all the human waves of the enemy continued their charge.

Yun-gu approached Hyŏn-t'ae, his dusky face wearing a concerned look.

"I had a weird dream last night."

Yun-gu had dreamed his stomach was grossly swollen and he had gone to see a doctor. The doctor had told him he was nine months pregnant.

"I think that means a bad-luck day."

Hyŏn-t'ae agreed and went to the platoon leader, who excused Yun-gu from combat that day. For whatever reason, on many an occasion a man had died in action after reporting a bad dream the previous night—thus the exemption. At the same time, rarely if ever did a man lie about his dreams in order to shirk combat. Exemption from direct combat was no guarantee of personal safety. In fact the men were convinced that nothing good would come of lying about their dreams. Such was the extent to which men held to their principles when going to battle.

That afternoon the clouds built until they blanketed the sky. Night brought to the heavens an inky blackness bereft of stars. The steady stream of flare bombs and signal flares was ultimately obscured by smoke and dust from the explosions. At length bloody skirmishes at close quarters broke out.

Tong-ho's unit was one of those caught in the hand-to-hand fighting.

"Rifle and grenades are useless," Hyŏn-t'ae muttered as he unsheathed his knife in the dense gloom.

Swept up in the fighting, Hyŏn-t'ae and Tong-ho were separated. At first Tong-ho felt lost. All he could think was that he had to do something—anything. And then a hand reached for his head, grabbed his throat. Tong-ho instinctively produced his knife. Had he actually stabbed with it? All he remembered was grappling with his attacker on the ground and then, when the man clutched at him no more, realizing he was dead. Where had he found the strength to do that? He had closed his eyes, he had used brute force, and his actions had seemed to emanate from a power that was inconsistent with his mental state. From that point on, he first reached for the hair of anyone attacking him in the dark, and if that hair was closely cropped, he fought back mercilessy, stabbing, kicking, tackling.

At dawn the enemy retreated. The screams and moans of fallen soldiers, unnoticed during the fierce fighting, now became audible. One man cursed loudly and said, "Kill me! I don't want to suffer any more." Another called for his mother, then recited what sounded like a prayer. Another sobbed wordlessly. This was the scene that followed an intense battle. Only this time, owing to the suddenness and scale of the offensive, it had been impossible to evacuate the wounded.

Tong-ho ran into Hyŏn-t'ae again. The other man's elbows bore numerous wounds.

"You're bleeding pretty good."

"It's all right. What about you? Don't look like you got hurt too bad. Must have learned how to put up a decent fight. No one's born to fight, but anyone can do it if he's desperate enough."

Yun-gu appeared.

"Give me a smoke," said Hyŏn-t'ae. "Mine are ruined—see?"

From his shirt pocket he produced a blood-soaked mass of cigarettes.

"Forget that. You need bandaging—now."

"Uh-uh. First I'm going to have a smoke."

Yun-gu fished out half a cigarette and gave it to Hyŏn-t'ae. Since he always broke his ration of Hwarang cigarettes in two before smoking them, he was always the last to run out.

Hyŏn-t'ae lit up, sucked deeply, and slowly exhaled. "Not much of a cut," he joked. "Otherwise smoke would be coming out." He grinned, revealing his white teeth against the coppery tan on his face. "I tell you, they just don't let up. Soon as I took care of one guy, another showed up, then another."

From the lowering sky there came raindrops and then a downpour. The southeasterly wind was even stronger that day. The rain fell in great lashing sheets, shutting down visibility in every direction.

The enemy took advantage of the downpour to launch another assault. UN B-29s braved the weather to bomb the enemy supply bases. Desperate fighting broke out amid the bombing. Before long the soldiers were covered with blood and muck. The rain washed it off and away it flowed, as if the ground had soaked up all it could.

With his wounded arms Hyŏn-t'ae managed to take up his rifle. But then a dull, prickly ache made itself felt—perhaps the wounds were beginning to fester in the soaking rain—and ultimately he had to fall back.

Just as the rain gave signs of easing, the showers resumed and the reckless waves of humanity continued their assault. By evening the enemy had overcome bitter resistance to breach the ROK defense perimeter in two places.

At nightfall the wind subsided and the rain grew sporadic. And then a surprise: the sound of gongs and Chinese clarinets behind their backs. The men in Tong-ho's unit panicked; they were surrounded. Cut off from the chain of command, in desperate confusion they scrambled to escape.

Hyŏn-t'ae and Tong-ho found themselves separated from Yun-gu. After weathering two hours of concentrated fire the pair managed to break through the enemy lines. They arrived at a stream. From what they could see in the dark the water was some fifteen feet across. They heard movements on the opposite bank—a second noose being tightened by the enemy?

They stepped into the water. Fortunately the stream was deep enough to allow them to squat down to neck level before moving farther. The bottom was a jagged mixture of rocks and stones. It seemed that normally the bottom was mostly exposed, but the stream had swelled over it in the rainstorm.

The current was swift. Hyŏn-t'ae and Tong-ho waddled upstream. From the lay of the land they guessed that the stream flowed north out of Ch'up'a Pass.

Hyŏn-t'ae whispered in Tong-ho's ear: "I'll be damned—uniforms get washed, no more bloodstains, and we don't lift a finger!"

But with the enemy on the opposite bank, waddling upstream for any length of time with only their heads above water was grim work. And Hyŏn-t'ae's arms were useless. The bandages, rain-soaked to begin with and now sodden from the stream, hung from his arms and the infected wounds ached dully, so that he couldn't move his arms at all. This made it all the more difficult to work his way upstream in a crouch.

By the time they had covered a mere four hundred yards Hyŏn-t'ae's legs were cramping. He kept falling behind Tong-ho.

Tong-ho moved around behind Hyŏn-t'ae and pushed him forward. When that method proved inefficient Hyŏn-t'ae instructed Tong-ho to pull him forward by his belt.

They moved noticeably faster now.

Another shower began to pour down from the black skies.

And then, ridiculously, before either of them realized it, the area beneath the belt held by Tong-ho grew stiff and hard in response to the touch of the one man's hand on the other's abdomen. Tong-ho released the belt, amazed that this one organ in Hyŏn-t'ae's otherwise exhausted, wounded body remained vital at a time of mortal danger, despite the cold rain falling on his head and the stream that at night felt so chilly for mid-July.

"Why not grab onto me there?" Hyŏn-t'ae whispered. "Makes a great handle."

Another mile and a half and they were finally able to escape enemy territory. They climbed the bank of the stream.

"As long as my pecker's up, no need to worry about dying!"

And with that Hyŏn-t'ae relieved himself in a great noisy gush.

# 3

FOR THREE WEEKS Hyŏn-t'ae was treated in a field hospital near the Kumalli power plant in Hwach'ŏn. During that time his unit was relocated to a village called Sot'ogomi, some six miles north of Hwach'ŏn and nine miles south of the front at Ch'up'a Pass. An army truck delivered Hyŏn-t'ae to Sot'ogomi. He climbed down from the truck and looked about.

Sot'ogomi was north of the thirty-eighth parallel and thus was northern territory before the war. When Hyŏn-t'ae, Tong-ho, and Yun-gu's unit had pushed through here the previous year for the second time, the houses lying at the foot of the hill behind the village had been reduced mostly to ashes. It was now less than ten days since the armistice, and in that short time a scattering of shacks had appeared. There were even a few houses being built.

The canvas structures that made up the base were in plain sight to the right of the road. Hyŏn-t'ae, knapsack in hand, was about to set out in the steamy heat on the ocher-colored dirt path to the base when he heard a distant voice.

"Hyŏn-t'ae—that you?"

He turned and off in the distance saw a group of soldiers making repairs to their quarters. One of them raised a hand. It was Tong-ho.

"Hey, how's the poetry coming along?" Hyŏn-t'ae called out.

He went inside regimental headquarters to report, then joined Tong-ho.

"Is it all right to shake hands?" asked Tong-ho.

"Sure."

Hyŏn-t'ae gripped Tong-ho's small hand painfully tight.

"That's good—I was afraid you'd end up with a bad arm. I heard the nurses had to spoon-feed you. Wish I could have seen _that_."

"You don't know the half of it. The worst part was the infection—set in so fast. So what's the word on our buddy Yun-gu?"

"Well, he's here."

"Yeah? I was afraid something happened to him that night."

"He was captured, but he managed to get away."

Hyŏn-t'ae snorted. "That'll give him something to talk about. So where is he?"

"I think he went to Hwach'ŏn—something to do with communications. It's four now, so he ought to be back."

Other friends had trickled over to shake hands with Hyŏn-t'ae and welcome him back. Hyŏn-t'ae noticed quite a few soldiers that he didn't recognize—reinforcements. Hyŏn-t'ae was forced to the realization that many of his comrades had died in the fighting preceding the armistice. As the men who had gathered around him recited the names of the casualties, gloom shaded their faces. But spreading beneath that gloom was an undeniable tinge of joy that they had survived. And what was wrong with that, so long as they kept the joy to themselves?

Yun-gu returned shortly before dinner. After the meal the men returned to their quarters.

"I was afraid something happened to you," Hyŏn-t'ae said to Yun-gu. "I asked some of the other wounded about you, but nobody knew anything. Thought we might have a little ceremony, help you rest in peace, so I bought these."

From his knapsack Hyŏn-t'ae produced two bottles of _soju_ and a few dried squid. "Instead we'll celebrate your safe return. I know it tastes better if you drink _before_ eating, but we'll each have a snort and then hear about the brave soldier's escape." Hyŏn-t'ae uncapped one of the bottles with his teeth and filled the cap of Yun-gu's canteen.

Yun-gu sipped as he began his account. "That night I figured I'd break through the enemy lines and head south toward the sound of our artillery. That was a mistake. I should have gone east instead."

The enemy had come from the west, then turned south and arranged themselves in several lines. Yun-gu would manage to break through one line only to find himself still in the midst of the enemy. The rain held up for a time but then resumed, and Yun-gu wandered through it all night long. At daybreak he took cover in a bomb crater filled with rainwater. Huddled there was Corporal Kim from his company, a man everyone called Trouble. The two of them crouched there, too tired to talk. After a time Kim muttered to himself, "If only our men can counterattack this morning." After another interval of silence Kim muttered again, "Long as we're going to be captured, better if it's the Chinks." Yun-gu agreed. One notable aspect of this war was the cruelty that Koreans displayed toward one another. The formalities for dealing with prisoners of war were disregarded; the usual practice was to execute them by gunshot—"direct disposition," it was called.

As luck would have it, it was indeed the Chinese Communists who apprehended Yun-gu and the corporal. They were taken to the rear of the enemy lines in the direction of Kŭmsŏng. There they were confined to a makeshift shelter thrown up against part of a bombed-out building. It offered scant protection against the elements. The straw mats spread on the ground were sodden with rainwater. The hut held some fifty prisoners. One by one they were interrogated.

Inside a smaller shelter at a beat-up table sat a man wearing the uniform of the People's Army and the insignia of a captain. He appeared to be in his early forties and spoke gently. The man asked Yun-gu's name and age. And then: "What is your rank?" "Private first class." Yun-gu had prepared for this, and the lie rolled easily from his lips. "Hometown?" "Seoul." "Same here. What about your parents?" "They passed on when I was young." "And?" "And I went to live with my father's younger brother." "Where is this uncle of yours now?"

"He and his family died three years ago in the September 28 bombing." A spark of sympathy appeared in the captain's eyes. "What did your uncle do?" "He sold insurance." "And what were you doing, Comrade, when the war broke out?" "I was going to school." "Majoring in?" "Commerce." The captain nodded. "Tell me—how was an insurance salesman able to send his nephew to college?" "He didn't. I worked my way through as a live-in tutor." "You must have had a difficult time," the captain said, nodding again. "When did you join the army?" "This spring." "You mean to say you didn't join up till you were twenty-four?" "I tried to keep out of sight before that." "Why didn't you volunteer for the People's Army when the war broke out?" Yun-gu was stumped. He couldn't very well tell the truth—that he had hidden beneath the veranda at the home where he was tutoring. He decided to stall, but then the captain smiled and said: "Would you care to volunteer at this late date?" Yun-gu hesitated here as well. "I guess I've put you on the spot. Take your time and think about it."

The captain changed the subject. "Tell me, Comrade, who are the officers among the prisoners here?" "None that I know of." Yun-gu understood the intent of this question. If the officers could be identified, military secrets could be extracted from them. During battle, though, the soldiers removed their insignia, and if they were about to be captured they would destroy their identification cards and dog tags, so that it became impossible to distinguish officers from rank and file or to determine who was senior among the latter. But the reason for Yun-gu's answer was not that he wished to protect officers. In fact he didn't know of any officers among the other prisoners.

For the first time the captain's expression hardened. "I don't think you're leveling with me. Not one, you say?" "Not one." "You're a tool of the capitalists!" the captain barked. "A commerce major, but you're not too good with numbers. This spring, eh? Off by two or three years, I'd say. You claim you joined up this spring, but you've been a soldier at least two years, no doubt about it. Your eyes give you away, Comrade. They look calm but they're always moving. One glance, and I knew right off. It's clear as day, Comrade—when the war broke out you were hiding somewhere, dreaming your reactionary dreams."

The first round of interrogation ended and each of the prisoners was fed a riceball. A People's Army soldier then appeared and called out a name. Every mouth ceased chewing the fluffy lump of steamed rice and barley and the hut fell silent. The name was called again, and a prisoner rose, a smallish young man. While following the People's Army soldier out, his adam's apple moved once, heavily, as he swallowed the remainder of his riceball.

That morning the rain stopped and the sky began to shed its overcast; by evening it had cleared. It was enough to make you want to remove your sticky clothes and air them out. The gorgeous sunset was oblivious to the prisoners in the hut. At dusk the prisoners were herded outside, lined up, and led away. The young man summoned earlier had not reappeared.

Each group of half a dozen or so prisoners was escorted by a guard with a submachine gun over his shoulder. Their destination was uncertain. The position of the stars was their only clue; they guessed they were heading north. About three miles along, they came to a narrow valley. Uncommanded, the men came to a halt one by one, starting at the head of the line. The prisoners assumed it was a rest break. They were not told to squat, however, but instead were ordered to produce all their belongings. "You son of a bitch, did you think we wouldn't find this?" Such could be heard at various points in the line. Yun-gu's wristwatch was discovered and confiscated. He had tried to hide it by tying it to his shirt tail and tucking it inside his trousers.

The line set into motion. Yun-gu counted the number of passes they had crossed thus far. The most recent one made four. At an isolated spot near the fifth pass the guards called a rest stop. They ordered the prisoners to squat, then smoked, concealing the lighted end of their cigarette with a cupped palm.

Again the march resumed. Another pass was crossed. At the following pass, a UN fighter suddenly roared overhead, machine guns firing, apparently aiming at the hill directly above the prisoners. Almost as suddenly, clouds reappeared obscuring the stars. And then, meteor-like, another fighter flew overhead, guns blazing, and yet another.

"Freeze!" the guards shouted repeatedly. But several prisoners ran off down the slope. Two of the guards, or maybe it was three, pursued them, submachine guns going *ratatat ratatat*. Presently the guns of the fighters stilled, and the silence at the foot of the slope was punctuated with more bursts of submachine gun fire. "Got three!" came a voice. A guard who had remained above counted heads and shouted down the slope, "There's one more—we're missing four!" Some time later the pursuers returned, bringing only the boots of the three dead prisoners. The guard who had flanked Yun-gu reappeared. He thumped together the pair of boots he had brought, dislodging dirt, then tied the laces tight and slung the boots over his shoulder.

At dawn the prisoners arrived at a hillside prominence. At the foot of the outcropping were several man-made caves, their entrances concealed by branches. Soldiers appeared from one of the caves. A change of guards, Yun-gu guessed. Roll was called, the names of the three shot prisoners and the one escapee were noted, and the list of prisoners was handed over. The guards with the boots removed their canvas footwear and put on the boots. The prisoners were given a riceball each, then ordered into two of the caves and told to sleep.

The prisoners lay their exhausted bodies across one another, legs over legs, on the grass-strewn ground, and soon fell asleep. Yun-gu found himself lying next to Corporal Kim. Realizing the corporal was still awake, he addressed him softly: "Who was that man who was called out yesterday?" Kim kept his eyes closed as he answered: "New rifle platoon leader." Kim, a soldier ever since his days in the constabulary, knew the faces of practically everyone who was a master sergeant or higher at the other bases, faces unfamiliar to Yun-gu. Who had squealed on the platoon leader? Might very well have been this man Kim, it occurred to Yun-gu, the thought prompted by the man's past, which had given rise to his nickname Trouble.

The previous year, shortly before he was to have been promoted from staff sergeant to technical sergeant, Kim had gone AWOL. Three weeks later he had reappeared. It was rumored that he had been helping his family with farmwork. But who could believe this, considering his reputation as a thug, his dislike of farmwork, and his background in the constabulary? Normally he would have been confined to the guardhouse and reduced in rank for such an offense. But in consideration of his many years of military service—he had enlisted directly from the constabulary—his only punishment was to have his promotion deferred. But then the previous winter, around the time he was transferred to the rear, he was caught stealing relief goods. He had used them to buy a girl, the story went. This time he spent a month in the guardhouse and was reduced twice in rank. Thereafter he had disregarded some inconsequential orders from a certain tech sergeant and had used plain speech in answering the officer—as if they were the same rank.

All this provoked Yun-gu's suspicion that Kim, depending on the situation, was certainly capable of informing on the platoon leader. But then the corporal, eyes still closed, said in an indifferent tone: "Probably a guy in his own unit turned him in, a new one who didn't know any better. Figured he'd get preferential treatment—maybe even one of us here. I'll bet he regrets it now."

At that point Yun-gu came to a realization. Suppose he himself had known about the platoon leader and been enticed by the possibility of the People's Army captain offering him a favor—could he state unequivocally that he wouldn't have informed? He was not so sure. Yun-gu was ashamed of himself for suspecting Kim.

The corporal opened his eyes almost imperceptibly and turned toward Yun-gu. "No use fussing over it now—we've got ourselves to worry about. Tonight's crucial. If we don't do something tonight, we'll end up too far north—then it gets real tough. Did you see those guys who tried to run off last night? Only one of them made it. The other three were too anxious, tried to run too far too fast, and look what happened. You only want to go a short distance, maybe five *kan*. Then when the sons of bitches leave, *that's* when you run away. Think about tonight, then get some sleep." And with that, the corporal's head sank back and he rolled over.

"And that's when I decided," Yun-gu continued. "I decided to go with Kim."

At dusk the men ate a riceball each and set out again. Yun-gu got into line a few places behind the corporal, near the tail end.

With the onset of the monsoons, low-lying, rain-swollen clouds were once again covering the sky.

As Yun-gu walked, he tried to pace off a distance of five *kan*. Five *kan* would be about thirty *cha*. Before they had set out, Yun-gu, using thumb and forefinger, had measured his foot—it was a bit longer than one *cha*. That meant five *kan* were not quite thirty footsteps.

Yun-gu counted six passes before they were allowed to rest. In spite of the darkness, Yun-gu knew that hills lay to the right and a precipitous slope to the left. *This is the place,* he thought. He fixed his gaze on Kim, squatting ahead of him. The guard standing next to Yun-gu went forward to the next guard for a light.

"Trade you my boots for your shoes if you'll give me a smoke," came the voice of a prisoner.

"Not till I see what those boots look like tomorrow morning," chuckled a guard.

Where the corporal had been squatting, a round bundle began rolling down the slope. Yun-gu hugged his knees to his chest and did likewise.

"Knock it off!" said the guards, thinking someone had set large rocks rolling to play a trick on them. Then they seemed to realize what was happening. The harsh report of submachine guns pierced the empty stillness between heaven and valley.

When Yun-gu guessed he was five *kan* distant from the *ratatat ratatat,* he grabbed a small tree branch and came to a stop. He was faintly aware of Kim lying prone a short distance away. Suddenly the place where the corporal lay broke free and slid downhill. Two guards thrashed through the undergrowth in pursuit.

Presently the *ratatat ratatat* of the submachine guns reverberated throughout the valley, followed by a shout: "Got one of them!" A short time later, from above: "Another one's missing!" Then Yun-gu heard Corporal Kim's boots being removed. "Huh, look at this son of a bitch—wristwatch strapped around his ankle," one of the guards muttered. Yun-gu heard the guards move farther off to search, then finally trudge back up to where the prisoners were, grumbling all the way.

When he was sure the prisoners had left, Yun-gu descended the slope. As he wondered where to go next, he heard a voice from the underbrush not far off. It was the corporal. He had fallen from a bullet to the abdomen and had somehow managed to play dead. The way he talked now, you wouldn't have thought he was about to die. "Feel like I was on a roll and they cut the game short. What's a guy to do?" The voice was unexpectedly calm. At the end, the corporal made a request: "I want you to send this to my family." So saying, he held out a closed fist to Yun-gu. Inside was a handful of dirt. "Make sure you send it. No letter. Just my name."

"And that's what this is," Yun-gu added. He brought out his knapsack, produced a hardtack wrapper, unfolded it. Inside the crumpled wrapper was dark ocher soil, less than half a handful by now.

"What's *that* supposed to mean?" asked a soldier with drink-reddened eyes. "Is there some gold mixed in with it or something?"

"Come off it," barked a soldier seated nearby. "Even if it was all gold, it wouldn't make up for the man's loss. He must have been raving when he died."

"I don't think so," said Tong-ho as he eyed the clumps of dirt in the wrapper. "It was his way of telling his family he had died. 'From dust to dust . . .'"

"That's pathetic," said Hyŏn-t'ae. "Get rid of that stuff. How come you kept it all this time?"

"Uh-uh," said Yun-gu. "It's my duty to see it delivered."

"After all it's a dying man's last wish. I'll go to personnel tomorrow and get his address, then send it off," volunteered Tong-ho.

"All right, you men do what you want." Hyŏn-t'ae poured another round of *soju* into his comrades' canteen caps. "But now, let's drink to our buddy Yun-gu for making it back alive. And to the memory of Corporal Kim. And to all our buddies who fought their last battle—rest in peace, gentlemen."

# 4

WAR SURVIVORS may suppress their joy behind a gloomy facade out of compassion and respect for their departed comrades. But those who contrive this gesture of respect may also disregard it. And among men it is often alcohol that induces the disregard.

With the Sot'ogomi base less than ten miles from the front, the men had to be in a state of constant readiness. This meant training and drills in the morning and camp cleanup and maintenance in the afternoon. Sunday was no exception. But in mid-September, on the conclusion of the prisoner exchange that was part of the armistice agreement, Sunday leave became available.

The destination of a group obtaining a Sunday pass depended on the depth of their pockets. Normally it was a drinking place or a "comfort station." Following hard on the heels of the armistice, clutches of opportunists had flocked to the bases to do business with the soldiers. Drinking places with hostesses began to increase. Licensed comfort stations came into being and pimps arrived, each with a stable of streetwalkers.

The usual pattern for an outing was *soju* or *makkŏlli* without the customary snacks—followed by a drunken brawl, which could break out at the slightest pretext, or a visit to a comfort station or brothel.

The alcohol-induced stimulation and the odor of a woman enhanced the men's joy at being alive.

Hyŏn-t'ae developed a knack for gaining Sunday leave for himself, Tong-ho, and Yun-gu.

"Well, what are we waiting for?" said Hyŏn-t'ae. "We've got more of the Governor's money to blow."

During his stay at the field hospital Hyŏn-t'ae had received spending money from his father. "The Governor" had been quite successful importing beef tallow for soapmaking, but the war had ruined this business. He had then managed to reestablish himself while a refugee in Pusan, this time in the sugar business.

They went to a drinking shack, and when Hyŏn-t'ae was suitably drunk he produced some banknotes from his pocket and pretended to sniff them. "What a sweet smell—never fails. Doesn't seem right to spend it on something that tastes so sour." He turned to Yun-gu: "Time for you-know-what. Got to stand up and be counted." And then he eyed Tong-ho: "Why don't you take this, buy yourself some caramels, and write a sweet little ditty while you're chewing?"

He dropped a few hundred-wŏn notes in front of Tong-ho, then left with Yun-gu. Yun-gu readily followed Hyŏn-t'ae at such times, his pleasure undiminished by the knowledge that it was made possible by someone else's money.

Tong-ho for his part was thankful that Hyŏn-t'ae, though he teased him about his fussiness toward women, didn't insist on including him in his outings with Yun-gu. Tong-ho bought a pack of cigarettes and had a smoke. Then he climbed the hill behind the base to where some pines had been felled to provide timber for camp repairs and fuel for the oncoming winter. He found a stump and perched himself there after covering the surface with undergrowth to keep the pitch from getting on his pants. Now he could retreat yet again into a world of his own, a world in which he entertained thoughts of Sugi.

The land beside the base had gone to waste, the elevated paths, barely visible, the only evidence that it had once been cultivated. Untouched for three years by plowshare or hoe, the earth was broken

in places to reveal the ocher soil. Weeds flourished; they had more of
a yellow tinge than when Tong-ho had last been here. The early October sun beat down relentlessly, toughening the berry seeds that lay in
the dirt and increasing their chances of surviving the winter.

He had consumed less than half of what Hyŏn-t'ae and Yun-gu had
drunk, but felt the alcohol warming his ears, as well as the pleasant
sensation of the breeze from the ridge cooling them. Perhaps it was
the imminent arrival of harvest season that brought to mind the
image of a peach as he thought of Sugi. But what kind of peach? It
wasn't a nectarine, with its bare skin, or a _sumil_ peach, with its fuzz
and soft flesh. Tong-ho didn't know the name of the variety, could
only sketch its appearance in his mind: white skin, short fuzz,
middling-firm flesh.

There was something unusual about Sugi's profile, and one day
Tong-ho had sat in different places to observe it—an experiment of
sorts. It didn't catch your eye if you looked at her straight on, but it
came into view if the angle and lighting were right. If the light source
was diagonally to the rear, or to the side and above, her face was
shaded except for the straight-sure bridge of her nose, and as you
sighted toward the perfectly rising tip you could make out a faint halo
about the tip and nostrils: a lighting effect you wouldn't ordinarily
notice. This halo was very much like peach fuzz, or the bloom on
grapes and persimmons, only softer and finer, making you want not
so much to feel it as to melt it with your breath. Tong-ho had discovered it that night two years previous in the Haeundae Beach hotel
room where they had stayed at Sugi's suggestion (and for which they
had emptied their pockets)—the memorable sendoff that Sugi had
planned for so long. In that secluded room, with thick snowflakes
falling outside, they had spent practically the whole night awake, and
the following morning, after a long kiss, he had caressed the tip of her
nose and her nostrils with his lips. It was that morning, clear and
bright, when they were laughing in childlike delight at the discovery
of the third fold in her eyelid, and the contrast it made with her other
eye, that Tong-ho had chanced to notice, in the sunlight streaming

through the window, that faint halo. "That's the most delicate peach fuzz I'll ever see," he had mumbled to himself. "And it'll never come off."

Tong-ho descended the hill and entered the grocery next to the base. A man of about forty was dusting the stock. He turned and approached Tong-ho.

"Can I help you?"

Tong-ho glanced at the piles of apples, pears, and persimmons.

"Um, aren't there several different kinds of peaches?"

A customer who asked incongruous questions rather than buying merchandise! The man was taken aback.

"It's something I've been trying to find out," explained Tong-ho. "What other varieties there are besides *sumil* peaches and nectarines."

"Well, . . . " said the man reluctantly. But then he reminded himself that his business depended entirely on the soldiers, and he seemed to realize he couldn't feign ignorance. "They say there are even more kinds of peaches than apples."

"Isn't there a peach that's like a nectarine only fuzzy all over?"

"Well . . . I guess we're talking about peaches that are hard to the touch. There's what they call the Ch'ŏn variety. Skin's red and so is the inside. Has a crease and comes to a point on top."

"Sounds like a *sumil,* too. . . . Is there one that's white and has a little fuzz?"

"Maybe you're thinking of the white peach. Short fuzz and firm flesh that's white as can be. Tastes good too. You know, I'll bet I have it in a can."

The man located a can on one of the shelves, gave it a swipe with his duster, and handed it to Tong-ho: "Here you are. Processed from the real thing."

The label had yellowed slightly. On it was a picture of two unnaturally round peaches, one overlapping the other because of the clumsy way the label was attached, accompanied by dark red letters identifying the product.

Tong-ho returned the can to the man. Not that he couldn't afford it. But when he realized that the contents were probably skinned and halved, he lost all interest. More poignant at the moment was the overlap of the man's description of the white peach with the image of the peach Tong-ho had sketched in his mind on the hill. *Peach season next year I'll check out that white peach but good.*

Tong-ho returned to the base to find Hyŏn-t'ae and Yun-gu already back. Yun-gu left without a word to wash his underwear and socks at the well.

Hyŏn-t'ae was stretched out in bed. "Hey, Poet," he said. "Been off by your lonesome all this time? Something on your mind? Well, bear up. Won't be too long before we're discharged, and then you can be with your sweetheart."

He displayed his arms.

"Want to hear a story? Damn, you should have seen the fuss my girl made over these scars. 'Just look at that new skin, how red it is, and smoother than the other—it's so pretty I could die!' She went crazy licking and sucking on it. So I told her, 'If you really think it's so swell, why don't I make you a scar of your own?' Know what she said? 'I already have them, more than I can count.' Good God! 'And they'll never heal, long as I live.' Now get this: 'If two of us with scars could have a nice life together, I'd never ask for anything more.' Give me a break! Who'd want to live with a wretched woman who doesn't know when to shut up? I wasn't in too good a mood after that. And I won't be in any hurry to see her again."

Tong-ho waited until Hyŏn-t'ae fell asleep, then wrote Sugi a letter. In the letter he wrote about peaches. And added that he hoped he'd be able to see Sugi Peach before the white peaches came into season the following year.

# 5

A CHILL WIND BLEW beneath an overcast sky. It was the following Sunday and once again Tong-ho, Hyŏn-t'ae, and Yun-gu had got passes and left the base.

At a small drinking place Hyŏn-t'ae and Yun-gu became pleasantly drunk before leaving to buy women. Tong-ho stayed behind, slowly sipping a fresh bowl of *makkŏlli* while mung-bean cakes were frying at the far end of the counter. On such a dreary day he was in no mood to go for a walk or climb his favorite hill. He hadn't started drinking until he joined the army and even now was not particularly fond of alcohol. He almost never drank without his friends, but he did so on this particular day, wanting to pass the time where he was rather than venture outside.

Tong-ho sat at one of three tables fashioned out of rough-cut pine planks. Those tables, sitting side by side, could accommodate perhaps a dozen men. Four soldiers sat across from one another at the next table. They seemed in no hurry to leave. One of them was describing how he had smuggled two blankets off the base in a pair of cans. The difficult part, he told the others, wasn't stuffing the blankets inside the cans but tugging them back out through the small opening. "Well, hell, how else am I supposed to get booze money?" he muttered, too

drunk to care what the others might think. It didn't seem to have
occurred to him that his pilfering might land him in the stockade. In
fact, the soldier's account of his misdeed bordered on bragging. And
in that account Tong-ho heard the delight savored by those who have
survived mortal danger on the battlefield.

As Tong-ho sipped his *makkŏlli* he felt the delight of the loud-
mouth soldier suddenly begin to warm his heart. And just as quickly
the warmth spilled out and circulated through him. This sensation,
along with the glow from an unaccustomed amount of alcohol, gave
a different cast than usual to the image of Sugi that now came to
his mind.

He was back in that quiet room in the Haeundae Beach hotel,
Sugi's face cupped in his palms. "They're so warm!" she said. Sugi
placed her hands over his. "Good night." Their lips met. Hers were
cool like a leafy plant. Only her breath was warm. But as that breath
was exchanged between them, her lips grew warm, and then her
cheeks and palms. "I can't breathe," she whispered, moving her head
so that her hot breath tickled his ear. Tong-ho felt an urge to warm
other parts of her body. He reached for her chest, but the quilt lay
tight across it. "Let's stop," she pleaded. Tong-ho was impatient.
"Not yet. Just a little more." "No, let's stop. I want this day to end
where we are now. Don't be foolish, Tong-ho. What does it matter?
This isn't like you. I'm all yours, aren't I?" Well, perhaps his desire
had indeed been inflamed by base notions.

And with that thought Tong-ho returned to his bedding. It had
been Sugi's idea to sleep separately. "Let's keep to our own beds. I'm
happy just knowing you're beside me tonight," she had said. Tong-ho
had willingly agreed. But when it came time to kiss her good night
and their lips rubbed together and they savored each other's hot
breath, his desire had flared in spite of himself. Tong-ho lay in the
dark, wide awake. The snowflakes swished and rustled against the
window. It was so rare—a heavy snowfall this far south on the peninsula. He tried to concentrate on the sound of the snowflakes disintegrating against the window, and gradually his mind cleared and his
desire cooled. Part of him felt incomplete, part of him tranquil. From

out of the darkness came Sugi's voice. "Are you mad?" she asked softly. Tong-ho didn't answer. It occurred to him that his feeling of tranquillity did indeed harbor faint anger. Was there something dirty about two people in love sharing a room for the night and engaging in the act? Again Sugi's voice: "I don't want you being mad." Tong-ho kept his silence. It was the best way to let her know he was angry. Maybe he wasn't being completely honorable, but then again he couldn't find anything shameful about his behavior. "You really are mad, aren't you?"

In the darkness Tong-ho heard Sugi turn toward him. Her hand reached out, found his, gently clasped it. Her palm was warm. His had cooled. He found himself taking a peculiar pleasure from knowing that if he continued to act indifferent, her resolve would waver and she would give in to his desire. And so he showed no reaction to the hand that held his. He could feel her pulse. Finally he drew her gently by the hand. She sat up and the outline of her face appeared distinctly in the darkness. He sat up, too, and cupped her cheeks in his palms. Her cheeks, like her hands, had remained warm. Her lips were hot. In no time his palms and lips felt as hot as hers. She gently nibbled his lower lip once, then put her mouth close to his ear. He felt her warm, panting breath. "Now lie down, I don't want you catching cold." But before she could ease him down he shrugged off her hands and plopped himself back. She drew the quilt to his chin and tucked it in. "Are you mad again? Foolish boy, can't you see this is my love for you?" She leaned toward him and her lips pressed down on his. "When I see you hurt, it hurts me too. But just for tonight, let's not. I'll always be waiting for you." A salty liquid flowed between their lips. Finally she straightened and returned to her bedding.

Again Tong-ho felt his mind grow calm. But he found it impossible to remain where he was. He approached her and softly touched his lips to her eyes. The lashes were wet and quivering. Very gently he sucked the moisture from them, first one and then the other. He lowered his lips to her cheek and found a trail of tears. Only her lips were dry. His lips forced their way between hers and tasted flesh that was

drinking bowl and poured Sŏnu a drink. "Can I bring you something to snack on? Mung-bean cakes, dried pollack—"

"Who needs snacks? Waste of money. Rather buy more drinks. . . . Pour that man a drink too," Sŏnu said, indicating Tong-ho's bowl.

"I think I've had enough," Tong-ho said politely, covering the bowl with his hand. "I'm not much of a drinker."

"So there *is* something wrong with me. Don't worry, I'm not going to stick you with the tab. Drink up!"

Tong-ho resigned himself and withdrew his hand.

Sŏnu's blurry gaze discovered Tong-ho's hand.

"My, my. Nice hands you've got there. Hands weren't just made for holding rifles. . . . Now look at mine." Sŏnu placed his hands on the table, fingers spread, and displayed them front and back. They were slender and tiny. "What do you think? They're tougher than when I joined up, but I'll bet they're smaller than most women's. . . . I've been ashamed of those hands ever since I was a kid. So I always keep 'em in my pockets—that way nobody can see 'em. . . . You know, I had a teacher, middle school, told me I had gynecologist hands. Oh, did I hate hearing that. . . . But I'll tell you something— these hands do a pretty good job of pulling a trigger. Watch. . . ." He demonstrated again and again with an imaginary rifle. "I'm as good a shot as anybody . . . maybe better."

Sŏnu drank a couple mouthfuls of *makkŏlli,* then let his bloodshot gaze wash over Tong-ho.

"Where you from?"

"Inch'ŏn."

"My home's closer to here—Yŏnbaek, Hwanghae Province. . . . Don't matter if it's close, though, if you can't go there. . . . And if you *can* go there, so what? Hometown—place where you're born, right? . . . Naw, it's more than that. It's a place where people are waiting for you, waiting to welcome you home. It's those people who make a hometown, right? . . . Got somebody like that, Sergeant Yun?"

Tong-ho hesitated, searching for an answer.

"Tell me about your parents."

"They moved to Pusan after the war broke out."

"Pusan, Cheju Island, doesn't matter where. Could be the other side of the thirty-eighth parallel. Long as you got at least one person waiting for you, you're all set. . . . But me . . . you know. . . ."

Sŏnu gulped the rest of his bowl, then turned and displayed the empty vessel to the tavern keeper.

"More!"

An sat patiently, waiting for the drunken ramble to end. Sŏnu thunked his bowl on the table in An's direction.

"Bastard—mouth off again and I'll rip out that yap of yours. Don't tell me you're worrying your poor little head about your parents because you left 'em up north. Don't tell me you'd feel better if you could have seen them pass away before you left. Damn you! Don't you tell me you're bitter because you didn't go through what I did. . . . You pray for your parents every morning and every night. Who am I supposed to pray for—myself? 'Father, I have slept well—and give thanks to you for watching over me. And I pray that today you'll shelter me in your warm embrace.' Something like that?"

From that point on, Sŏnu seemed to be talking to himself. He sounded like one of those drunks who won't stop chattering once they've started. "Sure, I used to say that prayer every morning and every night. . . . And then I took a different tack—prayed for God to take me instead. . . . Didn't work. Finally I realized God didn't exist. Actually I made up my mind that he didn't exist. Otherwise how could he let those things happen? Oh yeah, I know what you'll say: our heavenly father is testing us with one of his ordeals. Like he tested Abraham. . . . Well, I've had my fill of ordeals. When you get right down to it, people are weak. And God is cruel. We should believe a God like that exists? . . . But you can tough it out, can't you? Penance—it strengthens your belief. . . . That's why you're dogging me around and taking care of me when I'm drunk? To strengthen your belief? . . . Well, Jesus asked Peter three times, didn't he: 'Simon Peter, son of John, dost thou love me more than thou lovest these people?' 'I do, my Lord, thou knowest I do.' 'Then feed my young flock.'"

Sŏnu's lips curled into a scowl.

"You fancy yourself the shepherd, is that it? The shepherd who finds the one sheep that's missing from his flock of a hundred. And I'm that little lost sheep? Well listen, asshole, you have any idea what 'shepherd' means?... It's a dog... a breed of dog. But you're no shepherd—you're a crap hound, a dog that eats shit. And I've had enough of you following me around, crap hound, so get lost!... You like it when I bad-mouth you? An ordeal for the shepherd?... Okay, crap hound, let's try something. I want you to lick the sole of my boot. This boot that's walked hills soaked with blood. Come on!... What's the matter? Can't do it? Then how about this table? You can do *that*. This is where guys who escaped death get a little taste of joy at surviving. There'll be more of 'em in the future, right here at this table.... No? Can't lick it?... Then I'll show you—watch me."

Sŏnu proceeded to lick the wooden surface, then gathered his arms on the table and rested his forehead there. He shook his head, then lapsed into silence.

"His parents were slaughtered when the war broke out," An whispered to Tong-ho. "Father was a minister.... He drinks to forget it, and this is what happens."

The soldiers sitting nearby had left. Tong-ho could understand why. He was about to leave as well when Sŏnu suddenly looked up at An.

"Crap hound—what are you yelping about now? You think I drink because I can't forget? Wrong! It's because I want the memories sharper.... When I drink, everything comes back to life, even things I forgot.... All right, here's to remembering...."

Sŏnu poured himself another bowl of *makkŏlli*.

"It really is time to stop. What's the use of telling that same story night and day?"

Ignoring An, Sŏnu drank the entire bowl.

"Lookie here, Sergeant—it's Yun, right?—drink.... Drink and remember. All the way back. Sucking on your mother's tit. Or anything else you can remember."

And then he lifted his drink-reddened eyes and fixed them on a point in space.

"I can see it—it's all very clear—how they looked when I got out of that cave where I was hiding with the others—Mother and Father soaked in blood—the color of it. I wanted to see the blood of the sons of bitches who bloodied them. . . . But no blood I took could ever make up for the blood of my mother and father. . . . Every single night I prayed. Prayed I wouldn't wake up the next day. And every single morning. Prayed I'd be called to heaven that day. . . . Every time we went into battle I was out in front. And all I have to show for it is a special promotion. This is God's will? Claiming the blood of my mother and father? Damn cruel, that's what it is."

Shortly after the outbreak of the war a pit had been dug on the hill behind Sŏnu's home village. In the middle of the night some twenty villagers were herded there and machine-gunned, Sŏnu's parents among them. It happened that his father survived, the hail of bullets having missed his vital organs. Desperately thirsty from loss of blood, he crawled down the hill, found his way to a house, and asked for water. By a terrible coincidence that house had been taken over by the Public Safety Force. The men there, seeing that at least one of the villagers had escaped death, returned to the pit, and nearby they found two other survivors hiding in the bushes.

"You tell me. Was it God's will that out of all the houses in the village it had to be the Public Safety Force that my father went to? And those two who died because of my father . . . is that what you mean by 'God's profound will, which we humans in our wisdom cannot fathom'? My father devoted his entire life—sixty years—to God and the church. . . ."

Sŏnu's breathing grew rough.

"Don't ever tell me it was God's will!"

He hoisted himself to his feet and managed to stagger clear of the tables. Then he hesitated, stopped, and ever so slowly twisted to the right so that he was facing An and Tong-ho. His face wore a fleeting grin.

Tong-ho felt a chill. The man's expression was incongruous.

"How's that?" said Sŏnu.

Though he was facing them, Sŏnu seemed to be talking to himself.

When he could hold the pose no longer, he placed a hand on a table
for support and seemed about to collapse. But then he straightened.
"I'm not drunk, no sir, not me! . . . What's the tab?"

An was about to say something to Tong-ho but ended up scurrying
after Sŏnu and helping him outside.

The next time Tong-ho saw Sŏnu was at the battalion canteen. The
two men belonged to separate units, and if not for a place like the
canteen, they probably would not have encountered each other again.

Hyŏn-t'ae had received money from home that day. "Might as well
keep it in circulation," he announced to Tong-ho and Yun-gu, and
they dropped in at the nearby canteen. There, over drinks, they were
having a casual conversation about their plans for civilian life when
Sŏnu walked in.

If you first meet a man when he's drunk, he may seem completely
different sober. And that was Tong-ho's impression of Sŏnu now.
Sŏnu's tanned face, absent the liquor flush, looked paler. His cheek-
bones were more pronounced. The eyes glancing their way were
limpid and gentle. Sŏnu briefly made eye contact with Tong-ho, then
looked away with a strained expression. Whether by design or chance,
he sat down with his back to them.

Hyŏn-t'ae, mildly intoxicated, was holding sway: "Now our friend
Yun-gu the commerce major is going to end up at a bank. Give him a
receding hairline and he'll be perfect for the job. Don't know about
that wavy hair, though. In any event, if you're going to be a banker,
how about doing what you can for the Governor's business?"

"Just listen to this," broke in Tong-ho. "By the time this guy's a
banker you'll have inherited your father's business. What's the big
deal?"

"Hey, don't jump to conclusions. The Governor's in no hurry to
turn over his business to me. Sure, I majored in sociology because I
liked it, but the Governor went along with it too. Because if you're
going to run a business you have to have _vision_—that's what he
thinks. And take it from me, whatever I end up doing, I'm going to

go big and do it with style. Won't find me farting around with small change. I got a feeling things'll work out. Maybe I'm jumping the gun, but you know—"

Hyŏn-t'ae broke off when he saw Tong-ho glance up at An, who had just entered the canteen. An approached Sŏnu, who sat slumped over, close to the table, and seemed to speak. Sŏnu, concentrating on his shot of *soju,* utterly ignored him. From what Tong-ho and the others could see, his only drinking snack was kimchi—not much of a buffer against hard liquor.

How odd it was, thought Tong-ho, that An would follow Sŏnu around and put up with his insults. Granted the two of them were friends and had survived the outbreak of war in the North by hiding in a cave. But even so—

"You know him?" asked Hyŏn-t'ae.

"Sort of."

"Anyhow," resumed Hyŏn-t'ae, "don't think he's just going to hand over control to me. The Governor's a born businessman and it takes a lot to satisfy him. Damned if he didn't go down to Pusan after the war broke out and start over empty-handed—and now I think the business he built is bigger than the one he had in Seoul. In the letter I got today he says he was in and out of Seoul making preparations even before the cease-fire. Looks like he moved back there as soon as it was announced. And another thing—he's incredibly stubborn. Doesn't want anybody meddling in his affairs. Back when he ran a trading company my mother tried to get him to hire some relation of one of her college classmates. You think he'd listen to her? Not on your life. If he wants to hire someone, he puts an ad in the paper and screens the man himself. That's the procedure, and he doesn't bend it for anyone. Well, that works for some people. But if I worked with the Governor, I'm sure we'd be at each other's throats."

"Yeah, yeah, yeah," said Yun-gu, a twinkle in his eye. His swarthy face had taken on a purplish cast as he drank. "That's a pretty long-winded speech—like you're trying to shut us up before we ask you for a job."

"Ha—just like you. Well, I can see how you might look at it that

way. Don't worry—if you can't make it as a banker and you're down
on yourself, whatever I'm doing I'll make a place for you.

"Now for our friend Tong-ho. He'll be a Korean lit scholar. And
turn out a poem now and then. That's right, didn't you say your
Governor's a teacher? What is it he teaches? . . . Korean? Sure, runs in
the family—something to be said for that. But if you're going to be a
scholar I'd recommend glasses. With dark rims—got to have dark
rims. What are you scowling for? Okay, so maybe you're eyes aren't
bad. But you need to wear them anyhow. And make sure they have
great big lenses. Small ones are no good—they'd look miserable on
that thin mug of yours. Let's make the frames a bit thicker than usual.
And—"

"All right, all right! Enough is enough. Let's talk about you for a
change. You're going to be a company president, but you'll still want
to look like a sociologist. How do you accomplish that? . . . Okay, I've
got it. You grow your hair down to your shoulders and let your beard
grow out. And you'll need a walking stick—made of wisteria. Even if
you make company president and have your own car. What do you
think?"

Hyŏn-t'ae snorted. "Except for the walking stick, that sounds just
like a crazy guy I used to see when I was young. Now this crazy guy
had style. Never knew what he'd say next when he saw us playing. His
hair stuck out every which way and he'd point to it and say, 'Don't
you want to come in and play—I've got all sorts of flowers blooming
here.' We always had fun throwing rocks at him. But you know, for a
crazy guy he sure had style. And that's how you want me, a madman
with style? I'm overwhelmed! It's a rare occasion when I'm granted
something by the poet. All right, how about a toast to our future
appearance—"

Hyŏn-t'ae was interrupted by a thunderous roar from Sŏnu.

"Get lost, asshole!"

Hyŏn-t'ae's hand holding the bowl of _yakchu_ halted at his mouth.
His eyes reflected the light from the carbide lamp. He sensed Sŏnu
was trying to pick a fight with them. Yun-gu's purplish face tensed
and he glared at Sŏnu out of the corner of his eye.

"Relax," said Tong-ho in an undertone. "That's his friend he's shouting at." Tong-ho then gave a brief account of his previous encounter with Sŏnu. "Looks like he's good and drunk again. Says he drinks to remember, but it's obvious to me he wants to forget."

Sŏnu thumped his empty *soju* bottle on the table and called for more. It was the second twelve-ounce bottle he'd finished.

The canteen manager approached and showed Sŏnu several slips of paper. "Sergeant," he said respectfully, "you're a hundred forty hwan over."

The cost of the drinks, recorded on these chits, had exceeded the sergeant's salary. But advances could be obtained from the manager so that a soldier didn't exceed his monthly salary. Sergeants and higher just had to sign for an advance; lower ranks needed the senior corporal's signature.

"Oh? Right. So you can't give me any more. Well, that's the way it goes."

Sŏnu signed the slips, then rose to his feet. Wheeling about unsteadily, he caught sight of Tong-ho. Sŏnu's pale face had turned ruddy with drink and his eyes were bloodshot. When his eyes met Tong-ho's he fixed him with his gaze, unlike when he had entered the canteen. Then he drew near.

"Ah, Sergeant—what was your name again?—don't suppose you'd buy me a drink, would you?"

An rushed over.

"Don't tell me you're going to start in again. You've had enough—it's time to go."

"Go bark somewhere else, crap hound. Go to your master and bark your head off. . . . 'Lord, grant me thy boundless grace and safe passage through this world of confusion. . . .' Yeah, bark on, whatever you want. . . . Mind if I join you brave men?"

Hyŏn-t'ae and Yun-gu reacted with stony expressions but Tong-ho made room. He called for another glass and filled it for Sŏnu.

"Hooie—*yakchu!*"

"You don't want to mix that with *soju*," said An with a concerned look. "Come on, let's get up."

Sŏnu ignored him and drained the glass. "Sounded pretty interest-ing, what you were talking about. Why don't you continue? . . . Hey, don't let me spoil the fun. . . . Long as we're all putting our life on the line, can't we be friends? . . . How about telling me what _my_ future looks like?" Sŏnu's bloodshot eyes looked in turn at each of the three faces.

Tong-ho told himself there was no need to feel awkward now that they were sitting together. He spoke first.

"Oh, we were just shooting the breeze, sir. . . . Maybe you could start out by telling us your plans for when you're discharged."

"Damn good question."

"We need to know, sir, if we're going to talk about your future."

"Lookie here, Sergeant . . . Yun, that's it, Sergeant Yun. How's about we forget we're different ranks and drop the damned 'sir'? We can do that since we're about the same age, eh? . . . What do I figure on doing in the future? . . . Well—one thing's for sure. I don't have anyplace to go when I get out—not like you men. And as far as stay-ing on as a lifer . . ."

"Then we'd better make you look like a general."

"Well, I could spend the rest of my life in the army without much hope of making general. . . . But let's suppose I did. . . ."

"Okay, first thing you'll need is gloves. In winter, of course, but summer too. Big and thick as can be."

"Hmm. Fine. My little gynecologist hands don't exactly strike fear in the hearts of the men. Okay, what next?"

Tong-ho looked to Hyŏn-t'ae, tacitly asking him to join in and relax the atmosphere.

Hyŏn-t'ae, noting Sŏnu's absolute candor, felt less constrained in responding, even though this was his first encounter with the man: "The way I see it, your face needs a more commanding presence— have to add something to it. And the mustache looks odd. Instead of the mustache, get your mouth to twitch. Especially when you're upset about something or you need to think something over. Don't say any-thing, just do the twitch a few times. What do you think?"

"Sure."

Sŏnu took two mouthfuls of his new drink, pondered a moment, then spoke.

"You know, something struck me when you men were talking just now. What if we took everything each of you mentioned and put it all together? Receding hairline, hair down to the shoulders, beard growing out, big glasses, long walking stick. . . . I can see a face there . . . a face that looks like Jeremiah. Now there's a man I'd love to meet. The great prophet Jeremiah. . . . If we could bring Jeremiah here, I'll bet that's what he'd look like. So outwardly he'd have a different appearance from before, but inwardly there'd be a difference too. The Jeremiah back then was given revelations by God and uttered prophecies; the modern-day Jeremiah wouldn't do that. Know what he'd say? He'd say you can't prove that God exists, and you can't prove he doesn't. In other words, you can say he exists and you can say he doesn't exist. To the ones who believe in him he exists; to those who don't, he doesn't. We're all free to choose—it's up to you. People aren't controlled by the will of God. . . . Know what I mean?"

"That's a pretty far stretch. You fancy yourself a modern-day Jeremiah, Sergeant Sŏnu?"

Sŏnu transferred his vacant, bloodshot gaze to Hyŏn-t'ae: "No way, not the likes of me. A guy who needs gloves and a twitching mouth to do even a half-assed job of maintaining authority—a guy like that can't be a Jeremiah. . . . And another thing: If I'm going to take your suggestion and wear gloves, it won't be to strike fear in the hearts of my men. It's to hide what these hands have done. . . . And if I'm going to make my mouth twitch, the look of authority is the farthest thing from my mind. Because that twitch reminds me of something I never want to see again. . . . And you think a damned fool like me could be a Jeremiah? A modern-day Jeremiah would have to be someone who could act on his convictions, someone who didn't have an ounce of regret about anything he ever did, someone without any lingering attachments."

"But Sergeant, you look like a man who doesn't believe in God and acts on his own convictions."

"You're right about not believing in God. . . . I started thinking like that a while back. Only way I can put my mind to rest. Too many inconsistencies if you say that God is the master of this world. Better for my peace of mind to believe he's not there. . . . Anyhow, the guy you're looking at here isn't going to make a modern-day Jeremiah."

Sŏnu finished his drink, then rose and announced he was going to the toilet. He lurched toward the door, but then came to a stop. Ever so slowly he turned at the waist and looked back at the three men. His face wore a fleeting grin.

Tong-ho felt a chill, just as he had at the drinking place where he first encountered Sŏnu.

Hyŏn-t'ae and Yun-gu stared at the man's odd posture and expression.

"Not bad, eh? What do you think?"

As before, Sŏnu's question was directed to himself more than anyone else.

"Plastered again," An muttered to himself. He had been sitting silently next to Tong-ho waiting for Sŏnu's drinking spree to end. "Unless he's drinking he'll hardly say hello to you these days, much less get into a conversation."

Sŏnu jerked himself straight and lurched out the door.

"Apparently he shot a man who was cozy with the enemy," An said to Tong-ho in an undertone. "Told me he marched the man in front of him and shot him in the back. The man kind of twisted around with a grin—like my buddy did just now—then went down. I doubt if the man was actually grinning, but I guess it looked that way to my pal. So when he gets juiced up like this he mimics the man. One of these days he's really going to screw up, and that's why I follow him around. . . . He gets loaded and calls me a crap hound, every name in the book. Of course I know deep down inside he doesn't mean it, but I'm really afraid of what might—"

They were interrupted by the sound of vomiting outside the door. An rushed out and was then heard chiding Sŏnu about his drinking. Tong-ho pictured An rubbing Sŏnu's back to make him feel better. The sound of retching continued.

"Back off, crap hound! Don't want your help! Get away from me!"

Presently Sŏnu reappeared at the door, wiping his mouth with his handkerchief. An took hold of his arm from behind, but Sŏnu shook it off.

"You asshole, for the love of God will you get lost!"

Sŏnu tottered back to the table and sat down. Moisture had gathered in his dull, bloodshot eyes. It glittered in the light of the carbide lamp.

"Looks like *soju* plus *yakchu* equals one upset stomach," said Hyŏn-t'ae.

"Naw, I'm fine now—all cleaned out and ready for more."

So saying, Sŏnu filled his own glass, instead of waiting for one of the others to pour for him, and promptly drained it. Then, taking in the others with his moist, red eyes, he said: "You fellows know the difference between men and women when they die? When they drown, men end up face down, women face up. . . . Same when they're shot. The men pitch forward—"

He paused to pour himself another drink, and downed it immediately. The others waited for him to continue. But instead he served himself still another drink and rose without a word of explanation. He staggered toward the door, more unsteady now, and came to a stop. He managed to steady his swaying body, then slowly twisted to the right, his face displaying the same fleeting grin. But before the "Not bad, eh? What do you think?" could escape from his lips, he bent at the waist and toppled over.

An rushed to his side.

Cheek against the floor, Sŏnu screamed desperately, "Leave me alone, all of you! . . . Turn off the lights—now! . . . It's too bright! . . ." His arms flailed in the direction of the light. "Turn off the lights."

Yun-gu, gnawing on a piece of dried squid, broke his silence: "Not a bad performance."

A letter arrived from the family of Corporal Kim, the man who had died attempting to escape with Yun-gu.

Yun-gu had just returned to regimental headquarters from the Ch'up'a Pass area, where he had been sent to check on communications. The soldier who sorted mail for the various posts set aside a letter saying the recipient had been killed in action. Yun-gu realized it was a reply to the envelope with the dirt that had been sent at the request of the dying corporal to his family. He notified Hyŏn-t'ae, who then obtained permission from the senior corporal to open the letter.

The writing on the envelope appeared to be that of a grade school student. Inside were four notebook pages filled front and back. Judging from the contents, the letter had most likely been dictated by an adult. At intervals the writing was thicker where the writer had moistened the lead of his pencil with saliva. A few passages had been erased and corrected. The letter began with an inquiry about the corporal's health and reported that everyone at home was well:

*Strange things happen in this world. No sooner did your mom have a dream about you than we received your communication. I opened the envelope and knew right away what the dirt meant. We did what you told us with what you sent us last winter: we wrapped it up and placed it under the pot for the guardian spirit of our home, and we've kept it there until now, when we heard from you again. As you know, your dad has never known anything except working the land. The only thing I have ever wished for is to farm well enough so that our family will have no worries about food and will always be able to eat their fill. You used to complain that living off the land was the perfect way to starve, and that your dad was proof of that. Day and night you always looked for a place to gamble. You gave your mom and dad such a hard time. And so, to see that you finally seem to have got some sense in you makes us happy. Even last summer, when you came home to help out with the farming, you grumbled that farmers were the most pitiful creatures in the world. But your dad wouldn't survive for a moment if he had to leave the land. It's the happiest thing that even at this late date you finally understand how your dad feels. The divine spirits must have been aware of your state of mind, because Ch'un-bo and his family decided to sell their land.*

There followed a lengthy passage about Ch'un-bo. It appeared that this farmer had become the talk of the villagers, for he and his family had had to move to where his father's cousin lived in Kangwŏn Province. The cousin had persuaded Ch'un-bo's family to move, saying life was good there, but in such cases the truth often turns out otherwise. And no matter how many people might say that life is good in a particular place, how can a farmer be expected to uproot himself from his native area? The year before last, Ch'un-bo's father passed away—he had been bedridden for years—and last year his younger brother was killed in action. And that was just the start of a rough period in which the family accumulated quite a few debts. When the proceeds of their harvest this year couldn't even pay off the interest on the debts, they were helpless—the only thing to do was sell off their land and move.

> *Ch'un-bo's family worked the land here for generations. I feel awful bad that they had to leave. But I figured that as long as he was going to sell his land I might as well buy a parcel of it and no one could say I was taking advantage of someone's bad luck. The long strip across the stream from the stepping stones, they gave to Shin Ch'am-bong to pay off a debt. And the little patch below Eagle Pass, that's the one we bought. The land itself isn't all that choice, but making it ours is like a dream come true. This may sound strange, but the color of the soil on that land we bought is the same dark red as what you sent us. I guess this letter's running long what with your dad rejoicing over that land. This letter was quite a production—I made your little brother write it all down. You take care of yourself now. I'm sure you had a reason to send that dirt without a letter, but be sure to write soon.*

Tong-ho looked up from the letter.

"What do we do now? We never should have sent that dirt without an explanation. Even if it *was* his last wish."

"Who would have thought it would get there before the death notice?" said Hyŏn-t'ae.

"Shouldn't we tell them what happened?" ventured Tong-ho.

"What's the use? I'll bet the death notice was waiting for them when they got home from the post office."

"Their dream is going to be shattered."

"What's so special about the dreams of poor people? Sounds like their son means less to them than having a patch of farmland they can call their own."

"Last winter he made a killing selling all those supplies," Yun-gu broke in. "Wonder if he sent all the money home. I thought he'd pissed it away on some bargirl."

"That's what I thought too. He liked fancy living, but I guess he was realistic too. Anyhow, if he was alive, he'd be jailbait if he'd sold that stuff. . . . You can figure out everything from the letter. Simple old man out in the sticks—what could he know? But for a simple guy, he surprises me. How did he get it in his head from seeing the dirt in that letter that it was a message for him to buy land? They sound pretty practical, both of them. Though land always has been a practical item."

"It's practical, all right. But shouldn't the people who walk that land have a dream?"

Hyŏn-t'ae snorted.

"What for? A surprise for dinner instead of the usual stuff? More fun the next time we get leave? Come on, give me a break!"

# 6

"WOW!" Tong-ho crinkled up his nose at the pungent odor of freshly turned soil. It seemed the mud walls hadn't had time to dry properly; the sheets of newspaper covering them had bubbled and shriveled.

They were at a place just off the road between Hwach'ŏn and Ch'up'a Pass. The large interior had been sectioned off into half a dozen cubicles back to back. There appeared to be about the same number of young women working there. The place seemed to cater not only to the units stationed at Sot'ogomi but to soldiers in transit as well. Hyŏn-t'ae had brought Tong-ho here to show him a "good" drinking place—one with women to serve them and sit beside them.

"That famous nose of yours," joked Hyŏn-t'ae. He turned to Yun-gu: "Remember that godforsaken place where they shipped us from the front? Nobody in sight, and our pal here claims he got a whiff of face powder. I ask myself, now what the hell is he talking about? And damned if a woman doesn't show up on the road! Made a believer out of me. Never seen a man with a nose like that." He turned back to Tong-ho: "Well, if the smell of dirt bothers you we'll sit this girl next to you and she'll neutralize it."

So saying, Hyŏn-t'ae told the woman sitting between him and Yun-gu to move beside Tong-ho.

"Don't bother. Like you say, I can smell just fine from where I am."

"Why don't we call more girls instead?" said the woman.

"Yeah, do that," said Hyŏn-t'ae. "Doesn't look like you've got many customers."

The woman clapped her hands and called for two more women. Like the first woman, the two who now appeared wore shabby, ill-fitting traditional costumes appropriate to their soldier clientele. The white collars alone stood out.

Of the three women, two had a fleshy, healthy appearance but were plain-looking. The third, sitting next to Tong-ho, had a narrow oval face, sharp nose, and slender neck. The faded yellow of her jacket made her seem somehow unhealthy. Her square forehead and dark, clear eyes were the only features to dispel the impression of indecency given by this sort of woman.

"Where you ladies from?" asked Hyŏn-t'ae as he stuck a cigarette in his mouth.

"Goodness, we forgot to introduce ourselves," said the first woman, who sat beside Hyŏn-t'ae. She gave her name and said she came from the city of Ch'unch'ŏn. The woman beside Yun-gu hailed from P'och'ŏn, and Tong-ho's companion was from Seoul.

"Seoul, eh?" said Hyŏn-t'ae. "That's quite a hop from here."

"Not really. One of the other girls is from Mokp'o."

"Yeah? She must be a real trooper."

A stew of sliced pollack and bean curd arrived, along with a kettle of _makkŏlli_. After some drinks and jokes with the girls Yun-gu turned to Hyŏn-t'ae. "So you think it might be a while yet before we get out?"

"Afraid so. The word was that student recruits like us would get mustered out soon, but it doesn't look that way. Now I hear it won't be till next spring."

"You think it's true they'll swap us with a frontline unit in late November?"

"That's what they say. That means spending the winter buried in snow at Ch'up'a Pass. Too bad for our buddy Tong-ho. Who knows, though? Maybe he likes counting the days till he sees his sweetheart. Anyhow, long as we're not at the front we might as well booze it up and have a good look at the ladies."

"May we have a drink too?" asked one of the women politely.

"Yeah, long as you don't get carried away. Last thing I want to see is a bunch of blithering women."

The woman from Ch'unch'ŏn took an empty bowl and filled it halfway. She drank it all, then offered the empty bowl to the woman from Seoul, sitting beside Tong-ho. With a hint of irritation the woman from Seoul shook her head.

The bowl found its way to the P'och'ŏn woman, Yun-gu's companion. She poured it almost full and finished it in several gulps, then screwed up her face the way a child would and shuddered.

"Hey, there's a talent!"

"Not me. Ok-ju there's the best drinker," the P'och'ŏn woman said, indicating the woman beside Tong-ho. "Ok-ju, how come you're not drinking?"

"I overdid it last night and now my stomach's killing me—I'm full of gas."

"That reminds me," said the P'och'ŏn woman, "remember those soldiers last night? They said the night before last a soldier went off the road near the power plant and got himself killed."

"You mean the Kumalli plant?"

"Yes, he was driving a jeep. Sounded like he went in the water."

There had been a similar accident when Hyŏn-t'ae was recuperating at the field hospital at Kumalli. A road ran along the embankment of the reservoir that extended some ten miles from Kumalli to Oŭmni. Several yards below the dike was dark-blue water that was dozens of fathoms deep. The slightest mistake, and vehicle and driver ended up in the water. In such cases it was difficult to mount a rescue.

"Another land, air, and sea operation!"

"Land, air, and sea?" said the Ch'unch'ŏn woman. "What's that supposed to mean?"

"Don't you know? Driving a jeep, that's the land part. Flying down the bank, that's air. And into the drink, sea. So—land, air, and sea."

The women from Ch'unch'ŏn and P'och'ŏn laughed as if this were the craziest notion. But the woman from Seoul didn't crack a smile.

"I'd like to try that," she said.

"Try what?"

"Drive a jeep fast as I could and fly through the air into the water. It would be so . . . tidy. They'd never find me."

"You'd want your boyfriend along with you, though. . . ."

"Yes, that would make it better. . . . But if two people *really* loved each other and then found they had no future, killing themselves wouldn't be much fun. Better if two people who shouldn't have fallen in love killed themselves the moment they realized they were inseparable."

Hyŏn-t'ae snorted. "Let's not get sentimental. Sappy talk doesn't go with booze. Not in today's world. If you're going to tell a story when people are drinking, then it ought to make the booze taste better. Hell, I'd rather play rock-paper-scissors and make the loser drink. That would be a lot more fun than a sad story."

The empty kettle was refilled. The Ch'unch'ŏn and P'och'ŏn women offered each other an occasional drink.

The woman from Seoul took two cigarettes from the pack on the table. One she lit and passed to Tong-ho, the other she lit for herself. Before putting the cigarette to his mouth, Tong-ho furtively pinched off the lipstick-stained portion under the table.

The woman from Seoul sucked deeply on her cigarette and exhaled forcefully. Then, as if she had suddenly remembered something, she picked up the bowl that lay in front of Tong-ho, took a quick swallow, and offered him the rest. Tong-ho took a sip, avoiding the place on the rim where the woman had drunk, and returned the bowl to the table. He realized that today as usual he was barely emptying one drink for every two that Hyŏn-t'ae and Yun-gu finished. He just couldn't understand Hyŏn-t'ae's propensity for visiting places like this. It was all he could do to wait till they left for the next place.

The woman from Seoul asked Tong-ho to drink up. It seemed she wasn't interested as much in urging drinks on a customer as being offered a drink in return. Tong-ho resigned himself and drank.

"Attaboy! You won't see him refusing a drink from a lady," Hyŏn-t'ae bantered, his teeth looking all the whiter in the grin creasing his coppery face.

Without waiting to be offered the empty bowl, the woman from Seoul snatched it from Tong-ho's hand, then held it out and asked him to pour. She proceeded to gulp the *makkŏlli*, then returned the bowl to him. When Tong-ho gave no indication of drinking, she took it back and drank again. Tong-ho glanced at her out of the corner of his eye. The veins of her temples stood out and the area around her mouth and eyes was flushed. It was a mystery to him why someone who complained of stomach gas from overdrinking the previous night was now emptying one drink after another.

When the second kettle of *makkŏlli* was almost empty Hyŏn-t'ae went outside, apparently to go to the toilet. The Ch'unch'ŏn woman followed.

The woman from Seoul filled her bowl with what remained in the kettle. "Shall I bring some more?"

Tong-ho looked at Yun-gu: "What if we call it quits?"

"Well . . . let's see what Hyŏn-t'ae wants to do. . . ."

Yun-gu rose and went outside. The P'och'ŏn woman followed.

Shortly thereafter the Seoul woman was summoned. By now the edges of her mouth and eyes were scarlet. Her head perked up, displaying a hint of irritation, and she went outside.

Tong-ho gazed vacantly at the mess on the table as he waited for Hyŏn-t'ae and the others: pollack bones, spilled stew, cigarette ash, and dripped *makkŏlli*. He heard murmuring in the yard and then the door softly opened and the woman from Seoul poked her head inside.

"Come here for a minute."

Tong-ho went out, wondering if something had happened.

The woman led him past a room of boisterous drinkers and around to the back of the building. Tong-ho wondered if his friends were playing a trick on him. Perhaps they had moved the drinking party to another room.

The woman came to a stop at a door and opened it. Placing a hand on Tong-ho's back, she ushered him inside. Tong-ho felt the woman at his back and heard the latch being secured.

The room had only this one rice-papered door and was poorly lit in spite of the broad light of day outside. The smell of fresh moist earth stabbed at his nostrils, as if sunlight never reached this room. Tong-ho was bewildered. Eventually his eyes made out a sleeping pad on the floor. On it lay the woman, naked from the waist down. Finally it all began to make sense.

It was so peculiar: the thin, oval face and slender neck gave the woman a general impression of unhealthiness, but the body that gradually came into focus was well developed. The breasts rising beneath her thin shoulders and the ample hips below her narrow waist seemed all out of proportion to her slim build. Suddenly the image of Sugi came to mind. Tong-ho dismissed it, pledging never to think of her in a place like this. He should leave at once, he told himself.

As his eyes grew used to the dark he noticed the woman's upraised knees and then the blackness between her thighs. *Filthy!* A wave of disgust surged inside him. *Turn and leave,* he said silently.

The woman bolted to her feet, came close to Tong-ho, and thrust out her chin. "I don't please you, is that it? I look dirty to you. Just like back there. I saw you ripping off the tip of that cigarette. Didn't want that dirty part my lips had touched, did you? . . . Well, I could care less what you think."

The smell of cheap cosmetics and the odor of her flesh washed over Tong-ho's face. She gripped him tightly by the arm and pulled. The scarlet flush around her eyes and mouth disappeared. He had to free himself. But his will was paralyzed by the desperate force with which she clung to him, and he allowed himself to be led.

Tong-ho let his mind wander. *She must be cold, wearing nothing down there. And the floor's not heated. . . .*

The woman unbuttoned his pants. He let her pull him to a kneeling position. And then she took him. Afterward she pushed him aside, rose, gathered her clothes, and began dressing.

"That's all. You're free to go. Those other two said they'd pay." Her tone was businesslike. And then she left.

Tong-ho considered. *Hyŏn-t'ae must have joked to her that if she could get me in bed, then he'd pay. He obviously assumed no woman had a chance with me.*

Outside, Tong-ho avoided the room where they had been drinking. He left through the plank gate and headed back toward the base. As the cool breeze blew against his face, it occurred to him with certainty that he had just been violated by a woman. It was a ludicrous notion, but he found himself unable to laugh. Instead he told himself that part of his body was soiled. He stopped, urinated, and attempted to clean himself. But this only made him feel that the filth had spread. He lit a cigarette. After a few puffs, a wave of nausea rose from deep inside him. He squatted beside the road and tried to vomit, but little came up. Fits of retching shook him all over.

He heard someone behind him, and then Hyŏn-t'ae's voice.

"Hey, what's the rush? You left something behind."

Hyŏn-t'ae placed Tong-ho's hat on his head. But it came loose as Tong-ho continued to retch. Before it could fall off Hyŏn-t'ae repositioned it, while with his other hand he rubbed Tong-ho's back.

"Hey, I lost my bet with that bitch! You *can* get it up after all!"

"Leave me alone."

Yun-gu approached, fashioning a paper mouthpiece for one of his cut-in-half cigarettes.

"'Leave me alone'?" said Yun-gu. "You've been hanging around that guy Sŏnu too long. You can spare us the lights-out routine. It's one thing with a carbide lamp, but you can't very well turn off the sun."

When Tong-ho's retching had subsided, Hyŏn-t'ae looked down at him with a smile. "We have had one hell of a time making a man out of you."

# 7

IT CAN HAPPEN to anyone. You try to jump a ditch, but you fall short and one foot ends up in the water. You're disgusted with yourself. The feeling is all the worse if there's mud or sewage in the ditch. And if you're wearing new shoes, it's a struggle to keep from losing your temper. Why didn't you start running farther back, you ask yourself. Then you could have made it. Ah hell! you finally think. You let your anger run its course, and by that time you feel like sticking your other foot in the ditch and getting it mucked up too.

Which was precisely Tong-ho's state of mind. Back at the base that night, he lay awake tormented by regret. It was so unexpected, what had happened that day. To an extent he'd been a passive participant. But no matter how unforeseen the incident, no matter how unplanned on his part, wasn't it a fact that he could have avoided it? He was forced to the conclusion that he lacked moral fiber. Remorse gnawed at his heart.

The following day at target practice he had trouble concentrating. At first he was able to sight in on the target and fire. But then the target seemed to turn into the part of himself that had been dirtied. And when images of Sugi and then that woman began to superimpose themselves, Tong-ho found himself firing blindly.

"You been eating army food how many years now, and that's the best you can do?" shouted the platoon leader from behind. "You can't shoot slouched over like that! Come on, aim steady, one round at a time. Get yourself together and fire!"

But within a matter of days Tong-ho had grown displeased with himself for suffering so—it was absurd! He'd only done what any other man might have. He was *so* timid, and this realization brought with it an intense self-loathing. Why couldn't he put that incident behind him as others might have? Well, perhaps it wasn't so ordinary after all, something he could simply gloss over. And wasn't his love for Sugi as pure as ever? In fact, didn't he long for her now even more? What it amounted to was his damned fastidiousness, he told himself. Why did he cling to it? Prissy like a girl, Hyŏn-t'ae had once called him. And now Tong-ho found himself agreeing. It was embarrassing. And it was high time he killed off that part of himself.

The next time they had leave, Tong-ho suggested returning to the same place.

"History in the making!" Hyŏn-t'ae responded. "First time you've ever been hot to go to a place like that. So we return in celebration to where we made a man out of you!"

They arrived at the plank gate and its scrapwood border. Inside they were greeted by the woman from P'och'ŏn, Yun-gu's companion from the time before.

"Come in," she said, obviously delighted. "I was wondering if we might see you today."

They entered the room with the familiar dirt smell and settled themselves. Hyŏn-t'ae's former companion, the Ch'unch'ŏn woman, sat beside him and placed a hand on his knee. She seemed beside herself with joy.

The Ch'unch'ŏn woman's winsome smile revealed a gold canine tooth. Tong-ho had noticed it the previous time but didn't remember it being so dark and lusterless. There must have been a lot of copper in the alloy. He was gratified to realize that, unlike before, he now had the presence of mind to note a detail like this.

"What can we offer you? *Yakchu* to start off? Then a stew, stir-fry vegetables and potato noodles, or something grilled? There's lentil jelly, too, or we could batter-fry something. Whatever you'd like."

"Let's try the noodles and jelly. But first. . . . Guys?" Hyŏn-t'ae looked in turn at Yun-gu and Tong-ho. "What do you say we get some different girls?"

Yun-gu nodded in agreement.

Tong-ho was quick to answer: "The one I had last time is fine by me." He himself wasn't sure why he would insist on picking the woman who had caused him to suffer for days.

Hyŏn-t'ae turned to the woman beside him. "The girl you said came from Mokp'o—bring her and the one from Seoul who was with our buddy here, and anyone else you want."

The Ch'unch'ŏn woman immediately grew sulky: "What's the matter? Did I do something wrong last time?"

"Naw, we just feel like a change of scenery—that's all."

"Well, the other girls are with other customers."

"Fine—we can wait."

"Come on—I'll be extra nice this time."

"What about me?" said the P'och'ŏn woman, looking up at Yun-gu with inquiring eyes and forced cheer.

Yun-gu maintained a noncommittal silence. He was happy to let Hyŏn-t'ae make the decisions.

"What's the matter with you two?" said Hyŏn-t'ae, his tone louder and icier. "You want me to call the owner?"

Any other time, Hyŏn-t'ae's tone and his lack of concern for the women's pride would have sounded cruel to Tong-ho. But today he found himself envying Hyŏn-t'ae for the willpower evidenced by his usual decisiveness.

The two women marched out with sullen faces, the hems of their skirts trailing along the floor.

"They aren't worth a second roll," said Hyŏn-t'ae. "Not to say the others are any better." He produced a lighter and lit a cigarette.

Presently two other women arrived with a tray bearing a kettle of *yakchu* and drinking bowls.

"Which one of you's from Mokp'o?" asked Hyŏn-t'ae.

One of the women nodded almost imperceptibly and approached Hyŏn-t'ae.

"Naw, sit over there. From the looks of you, you're my buddy's type."

Yun-gu drew the woman by the wrist to his side.

To Tong-ho the Mokp'o woman looked older than any of the others he had seen there. But her egg-shaped face was in no way ugly and her thick lips gave her a caring impression. Tong-ho recalled Hyŏn-t'ae's observation that when it came to buying women, crafty Yun-gu chose older ones so that he'd get more loving. Tong-ho found himself agreeing.

The other woman said she was from Kangnŭng. She was missing a few teeth, which gave her chin an upward tilt.

Tong-ho took a drink, mustered his courage, and spoke: "Where's the other one?" He realized that the pitch of his voice was unnaturally high. *Can't you control yourself and act more relaxed?*

"Who do you mean?" asked the Mokp'o woman.

"Um, isn't there one from Seoul?"

"Oh, of course, you mean Ok-ju. She's with another guest now."

Tong-ho may have heard the name the previous time, but now the realization that her name was Ok-ju imprinted itself in his mind.

The first kettle of *yakchu* disappeared amid random conversation, and Ok-ju still hadn't arrived.

"Ought to call one of the other girls instead, what do you think?" asked Hyŏn-t'ae.

"Don't bother," said Tong-ho.

"You chump, you've fallen for her. Oh well. Hey, Mokp'o lady—go pry the Seoul girl loose for a minute."

The woman clapped her hands and an errand girl appeared. The message was conveyed and another kettle of *yakchu* ordered. Presently the girl returned with the *yakchu* and reported that the guest in the other room was about to leave.

Tong-ho was seized by a peculiar thought. What if Hyŏn-t'ae and Yun-gu got drunk enough and left with their girls and Ok-ju still hadn't appeared? Wouldn't it be much better that way? He could simply sneak back to the base. But the next moment he realized this was not a solution to his problems. Instead, his insufferable prissiness would continue to shadow him—a constant nagging reminder. Now that he had the opportunity, better to root it out once and for all. He should wait for this woman Ok-ju. Regardless of his relations with her, his love for Sugi would remain pure.

Tong-ho finished his _yakchu._ "Have a drink, you two." He offered his bowl to the Mokp'o woman and filled it. "Did you come straight here from Mokp'o?"

"Naw," she drawled. "I made a few stops along the way—Chŏnju, Pusan, Taegu."

"And where to next?"

"Good question. One thing's for sure: I can't go any farther north than the thirty-eighth parallel."

She returned the emptied bowl to Tong-ho and poured him another drink. Tong-ho drank, making no effort to avoid the place he presumed her lips had touched. And then it was the Kangnŭng woman's turn to accept a drink from him.

"Look at this chump! Not bad for a guy who had such a long face all week." Hyŏn-t'ae's tone was edged with cynicism.

The words momentarily stung Tong-ho. He realized he was making a conscious effort to act as loose and free as anyone else in a place like this. _Have to drink more!_

A woman was singing in the other room.

"Ok-ju," said the Kangnŭng woman, tilting her head in that direction. "That guy still hasn't left."

Her voice was thick and husky when she sang, Tong-ho observed, unlike her speaking voice. An image of Ok-ju's large breasts and fleshy rump, which looked so unbalanced on her willowy build, filled his mind's eye. He took another drink.

A man took up the song Ok-ju was singing. Unfamiliar with the songs one might hear at a drinking place, Tong-ho couldn't very well pass judgment on the singing, but he did think the man had a good voice.

"That's the head of the Youth Corps," the Kangnŭng woman volunteered. "He lives in that village back up in the valley."

If you went around the bottom of the hill to the right of the base and far up a narrow valley you'd come to a hamlet of some thirty homes. It was at a distance from the main road—probably the reason it hadn't been reduced to ashes during the hostilities of the last three years. Those who had fled returned after the cease-fire and now the village was pretty much the way it had been before the war.

"Is he a regular customer of Ok-ju's?" Tong-ho asked the Kangnŭng woman.

"Better not ask. That's a no-no," broke in the woman from Mokp'o. "Why don't we sing too?" she proposed in an effort to inject some life into the gathering.

"Fine by me," said Tong-ho. "You first."

Except for her moist eyes the Mokp'o woman showed no signs of the alcohol. She began singing "Tears of Mokp'o":

> The boatman's song grows distant,
> Waves steal over Samhak Island's shores,
> Tears of farewell mottle the skirt
> Of the bride on the wharf

Tong-ho recognized the song and followed along silently.

"All right, that's enough," said Hyŏn-t'ae. "No weepy songs. Pick something else."

The Mokp'o woman seemed unfazed by this request. "How about 'Kangwŏndo Arirang'?" she said to the woman from Kangnŭng.

The Kangnŭng woman's face and ears showed a liquor flush. She began to sing:

> Castor-oil plant, camellia, blossom not
> Lest the maidens in the hills
> Get lustful thoughts . . .

Tong-ho observed the woman's sunken mouth and found himself thinking she didn't do a bad job with this flowing melody.

> *Arirang, Arirang,* arario,
> *Arirang Pass . . .*

"Hold on a minute."

Before the Kangnŭng woman had finished, it occurred to Tong-ho that he could no longer hear voices from the other room. Nor did the song resume. Tong-ho wondered what had happened after the song ended. More drinking? Was the visitor preparing to leave? Or were the man and woman about to move to a different room? An oppressive feeling came over Tong-ho.

And then he heard someone emerge from the other room. He strained to listen. It sounded as if the visitor was leaving. Presently he heard the scuffing of a woman's slippers. He managed to restrain a sigh and drank from his bowl of *yakchu.*

Hyŏn-t'ae, puffing on a cigarette, noticed.

"What's got into you, drinking like that?"

Ok-ju entered. As before, her eyes and thin lips were reddened by drink. Only the sharp tip of her nose remained pale. Tong-ho suddenly felt ashamed of himself and glanced away. Ok-ju, utterly calm, surveyed the three men. "Hello." She sat beside Tong-ho. Then, as if to augment her cursory greeting, she mechanically poured each of the men a drink. Her complete lack of emotion gave Tong-ho a feeling of tranquillity.

Hyŏn-t'ae finished his drink and filled the empty bowl for Ok-ju.

"Here's to you. For making a man out of our buddy."

"Nice joke." Her thin lips displayed a fleeting, perhaps sardonic smile. Against custom she accepted the bowl with her left hand, prompting Tong-ho to consider that maybe she was left-handed. The second kettle of *yakchu* was emptied and Tong-ho ordered a third.

"Are you all right, chump?" asked Hyŏn-t'ae with a look of surprise.

"Of course. If I have a mind to drink, this stuff's not going to bother me."

"Spoken like a rookie," said Yun-gu. "He'll know better once he develops a taste for the stuff."

In fact Tong-ho had never drunk so much before. But his head felt perfectly clear. He glanced at the woman beside him. "Ok-ju," he said, as if he had just thought of it, "how about doing that song you were singing in the other room?"

"Which song was that?" Her face remained dead still as she spoke, the tip of her nose looking impossibly sharp.

"You know: 'You wind, you raging wind'—something like that."

"That Cheju song, remember?" said the Kangnŭng woman.

Ok-ju sat silently a moment, then lit a cigarette and took a drag. She began to sing:

> Gone, my husband, out to sea
> Blow, you wind, you raging wind,
> Blow three months and ten . . .

The other two women joined in, tapping chopsticks against the table in time.

> And now it's time for you and me,
> Day by day and night by night,
> Our true and steadfast love . . .

*Yeah, that's it,* Tong-ho muttered to himself. His lips were violently flushed. *Husband's out to sea. . . . You wind, you raging wind. . . . It blows for . . . yeah, three months ten days, that's right. Now I get it.*

When the new kettle of *yakchu* had made the rounds a couple of times, Hyŏn-t'ae whispered something in the Kangnŭng woman's ear and the two of them rose and left. Yun-gu then nudged the Mokp'o woman and they followed suit.

*It's that simple,* thought Tong-ho. But here he hesitated. What now? Why hadn't he followed his friends without so much as a backward glance at Ok-ju? That would have been the easiest, most natural way. He grew impatient. And the more impatient he became, the harder it was to overcome his inhibitions. *Maybe I'll just have to wait here till they get back.* But this thought barely registered before a louder voice called out inside him: *You have to do what you came here for. Else you'll never be able to forgive yourself for your indecision.* He brought his drink to his lips and realized his mouth was bone dry.

"Well?" said Ok-ju, her voice soft and subdued. She was completely different from the time before. Then she had seemed defiant and rebellious. Her quiet tone gave Tong-ho courage. He rose and tapped her slender shoulder, then helped her to her feet.

Ok-ju led the way to the room and opened the door. This time she entered first. Tong-ho followed and she secured the latch. In the damp air of the room the odor of fresh earth stabbed at his nostrils.

This time it was Tong-ho who unbuttoned his pants after the woman had reclined on the spread-out sleeping mat. And this time he knelt unassisted between her legs. Afterward the woman, unlike before, did not thrust him aside. Silently she rose and began to dress. For Tong-ho it was a letdown. Was it for this that he had struggled with himself for so long? It was absurd.

Tong-ho watched the woman finish dressing, then produced half a dozen hundred-hwan notes and offered them to her.

"I'm sure the other gentlemen took care of it."

"Take it anyway, will you?"

The woman tucked the money in her palm and left without a word. Watching her slender shoulders Tong-ho experienced an unaccountable feeling of loss and unfulfillment.

Starting the next day, Tong-ho focused intently during target practice and summoned all his energy for the hand-to-hand combat drills. He was a faithful participant in camp cleanup and repair. Break time he passed in small talk with his comrades. The important thing was to avoid being alone. At any such moment Sugi might intrude upon his thoughts, and he found that prospect forbidding.

He refused to admit that a crack might have opened in the armor of his love for Sugi. He tried to convince himself that his love for her was unchanged and that he continued to hold it dear. But apart from that precious love, he simply had to make sense of the confusion in his mind triggered by the infiltration of that one unexpected incident into his life.

He wrestled with himself for hours about his fastidiousness. In the end he found himself tormented anew by the realization that despite the meaninglessness of their relations the sight of Ok-ju's slender shoulders receding from view had left him with a feeling of incompletion that he could ignore only at the peril of losing his peace of mind.

On their next day of leave the three men got drunk at a ramshackle drinking house. Hyŏn-t'ae and Yun-gu announced their intention of getting a "tuneup." Whereupon Tong-ho went off by himself to see Ok-ju.

He arrived at the plank gate bordered by the scrapwood enclosure just as a man emerged from the drinking house. The man looked about forty and seemed tipsy. He brushed by Tong-ho, who noticed his olive-colored fatigues. Something prompted Tong-ho to turn and observe the man. He had a squat, chubby build and a slew-footed gait, but what really caught Tong-ho's eye was the exaggerated way he threw his arms out as he walked.

Ok-ju happened to be visible through the open door of a room she was clearing of drink and food. Seeing Tong-ho enter through the gate, she produced an odd smile, her eyebrows raised.

"Come in."

"What's so funny? Me being here by myself?"

"No, it's nothing. Come on in." She called the errand girl and had her finish cleaning up. "It's just that you looked so stiff coming through the gate. Kind of a funny way to walk when you're out drinking."

Tong-ho had felt emboldened by the drinks he'd consumed with the others a short time before. Now he was bothered by the realization that this bravado had made him appear unnatural to Ok-ju. To restore his spirits he would have to drink more.

"Ask her to hurry up with the drinks," he told Ok-ju.

A kettle arrived and Tong-ho finished two bowls in rapid succession. He then passed his bowl to Ok-ju and filled it. But instead of taking a healthy swallow she merely touched the bowl to her lips.

"What's the matter? I thought you had a pretty good capacity."

"I'm already drunk. It's still daytime and I can't afford to drink any more than this. I'll have other guests too by and by."

Tong-ho finished the kettle more or less by himself.

"Another one?"

Shaking his head, Tong-ho took her by the wrist and rose, wanting the privacy of the other room. This desire, and the act of taking her by the wrist, felt completely natural.

"You'll need to pay up."

Tong-ho produced the cost of the drinks.

"And . . ."

He gave her some seven or eight hundred hwan—what was left from that month's pay.

In the other room Ok-ju was loosening the ties to her blouse when Tong-ho beckoned her to stop. She looked at him, puzzled.

"Ok-ju, are you, ah, left-handed?"

The question baffled her.

"What if I am?"

"That's what I mean. I wanted to know a little more about you."

"I don't understand."

"Well, for example, what kind of woman you are."

Ok-ju erupted in laughter yet seemed vexed.

"You're serious, aren't you? Well, if you really want to know, I'll tell you. My real name is Ch'oe Myŏng-ae, I'm twenty-three, I was born in Seoul, married at twenty-one—"

"It's the present I'm interested in, not the past."

"Oh, the here and now. Well—as you know, my name is Ok-ju, I'm a cheap barmaid . . . and I sell my body for five hundred hwan, or maybe three hundred."

"What I meant was . . . don't you have a man in your life?"

"A man. Indeed I do. Every one of them who buys me."

"I wish you wouldn't be sarcastic. . . . Ah, that visitor you had before I arrived—isn't he the head of the Youth Corps?"

"What about him?"

"I was just curious. He was here the last time too, so I thought maybe he came here every day."

Again she burst out in laughter. And then, regarding Tong-ho as she would have a little brother: "Is there something wrong if he visits me every day?"

"No, that's not what I meant."

"Well, then, let's stop the talk and get on with it. If I'm out here too long I'll catch a scolding."

She began to undress. Tong-ho noticed the swift movement of her hands.

"How much for the night?"

"All night long, you mean? Two thousand."

Again the act was perfunctory. But this time, as he gazed at her body after she had dressed, Tong-ho felt a kind of familiarity with her.

Outside the fresh air swept over him and his mind seemed to clear. At the same time, the satiation of his desire, the dissolution of tension, had left him empty and once again he felt the effects of the alcohol. It was not an unpleasant feeling. He was a bit unsteady on his feet. He realized he was humming to himself.

> Gone, my husband, out to sea
> Blow, you wind, you raging wind
> Blow three months and ten . . .

> Blow, you wind, you raging wind
> Blow three months and ten . . .

A man was approaching. He stopped in front of Tong-ho.

"Sergeant Yun?"

It was An. Tong-ho lifted a hand in acknowledgment and kept walking. From behind he heard An ask where he was coming from. He didn't answer.

"You must be drunk."

"Yes, I am, and loving every minute of it."

"Ah, I don't suppose you've seen Sergeant Sŏnu?"

"Haven't the slightest."

"You really are drunk. That much liquor's not good for you."

Tong-ho continued on his way.

> Blow, you wind, you raging wind
> Blow three months and ten . . .

Hyŏn-t'ae and Yun-gu had already returned to the base.

"Listen, you two!" Tong-ho shouted. "I'm all cleaned out! Put a beautiful woman next to me and I won't even look at her—that's how cleaned out I am! Love, hate, all of those stupid qualities—I've washed 'em all away, I'm free and easy. . . . Blow, you wind, you raging wind, blow, typhoon, blow three months and ten, blow three years and ten, I don't care!"

Tong-ho sprawled out on his cot next to Hyŏn-t'ae's and presently was snoring. Thus began a complete change in his drinking habits.

The reconnaissance company to which Tong-ho and his friends belonged had never had a canteen of its own. And so the men had taken to using another infantry battalion's canteen. To remedy the inconvenience the company commander had arranged with regimental headquarters a few days earlier to open a separate club for his men. This canteen, such as it was, consisted of shelving assembled next to the mess area and offered only a few personal necessities, some inexpensive snacks such as cookies and dried squid, and a small selection of drinks.

Tong-ho, paying with chits, took to drinking there. Though he still accompanied Hyŏn-t'ae and Yun-gu on their outings, he preferred drinking alone at the canteen. There he discovered that domestic dry gin had more of an effect on him than *soju*—especially if he began with a bowl or two of *makkŏlli*. From time to time he brought a bottle of dry gin back to quarters.

Hyŏn-t'ae finally felt compelled to say something. "Look at you. If you're going to drink, do it right, chump!"

"Right or wrong, the point is to get drunk, isn't it? And this dry gin definitely gets the job done."

"And screws up your stomach along with all that squid you're gobbling."

"So you've turned into a health expert. Well, regardless of what it does to my stomach, dry gin's good for my mental health. For one thing, I get a good night's sleep. Whatever's on your mind, one sip and you're out."

One night Tong-ho returned from the canteen and rummaged through his knapsack until he located the bundle of letters from Sugi. Behind the barracks he placed them on the ground and touched a match to them. They curled up, giving off smoke that rose a few inches before blending into the darkness. Tong-ho remained until every last scrap was consumed. Back inside he muttered to no one in particular: "I want more of that free and easy feeling—more."

That night Tong-ho dreamed he was alone on a bus. He was on his way to Inch'ŏn to see Sugi. There was no driver and the bus rolled along by itself. The sound of the engine numbed his ears, and the various parts of the creaking wornout chassis produced a cacophony of noise. Tong-ho considered: What if the chassis was held together by a single screw and that screw came loose? The chassis would fall into pieces. And he himself would be scattered who knows where. The bus came to a downhill stretch and built up speed. Again Tong-ho thought: it was the speed of the bus that was preventing the aging chassis from disintegrating. The moment it slowed to a stop the chassis would crinkle and collapse like a heap of ashes. But wasn't this incline none other than the dangerous downhill of Wŏnt'aei Pass? If it was, and the bus failed to make a curve, it would overturn.

"Wŏnt'aei Pass!" Tong-ho cried out. "It's Wŏnt'aei Pass!"

"Hey, pal, what are you hollering about? Wake up!"

Hyŏn-t'ae, next to Tong-ho, shook him awake. Tong-ho was soaked with sweat. Yun-gu, sleeping on the opposite side of Hyŏn-t'ae, also awoke: "Is this the guy who was telling us how well he sleeps after he drinks?"

Hyŏn-t'ae said to Tong-ho, "What the hell is Wŏnt'aei Pass?"

Tong-ho gazed into the darkness before replying, "It's between Seoul and Inch'ŏn."

"So what about it?"

Instead of responding, Tong-ho found the bottle of dry gin at the head of his bed and took several swallows. Then he rolled over in the opposite direction.

In a matter of days Tong-ho's face grew painfully haggard. His angular cheeks became sunken and his large clear eyes, bloodshot even when he was sober, were like hollows.

On a day marked by a hard frost Tong-ho received a letter from Sugi, his first contact with her in some time. On the back of the envelope was her Inch'ŏn address. She and her family must have returned home from their wartime refugee lodgings in the south. Behind the barracks he burned the letter without reading it.

"Not again!" said Hyŏn-t'ae. "You chump, that's what girls do."

"Letters can't solve the problem. I have to talk with her instead."

"What problem?"

"Better you didn't know."

The following Saturday afternoon Tong-ho approached Hyŏn-t'ae. "Could you finagle a pass for me?"

"How come?"

"Just get me the pass, will you?"

"Don't tell me you're hung up on old skin-and-bones."

"Aw, will you just—?"

"What's got into you? All you do anymore is slug booze, and I think I know why. But I also thought your mind was settled. Yet look at you."

"Actually I don't understand it myself. The only thing I know is I have to go out tonight."

"Give it up, chump, it's no use. Tomorrow we'll go someplace else and have some fun. You don't want to hang around with the same woman at a place like that. Beats me how you can get enjoyment out of it."

"Are you going to get me that pass or not?"

"Hell, have you looked in a mirror lately?"

Finally Hyŏn-t'ae arranged for a pass through the senior corporal.

"And front me three thousand hwan too, will you?"

That day, when he could wait no longer, Tong-ho left the base. To pass the time before sunset he had to wander about. It was late November and by evening a chill wind had risen. Whenever he passed a drinking place his pace slackened before he realized it. But then he would speed up and be gone. Today he would remain sober no matter what happened. For once he would confront her with a clear mind.

Headlights appeared on the army trucks passing by. Before long he would see her. Suddenly he wondered if it was really necessary to seek her out in this manner. He himself couldn't understand it. He only knew, with the certainty of established fact, that he must see her that night.

When full dusk had fallen he finally entered the plank gate. Briefly he wondered: What if she's with someone else? A woman was moving through the yard and Tong-ho asked her to call Ok-ju. The woman went inside and presently Ok-ju appeared. She approached Tong-ho and thrust her face forward as if looking into a mirror in the darkness. She reeked of cheap face powder.

"Well, who do we have here?" There was no indication that she had been drinking.

Tong-ho had already counted out two thousand hwan and he placed it in her hand.

"It's too early. Won't you come inside and have some *yakchu?*"

Without replying Tong-ho handed her the remainder of the money he'd borrowed from Hyŏn-t'ae. The extra payment appeared to release her from the obligation to entertain other customers. She led Tong-ho to the usual room, ushered him inside, then fetched an oil lamp. Then she left again, saying she'd light the firebox to warm up the room.

The lamp glass was coated with soot. A sign of neglect, it seemed to Tong-ho. He didn't recognize it, but somehow it wasn't unfamiliar. The pungent odor of fresh soil in the damp room as well as the sleeping pad laid out on the floor now seemed quite natural. Acrid smoke entered the room, telling him the firebox must have been lit. But Tong-ho found it bearable enough.

Ok-ju returned. She placed her slippers next to Tong-ho's boots and latched the door. But when she started to undress, Tong-ho stopped her.

"You can stay dressed."

Ok-ju regarded him quizzically.

"It's all right. You can lie down the way you are."

Ok-ju removed only her skirt and lay down on the sleeping pad. Tong-ho drew the quilt to her chin, rose, and extinguished the lamp. Then he lay down beside her, leaned over, and said: "Let's just sleep like this tonight. . . . And so. . . ." He brought his lips to hers. So cool. He cupped her cheeks and began to cover her face with kisses.

"_Ai!_ What are you doing?"

She turned away from him. Her breath on his ear carried no warmth.

He caressed her neck, then reached inside the quilt and slid a hand inside her clothing. Her arms sprawled atop the quilt, she made no effort to stop him. But he proceeded as if she were resisting, his fingers gradually pushing deep. His only sensation was the coarse feel of her skin; there was no smell of flesh. His hand pushed into the cleft between her breasts. Those breasts didn't feel as pliant as Sugi's. Suddenly his hand was snatched away.

"What is it with you?" She sounded vexed. "Can't we just get on with it?"

But Tong-ho felt no desire. He let his head sink back on the pillow. He reached in his pocket for a cigarette and lit up. His state of mind felt like the dark void before his eyes. He wanted very much to talk.

"Ok-ju, why is it so hard for people to break out of their own narrow walls?"

She lay where she was without replying.

"You know, it seems those walls are fixed when we're young."

"You're talking over my head. Let's get on with it and go to sleep."

But Tong-ho instead began to relate a story: "I must have been about eight. It was fall and I was doing my homework on the veranda when my cousin came by. Well, she offered me a bite of an apple. She'd already eaten about half of it. I shook my head, told her I didn't want it. My grandmother had just brought us a bunch and I'd had two. But my cousin kept that apple in front of my nose. The thing was, she wasn't being playful. She was younger than me but she looked like such a big girl—so grown-up. Well, what the heck, I took a bite. And another bite. And then another one. Suddenly she puts the apple down. And then she makes a face and starts spitting. I look at the apple and notice a spot of blood—must have come from my gums. Even way back then I felt ashamed letting someone see something about me that wasn't right. Ever since then I've been very careful about eating things like fruit unless it's been cut into sections first."

He had once told this story to Sugi. "That's so like you," she had said. "But with me you shouldn't worry about such things—please eat."

Ok-ju, though, had no response. She lay silently in the dark.

"I always think of that in connection with something else that happened," Tong-ho continued. This other incident concerned the same cousin. It was the spring of his fifth year of middle school, as he recalled it. He had returned home from school one day to find his cousin talking with his mother in her room. As he stepped up to the veranda he heard his mother ask, "Was it a lot?" He wondered what this meant. But when he slid open the door to his mother's room the conversation broke off. He noticed that his cousin's face looked thinner than usual. Before long he was able to make sense of his mother's question. He went to the toilet and saw, lying in the pit, a bloody wad of cotton. He aimed at the wad and the dark blood turned a vivid pink.

"It reminded me of flowers that had just bloomed." This story he had never told Sugi and he wondered why he was relating it to Ok-ju now.

"And then I met a woman—"

Ok-ju finally broke her silence.

"I was wondering when you'd get around to the subject of your sweetheart. Well, you can skip that part. Let's just get on with it and go to sleep. Or else have a drink."

She rose and lit the lamp.

"I'll be back with some *makkǒlli*."

Tong-ho searched his pockets. He gave her the hundred-odd hwan that was left.

She wrapped her skirt about her and left.

Tong-ho lit a cigarette.

Presently Ok-ju returned with a kettle of _makkŏlli_ and a small bowl of kimchi. No drinking bowls. She offered him the spout of the kettle. He shook his head. She brought the spout to her mouth and drank, took a breath, drank again, took another breath. She offered him the spout a second time. He shook his head. Again she brought the spout to her mouth.

"I guess my face doesn't have that big-girl look like your cousin. And maybe your loved one is . . ." A hint of a smile appeared and a pinkish liquor flush began to spread over her face.

Tong-ho concentrated on his cigarette.

Again she drank. She didn't touch the kimchi. After she had finished the entire one-quart kettle by herself she blew out the lamp.

"Just lie down like you did before."

Again she removed only her skirt before lying down. Her breathing sounded rough.

Tong-ho crushed out his cigarette. He cupped her face and put his lips to hers. The alcohol had warmed her cheeks and lips. But before he could kiss her face elsewhere she turned away from him.

"Don't waste your time. Just get on with it and go to sleep."

"You dislike me that much?"

"Listen, I know what's going on. You're looking for the one you love in me. Well, it's not going to work."

"No, you're wrong. There _is_ someone I love, but—"

"Spare me. Think about the first time you came here. You probably wished you'd never met me. You couldn't stand it here. Frankly, it wasn't very pleasant for me either. But that's fine. The main thing was to earn a few hundred hwan."

"You're right. I won't deny it. But it's different now."

"What do you mean, different?"

"The one I love is far away, too far."

"And so you're trying to look for her in me."

"No, I'm not."

"That's what you say. You think I don't know. . . . But it's no use."

She fell silent, lowered her underwear, and drew Tong-ho's hand to a spot low on her abdomen.

"Feel it. You know what that is?"

Tong-ho felt an incision in the soft flesh.

"It's all that's left."

"What happened?"

"That's where they operated. I was eight months pregnant and they cut me open and took out my dead baby. I'd just learned my husband had died in action. I guess I fainted, and fell off the veranda. . . . And there I was, helpless. Two weeks after we were married he went off to the army. I waited for the day of his return—it was all I ever wanted. We were in love, we really were. . . . Even in death he lived on inside me. He had a wart the size of a red bean in his left ear. I could see it clearly, right down to the color. No luxuries for a poor couple like us. Every once in a while we'd leave the city for a few hours. The feel of a soft breeze on my forehead, the comfort of leaning my head on his shoulder and closing my eyes, and when I opened them the reflection of sunlight on the leaves of the trees—those things were still alive for me. They kept me going."

She fell briefly silent, a still form in the darkness.

Tong-ho was amazed at this hidden side of her. She was different from the person he had thought of till now as Ok-ju the drinking house woman. As he listened to her he found himself concentrating on her breathing.

"And then those things began to lose their color. Those things I could see so clearly even when I started sleeping with other men . . . they started to fade—the wart in his ear, the shape of those leaves that reflected the sunlight. I tried to bring them back. But I couldn't. They just kept fading. . . . And now the feel of that soft breeze, I can't bring it back. And the comfort of putting my head on his shoulder, it's all gone. Only thing left is this little line on my stomach." She breathed once, deeply. "I've got to hand it to you. You made me spill it all out."

"I remember something you said once: 'Better if two people who shouldn't have fallen in love kill themselves the moment they realize they're inseparable.'"

She burst out in an irritated laugh. "Yes. And one of the gentleman you were with called me sentimental—said that in today's world snacks for drinking are better than sappy talk."

The vexed laughter of the previous moment died out and in a measured tone she said: "Love is silly. I don't hope for things like that anymore. You know something? There's nothing as heartless as the human body. This body of mine was able to rid itself of every last trace of that man." She paused for breath. "There's nothing as heartless as the flesh. Sometimes it scares me."

"I've felt that way myself."

"Your situation is different. You'll be on your way home before long, and when you get there everything will return to the way it was before. The one you love and everything else. . . ."

"Sometimes I'm not so sure."

"Of course it will. . . . Whatever it is you're scared of, it's only temporary. And I know how to get rid of it."

And with that she bent near and began to undo his pants. Her hands moved more gently than at any previous time. And even though the act itself was rather short, as always, she drew him to her more affectionately than ever before.

That night for the first time Tong-ho felt a kind of fulfillment.

Her breathing became even and regular. Tong-ho cautiously turned and observed her. Her angular features stood out in the dark. He looked for a glow, found none. He thought of Sugi. Strangely, enveloped in a kind of peaceful emptiness, he felt neither guilty nor apologetic toward her, and that was fine with him.

Before he could visit Ok-ju again his unit shipped out to the Ch'up'a Pass front.

# 8

IT WAS THE END of November but winter was already entrenched in the Ch'up'a Pass region. This area was no more than ten miles north of the Sot'ogomi base, but owing to the alpine location the difference in weather was dramatic. Wind stung the cheeks and the thud of boots against frozen earth hung in the air.

Keeping watch around the clock right at the front lines was inevitably stressful. But this kind of stress was different from having to march in temperatures in the minus twenties and thirties with the war going on all around. Perhaps this was why the cold seemed more intense here. It was necessary to stand a constant watch in these conditions to detect enemy movements and prevent spies from infiltrating across the cease-fire line.

Since Tong-ho and his comrades had arrived a week and a half earlier, heavy snow had fallen three times in the space of two days. Everywhere they looked it was white. In some areas the snow might melt only to be replaced by a fresh covering, while in shaded ravines it might linger till spring, when grassy shoots would push through it. Here, in this area entombed in winter's chill, Tong-ho's haggard body began to recover. Every day saw improvement. His face, stung by the wind, had a bluish tinge and looked swollen, but his eyes regained their clarity and luster. His drinking was under control, which meant his digestion improved and he slept better. The crunch of the sentries' boots on snow penetrated his slumber but served at the same time, curiously enough, to usher him gradually into a sounder sleep.

One day a soldier returned to quarters with a pheasant he'd captured by setting out bait at his sentry post. This was a rare event, and several of the men took the opportunity to nestle the bird in their arms and comment on it. One of them speculated that it couldn't fly because it had somehow been injured during the war; another wondered if it was blind. The same day, a liaison man returned from regimental headquarters with mail and documents. Among the letters was one from Sugi. Tong-ho had continued to receive letters from her at Sot'ogomi but these had gone unanswered. This particular letter was the thickest she had ever sent, perhaps reflecting her uncertainty during this interval.

The letter generated waves of emotion that dashed Tong-ho's composure. *Should I open it?* Granted he had made up his mind not to correspond with Sugi before his discharge. It had been impossible for him to describe in a letter the changes in his life that had taken place at Sot'ogomi. And his feelings now would not permit him to write about other matters. He preferred to wait until he could meet her in person. Afraid this most recent letter would resurrect his inner turmoil, he burned it instead.

The result, contrary to expectations, was that Tong-ho grew more troubled. What was in the letter? Wasn't it something he should know about? His decision to burn it began to seem much too hasty, cowardly even. He only wished that it was possible, in his present state of mind, to rush to Sugi and pour himself out to her. She would understand; she would forgive him. But Sugi was too far away.

He wished to forget the roiling of his emotions. If only he could be with Sugi and drink to his heart's content. It was at this moment that thoughts of Ok-ju surfaced. Said she who had treated him so gently: "Whatever it is you're scared of, it's only temporary. And I know how to get rid of it." He had had no chance to speak with her at the time of his transfer to the present post—not that he would necessarily have

taken advantage of such an opportunity. He thought the transfer
would end their relationship. And in fact he had almost forgotten her
in his four weeks here. But now that she had come to mind, he began
to waver. *I could lose these complicated feelings in that peaceful emptiness I felt with her. . . .*

Daytime leave was not permitted at the front, even on Sunday, and
overnight leave was out of the question. But Tong-ho felt compelled
to make a special request. And so he had to resort to Hyŏn-t'ae.

"You chump—are you out of your mind!" was the response.

"You've got to help me—today."

"Where is it you're off to?"

"Sot'ogomi. I'll be back tomorrow morning for sure."

"Sot'ogomi? You chump—you *are* out of your mind. Haven't you
forgotten old skin-and-bones yet, you idiot?"

"I know what I'm doing. Just get me a pass."

"Blockhead. What are we going to do with you?"

"I'll be back tomorrow morning—I promise."

"Wait a minute! You and me have hide-and-seek duty tonight."

"Hide-and-seek duty" meant standing watch at night at the edge of
the buffer zone between northern and southern forces.

"Well . . ." Tong-ho gestured with his chin toward Yun-gu, who sat
near the south-facing door mending a threadbare sock. "Yun-gu—
how about taking over for me tonight? I'll buy you a pair of socks."

Yun-gu was not enthusiastic. "Socks or no socks, two nights in a
row is asking a lot."

"Hey, don't count your chickens before they're hatched," Hyŏn-
t'ae cautioned Tong-ho. "Not even sure I can get the pass. . . . Talk
about a one-track mind. I ought to . . ." And with that Hyŏn-t'ae half-
seriously brandished a fist in Tong-ho's direction, then left.

A while later Hyŏn-t'ae returned with the pass.

"Here. And for the love of God don't pester me any more."

Tong-ho reached into his shirt pocket, extracted his pay envelope,
and counted what remained.

"Can you lend me two thousand hwan?"

"You chump." Hyŏn-t'ae produced some money he kept tucked

away inside his shirt. "Take it. It's my spending money—the whole works."

Tong-ho left immediately. The winter solstice was approaching and the sun was about as low in the sky as it gets. He walked some three miles along a twisty mountain road, and by the time he arrived at Four-Way Junction dusk had fallen. From this junction roads led east to Tongmak Village, west to Kǔmhwa, and south to Hwach'ǒn as well as north to Ch'up'a Pass. There was a checkpoint at the junction.

Displaying his pass, Tong-ho proceeded through without incident and began walking the road to Hwach'ǒn. He attempted to flag down any army truck that passed, but they all whizzed by—reluctant, apparently, to stop for a rank-and-file soldier armed with a carbine. But Tong-ho took no offense. Sot'ogomi lay no more than six miles away.

There appeared to have been a heavy snowfall here as well, and though the night was moonless the snow that flanked the road reflected the starlight and lit the way. Tong-ho thought about the woman he was going to see. Whether he really liked Ok-ju was secondary. The important thing was, she was his first sexual partner. And that thought gave rise to a vague excitement. Automatically he shifted his rifle from one shoulder to the other.

Before arriving at his destination Tong-ho purchased a bottle of gin and stuck it in his pocket. It would be nice to get drunk with Ok-ju.

As he entered the brushwood gate the errand girl caught sight of him.

"We have a guest!" she shouted toward the main room.

A young woman emerged. Tong-ho could see, even though her form was silhouetted against the lamplight leaking from within, that it was the Kangnǔng woman, the one with the missing teeth and puckered-up mouth. He asked her to call Ok-ju.

"All right," said the woman. Then, apparently unaware of her customer's identity, she went to a vacant room and opened the door.

Tong-ho remained where he was.

"Call Ok-ju for me."

"Well . . ." Finally the woman recognized Tong-ho. "Goodness—it's been quite a while," she said respectfully. After a moment's pause she added: "Ok-ju is with someone now."

Tong-ho scanned the other rooms. Two were lit and the chatter of women and guests was audible.

"Ask her to come here for a moment."

Again the Kangnŭng woman hesitated. "As I said, she's with someone." There was a brief silence. "But they should be done before long. Why don't you go in and have some *yakchu?*"

It finally registered in Tong-ho's mind that Ok-ju was entertaining a guest. He recalled the head of the Youth Corps—the man's squat, chubby build and slew-footed gait.

"It's cold out here—won't you go inside?"

"No, I'm okay here."

The Kangnŭng woman gave up and disappeared in the direction of the main room, hunched over against the chill. *Can't very well expect her to stay here with someone who doesn't appreciate her company.*

Tong-ho remained where he was for a moment, then went around to the back. None of the rooms was lit. It was utterly still. He approached the familiar room. Something told him it was the only one that was occupied. To be sure, this something was not a voice, for the room was as still as the others. It was instead a kind of living presence that seemed to emanate from that room alone. He stood silently before it. Suddenly, standing there like that, in his own eyes he seemed petty and cowardly. He should leave, he told himself. And then he heard the sound.

*Ah—ah—ah—ah*

It was a peculiar sound—a woman's voice, neither a scream nor a moan, but an urgent outcry, gradually rising, repeating itself. He began to walk away as if pushed by an irresistible force. Then just as quickly he became stock-still. Something was gnawing at him. *"There's nothing as heartless as the flesh—this body of mine was able to rid itself of every last trace of that man—sometimes it scares me."* He felt as if inside himself he was being chafed by sand. And in a flash that sand was transformed grain by grain into a burning heat. He was overcome with rage and his body tightened.

Tong-ho surveyed his surroundings. Nearer the building the ground was bare and dark; farther off it was snow-covered and not so dim. There—a small back gate next to a brushwood enclosure. He steeled himself, approached the gate, unlatched it. He drew close to the room, which was quiet now, and tested the lattice door. Locked. He smashed it in with the barrel of his rifle. Then leveled the muzzle and twice pulled the trigger. Whether the man with Ok-ju was the head of the Youth Corps didn't matter. Their mingled screams followed him out through the rear gate.

The occasional truck and jeep passed by on the road. At first Tong-ho was oblivious to them. But after covering some three miles he grew nervous realizing he was visible in the headlights. The vehicles approaching from behind were more worrisome. By now there had been ample time for the Kangnŭng woman to report the identity of the perpetrator. They could be pursuing him at this instant. He tried to keep as far from the roadside as possible.

Apparently the checkpoint at Four-Way Junction hadn't been notified, and he passed through without incident.

Steam rose from Tong-ho's face and neck. He was back at the Ch'up'a Pass base.

"What happened to _you?_ Your face is white as a sheet," said Hyŏn-t'ae. His watch was drawing near and he was preparing to go out. Eyeing Tong-ho dubiously, he added: "So you changed your mind and came back? Good idea."

Without a word Tong-ho returned the two thousand hwan he had borrowed.

"I guess you didn't get my socks?" said Yun-gu, who was likewise preparing to stand watch.

Tong-ho made no response. Crawling over the sprawled-out forms of sleeping soldiers, he located his knapsack and took out some writing paper and an envelope. Then he made room, sat, and settled himself.

Hyŏn-t'ae had not removed his eyes from Tong-ho. "Inspiration strikes and the chump has to write a poem. But hey—what's the hurry? There's no light over there—how can you see?"

The cramped quarters consisted of dried-earth walls and a single south-facing door where a tin can had been fashioned into a kerosene lamp. Except for a five-foot circle of flickering light, darkness filled the interior.

Hyŏn-t'ae donned his cold-weather hat. "Time to head out. You going to be all right, Tong-ho? Why don't you stay here and get some rest?"

Tong-ho, sitting silently in the thick gloom, folded the sheet of paper, placed it in the envelope, then stuck it in his shirt pocket. He rose and followed Hyŏn-t'ae outside.

The air was icy. With every breath Tong-ho could feel the hairs in his nostrils freeze. The perspiration on his body had not yet dried and sent shivers up and down his spine. He realized he had forgotten his gloves.

They passed the frontline sentry post and when they arrived at the buffer zone Tong-ho reached in his pocket and produced the bottle of gin.

"What have you got there?" said Hyŏn-t'ae.

Tong-ho silently uncapped the bottle, took several swallows, and passed it to Hyŏn-t'ae.

"So you made it to Sot'ogomi after all." Hyŏn-t'ae likewise drank from the bottle. "I figured you were gone too long to have turned back midway. I guess you didn't get to see her?"

"Uh-uh."

"Move on down the line, did she?"

Without a word Tong-ho took the bottle from Hyŏn-t'ae and drank.

"Those women don't stick around for long. Well, it's better that way—now you can stop worrying your little head."

Tong-ho brought the bottle to his mouth again.

"Hey, come on! You don't want to get tanked out here. You sit down and nod off drunk like that, you'll never wake up!"

"Hyŏn-t'ae, remember Corporal Kim, the guy we used to call

Trouble? Remember what Yun-gu had him saying—'Feel like I was on a roll and they cut the game short'? I think I understand what he was talking about."

"What do you mean?"

"I mean, what I'd like to know is, are we the victims or the victimizers?"

Hyŏn-t'ae gazed attentively at Tong-ho. The cloud of vapor issuing from his nostrils seemed to be more than just the result of alcohol.

"Did something happen to you today?"

"The way I look at it, the young people serving in this war are victims—no matter what they may have done. Okay, maybe 'young people' is too fancy a way to put it. But just look at the ones we've known—Corporal Kim for starters, and Sergeant Sŏnu, and . . ."

The pair of sentries on duty approached them, one from the left and one from the right. It seemed that Hyŏn-t'ae and Tong-ho were late. Hyŏn-t'ae and Tong-ho parted and set off in the directions from which the other pair had come.

Stars studded the sky, cold as shards of ice. The snow-covered ground lay white in the starlight, but the farther off you looked, the dimmer the light until finally it blended into darkness.

Hyŏn-t'ae heard the shattering of glass. He looked back, telling himself it was Tong-ho throwing away the gin bottle. _The chump, something happened to him today—the guy is such a simpleton._ Tong-ho's white parka had become indistinguishable from the snow, then had been swallowed by darkness; he could no longer be seen. Hyŏn-t'ae returned his gaze to the buffer zone and resumed walking. He knew this area was off limits for smoking, but for some reason he felt a continual urge to light up.

It was two hours later, when the next pair of sentries arrived, that Tong-ho's body was found. His blood, black in the darkness, had frozen on the snow. The artery in his left wrist had been severed. Half buried in the snow beside his left hand was a piece of broken glass. His face was white as the snow.

The body was placed in front of the men's quarters, a fire lit, and a vigil held for the remainder of the night. The corpse yielded a thousand-odd hwan and an envelope—the one he had stuck in his pocket before going out to stand watch. On the envelope was written the name *Chang Suk*. As one of the men was about to inspect the contents, Hyŏn-t'ae took the letter from him and slipped it into his pocket.

In early April, when meltwater began flowing in the mountain valleys, the first round of student-soldiers was discharged.

Yun-gu was the first to receive his notice. Though discharges were based on year and month of entry, the procedure took place rank by rank instead of across all ranks. The day he was to leave, Yun-gu bid farewell to the sergeants. "I'll write as soon as I'm settled," he told Hyŏn-t'ae, then said good-bye, a look of delight spreading across his swarthy face.

"You're going back to that family where you were tutoring? Good for you. Lucky SOB—unlike some of us," said Hyŏn-t'ae.

Yun-gu had lost his parents as a boy, then moved in with the family of his father's younger brother. But that family had been killed by a bomb during the war, and from that point on, Yun-gu was on his own. Yun-gu had been in touch with the family where he was a live-in tutor before the war, and as luck would have it they had written that they would welcome him back to look after the younger brother of the boy he had taught.

Yun-gu set down his knapsack and tightened the drawstring.

"If our pal Tong-ho was alive, he would have gotten out before me."

Hyŏn-t'ae, about to light a cigarette, responded: "That reminds me, I have that last letter he wrote to his sweetheart. What am I supposed to do with it? There's no address."

"The chump must have flipped out—how could a man forget something like that?"

"In his case a last letter couldn't be that important anyway. . . . Well, see you in Seoul."

"What the hell, it's all over now. And about frigging time too."

Hyŏn-t'ae put the lighter to his cigarette and spoke slowly: "We have our own lives to lead."

# Part Two

# 9

WHEN CHRISTMAS DAY arrives with a driving rain instead of
snow, people tend to expect a mild winter. But contrary to expectations the new year ushered in a cold snap and several days of intense
cold. Around five in the afternoon on one such day Yun-gu set out for
the Kwigŏrae Tearoom in Kwanggyo for the usual Saturday night get-
together. The date was January 5, 1957.

Sŏk-ki was already there. He was reading a newspaper, his forehead virtually touching the page. His hazy gaze rose at Yun-gu's
approach.

"Is that you?"

"Well now, what happened to your glasses?"

"Aw, they got broken last night. . . . Did you know Hyŏn-t'ae got
arrested?"

"He did?"

"They think he's a draft dodger."

"How could that be? What about his discharge notice?"

"That's just the thing."

The previous afternoon Hyŏn-t'ae and Sŏk-ki had watched a movie
at the Kukche Theater and then left for a billiard hall in Mugyo-dong
where, just as they turned down an alley, a policeman asked them for

identification. Sŏk-ki's guess was that Hyŏn-t'ae's appearance had caught the policeman's eye. Hyŏn-t'ae was a handsome man but his seedy looks betrayed this fact: the bushy, unkempt hair, the willful, scraggly beard, the shabby overcoat, the muddy shoes. At some point he had lost interest in grooming himself, and this tendency had grown more pronounced.

"I show the policeman my discharge notice," said Sŏk-ki. "No problem. But guess what our pal does—he pulls out his citizen's ID! 'Where's your discharge notice?' I ask him. He says he lost it somewhere."

"You two must have been boozing."

"Nope. Did that the night before and we were out pretty late. That's probably why he snored through the movie. But the funny thing is, when the policeman's about to take him away he says for me not to tell his family."

"So did you?"

"Well, sure. I had to say *something*."

"Okay, you did the right thing."

"Yeah, so I called the Governor and then I tried again this morning but they hadn't heard anything. I told them to keep checking, since he was arrested for sure. Think I should call them again?"

"Don't bother. Either he's still locked up or he's on his way here."

Sŏk-ki nevertheless rose ponderously, his frame looming large even without the help of an overcoat, and made his way to the phone on the counter. He picked up the receiver, brought his face close to the instrument, and dialed. At one time he had made a name for himself as a boxer and used to hold an amateur middleweight title. But during the war he had been wounded in the eye during a skirmish on the eastern front and now he couldn't distinguish objects even close-up without glasses.

Sŏk-ki returned, his squinting gaze accompanied by a frown. "They said he's not back yet. What in hell do you suppose happened to him?"

Yun-gu picked up the newspaper and said absentmindedly, "Well, so much for the Saturday gathering."

Since the previous spring, after Yun-gu had started a poultry farm on the Ttŏkchŏn Road outside of Ch'ŏngnyangni, he, Hyŏn-t'ae, and Sŏk-ki had been meeting every Saturday. By that time Hyŏn-t'ae and Sŏk-ki, friends since middle school, were drinking together every day. At first Yun-gu had declined out of respect for the family who employed him as a live-in tutor. Then, after becoming involved with the daughter of this family, he had occasionally gone out drinking with Hyŏn-t'ae. But the poultry farm now occupied most of his time so that he was unable to go downtown very often. For this reason he had set aside Saturday as the one time each week that he would see his friends. The gatherings had no other purpose than idle talk and drinking, and for some time had been taking place merely from force of habit.

So there they were: Saturday but no Hyŏn-t'ae. Granted the absence of any one of the three was bound to dampen the mood of the gathering. But especially so in the case of Hyŏn-t'ae. Even if it wasn't Hyŏn-t'ae who had suggested the gatherings in the first place, he was their nucleus, the one who kept the meetings alive by his willingness to assume practically the entire cost of the drinks.

Yun-gu was occupied with the newspaper headlines. On the front page: "Shooting of Vice-President Chang Probed"; "Assembly Team Launches Investigation." On the city page: "Clothes Stolen Off Child's Back"; "Food Shortage Affects 500-Plus Farm Homes: The Situation in Wando County"; "Food Shortage Affects 20,000-Plus Farm Homes: Statistics for North Kyŏngsang."

"So what are we going to do? You feel like waiting a little longer?"

Yun-gu checked the market prices for eggs on page 2, then folded the paper. "I don't think he's coming. But I'm sure he'll be okay. The Governor has some clout, you know."

"Well, that leaves you and me. So let's go have a drink."

Ever since Sŏk-ki had given up boxing as a result of his eye injury, he had found it an ordeal to pass an evening without drinking. His sturdy body, moreover, had endowed him with a tremendous capacity for alcohol.

They left for their favorite drinking spot, a place within range of the tearoom. It was a home, it had no sign, and those who managed to find it generally became regulars. A vacant room always awaited the three friends there on a Saturday evening. They emptied the first pint kettle and Sŏk-ki wasted no time ordering a second one from the serving boy.

Yun-gu observed the gleam of intoxication that had appeared in Sŏk-ki's hazy, listless eyes. "You must have outdone yourself with the booze last night. Breaking your glasses and all."

"Yeah, I was drunk all right. But a couple of guys provoked me and I had to nail one of 'em. They were saying that amateurs fix fights just like the pros. I can't ignore stuff like that. So somehow my glasses fell off but, hey, my punch was right on the money."

Sŏk-ki slowly brought his drink to his lips. "I hope that son of a gun's all right."

Yun-gu gazed at Sŏk-ki's broad shoulders and wondered if he should be getting into a drinking bout with this friend who normally looked so gentle and yet occasionally got violent when intoxicated. Another thought occurred to him almost immediately: He could pay for the drinks this once. Still, that wouldn't help him predict when his friend might be ready to leave. And what would he do if Sŏk-ki insisted on visiting the women on the third block of Chongno and who knows where else?

A third pint kettle arrived. Yun-gu made up his mind to leave when this kettle was empty. He poured Sŏk-ki a drink.

"That son of a gun isn't going to show up," Sŏk-ki sulked. "He must have really got himself in a pickle."

Yun-gu decided to voice his thoughts, though he doubted Sŏk-ki would understand. It was true that his well-known boxer friend was a former law student, but he was also slow-witted.

"Look, Sŏk-ki, here's what I think. Even if our buddy was released I don't think he's coming here. He says he's lost his discharge notice, he says not to tell his family, he's nice and obedient when the policeman leads him away. You know what? I think it's all an excuse. I think what he really wants to do is quit getting together on Saturdays. We're just meeting out of boredom, and he wants out. See?"

Sŏk-ki directed a slit-eyed frown at Yun-gu but remained silent.

"Fact is," Yun-gu went on, "we should have called it quits earlier. Dragging things on till now isn't making us better friends. We do this out of habit, that's all."

Sŏk-ki took in Yun-gu's gaze and finally he answered, gesturing with his drink for effect: "You make it sound so complicated. Three friends who think alike and we need a list of reasons to go out once a week for drinks. Is that what you're telling me? I've heard enough. Come on, let's take today for what it is and have ourselves another drink."

"Fine. Help yourself. I've had my fill."

"Don't be a chickenshit. Tell you what—drink up the cost of a dozen eggs and then you can go."

They sat silently, emptying their drinks. And then the door creaked open and Hyŏn-t'ae's head poked inside.

"Hah! Wouldn't you know it!"

"You son of a gun!" Sŏk-ki's slit eyes gleamed. "Get in here, you no-good!" he called out in genuine delight.

"What in hell happened to you?" asked Yun-gu, his face purple with drink.

"Gentlemen, if you want an answer, you'll have to give me a snort. I'm dying of thirst."

Hyŏn-t'ae promptly emptied the drink Yun-gu poured him, then turned to Sŏk-ki: "You bum, I told you absolutely not to say anything to my family. . . . You two think I didn't show my discharge notice because I lost it? Well, that's not how it happened. I _planned_ it that way."

Sŏk-ki produced a weak smile. "That's a new one. You son of a gun. But there was no way I could keep my mouth shut."

"So why did you do it?" Yun-gu added.

"I felt like giving up drinking and it seemed like a good idea at the time, going to jail. Can't very well quit when I'm with you two."

"So a lot of good it did you getting out. Did the Governor himself show up to bail you out?"

"Uh-uh."

Hyŏn-t'ae went on to explain. He had been taken to a detention center for draft evaders. After a time someone had called out his name and asked him to come forward. Hyŏn-t'ae realized then that his father had sent someone for him. But he had ignored the summons, sitting silently in a corner, face turned away. That morning his name was announced again but he pretended not to hear.

"But when it got close to five o'clock I felt antsy—didn't want to sit there anymore. So I showed them my discharge notice."

Yun-gu fitted a cigarette into his holder. "Of course. You couldn't stand to miss the Saturday get-together, right?"

Hyŏn-t'ae grinned, his white teeth showing through his long, sparse growth of beard. His face was haggard.

"Don't kid yourself. I figured you two wouldn't show up. So I thought I'd have a drink all by myself right here in this room."

"Cut the crap and bottoms up."

"Hey, what happened to your glasses? I'm gone for one day and look at you!"

Several rounds of drinks were consumed. Now that Hyŏn-t'ae had cleared the air and showed an inclination to take charge of the gathering, Yun-gu was able to relax. He felt the drinks spread a warm glow throughout his body as he listened to Sŏk-ki give Hyŏn-t'ae a blow-by-blow account of his fight the previous evening.

After Sŏk-ki had returned to his drink, Yun-gu asked Hyŏn-t'ae: "How many got hauled in last night?"

"Quite a few—probably thirty in my group alone. I imagine they'll ship 'em down to Nonsan tomorrow." And then Hyŏn-t'ae seemed to think of something. "It was kind of a rough night, but one good thing came out of it. One of the other guys was a friend of mine who's got an orchard outside the Chaha Gate. He told me an interesting story. He said plants have instincts. Fruit trees, anyway, definitely have an instinct to preserve the species. So when you prune them, what you're actually doing is taking advantage of that instinct. If you don't prune them you get mostly leaves and less fruit. It's like the tree is thinking, 'Well, since I'm strong and healthy, I can take my time producing.'

It's only when you prune it that you get it to thinking, 'Damn, they're chopping off my branches, there won't be much fruit, I'd better start producing, keep the species going.' And that's when you get it to bear. Well, with people it's exactly the same. Generally, you don't find many children in a well-off family. But a poor family will have lots of children. The same instinct's at work. Now how about that? Makes sense, doesn't it?"

*Drunk again,* thought Yun-gu. *Listen to him rattle on.* His cigarette had burned down to the holder but he continued to puff on it. After his discharge he no longer cut his cigarettes in half. Instead he had bought the holder, made of artificial ivory, so that he could smoke his cigarettes to the very end.

"And so I have an idea—I'm going to write a research paper. I'll call it 'The Pruning of Fruit Trees and the Future of Mankind.' What do you think? First I'll argue that with humans there's one class that has to be pruned and another class that can be left to grow at their own pace. And then I'll suggest that unless these two classes are handled the right way, the day will come when the human race dies out. Now there's a paper that ought to generate some interest, eh? Even if you two probably can't appreciate its true value."

Hyŏn-t'ae paused to wet his throat, then continued.

"I want to write a preface too. I want to say that my motive for writing this essay is to bring to light the contributions of our Saturday Club. Actually the Saturday Club members themselves represent a class that needs spiritual pruning. Thing is, though, this essay is going to be huge. I'm not so sure I can finish it in my lifetime."

"Sounds like you're talking yourself into believing you won't write it in the first place," said Yun-gu.

"It's not a matter of whether I write it or not, but whether I can remember what I just said and get on with my life."

An alcohol-induced gleam escaped through Sŏk-ki's narrow eyelids. "Don't get serious with us, you son of a gun. Are you saying you want to break up the club?"

"Not the club, but me myself, the way I am now."

"What's that supposed to mean?"

"Just as well if you don't know. All right, give me that glass and fill 'er up."

It was after ten when they left. Sŏkki lived in nearby Kwanhun-dong. When they reached the broad avenue of Ch'ŏnggyech'ŏn he turned to Hyŏn-t'ae.

"Hey—let's go to that place, the one with all the good girls."

"Not today."

"Then how about another drink?"

Yun-gu checked his watch and said, "Let's call it a night instead."

"You sons of guns are breaking up the club and I'm not going to forgive you."

"What you need to worry about is getting yourself home in one piece," said Hyŏn-t'ae. "And don't get hit by a car."

"If I do, the car will get the worst of it."

"You dimwit! I'm going to have to buy you a new pair of glasses."

"Yeah?"

"Meet me at the Yangji around two tomorrow."

Sŏk-ki trudged off. Hyŏn-t'ae and Yun-gu set off in the direction of the Hwashin Department Store.

"Guy's walking even slower than usual. Probably can't see where he's going. He's always been kind of a slowpoke anyway. Can't figure out how a guy like that ever became a boxer. Though I have to admit I never saw him in the ring. . . . Anyway, he's got his good points."

Hyŏn-t'ae imagined the massive Sŏk-ki flailing at the air with his fists. *You get an explosion right in the face, sure does make you loopy—knocks you down.* Sŏk-ki had talked about his eye injury at the front as if it had happened to someone else. *Never took a punch like that before. Not going to stay down, though. Back on your feet, but everything's dark, can't see a thing. Start flailing away, don't connect once. Pound at the air for a while, then down for the count.* Though Hyŏn-t'ae had never seen Sŏk-ki box, he found it easier than he imagined to reconstruct the scene.

At the first block of Chongno they arrived at the bus stop for Chungnyanggyo.

"How about a hot drink?" said Hyŏn-t'ae. "I need to talk to you for a minute."

Nearby was a second-floor tearoom. Hyŏn-t'ae led the way up. Yun-gu checked his watch again—a little past ten-thirty. Still time before the last bus. As he followed Hyŏn-t'ae up the steps he tried to guess what his friend wanted to talk about. For a fleeting moment he wondered if it was Hyŏn-t'ae's relationship with Mi-ran, the daughter of the family that had taken in Yun-gu as a tutor. Perhaps it was Hyŏn-t'ae who had made Mi-ran the way she was.

Cheerful Mi-ran: always ready to tell Yun-gu she liked Hyŏn-t'ae. Although she had given herself up to Yun-gu at the time, she was not the sort to keep quiet about her liking for another man. Instead you'd expect her to express it in some form of action. What had been Hyŏn-t'ae's attitude, though? Was that what he wanted to talk about now?

After they had ordered, however, Hyŏn-t'ae asked if a woman had visited Yun-gu in the past day or two. Yun-gu said no. Hyŏn-t'ae lit a cigarette.

"Well, Tong-ho's old girlfriend showed up. Sugi—remember? She looked me up a couple of days ago. Tong-ho must have told her about us in his letters."

"That would have been more than three years ago. He died the winter after the cease-fire. What do you suppose she wants now?"

"You never know with women. From the looks of her she isn't married."

"That makes her an old maid—she's close to thirty for sure. And those are the ones who have their noses in the air."

"Her case is different. After three years she wants to know about her boyfriend. Said she has to find out why he killed himself. I told her I didn't know and sent her on her way."

"What about that letter you found on his body?"

"What good's that piece of paper going to do her now? I can't even remember what I did with it. And I don't see the need for her to be digging up the past and making a nuisance of herself. What's there to gain? So I said I didn't know, and so long. But she has your address, so maybe you're next on her list. I wasn't going to give it to her. But then I figured I might as well since she'd probably manage to find you anyway. If she does find you, probably best to tell her something that sounds reasonable and then send her on her way."

After leaving the tearoom Yun-gu caught the bus for Chungnyanggyo while Hyŏn-t'ae crossed the streetcar tracks and turned toward Insa-dong. Hyŏn-t'ae's home was in nearby Chae-dong.

A few steps up the street to Insa-dong Hyŏn-t'ae decided, as was his wont from time to time, to see Kye-hyang, the dull-witted girl at the Pyongyang House. And so he turned down the alley that led to Nagwŏn-dong. Absolutely no emotion played on the powdered face of this nineteen-year-old girl; it all seemed stored up in the chill, absolute white of her complexion. When she was somehow able to manage a smile, it gave the impression that the slight spread of lips was something mechanical, an external phenomenon that bore no relation to her inner emotions. It simply made her small, white, densely spaced teeth appear even colder. Hyŏn-t'ae found this characteristic to his liking, but he could not have explained why.

It was after eleven when he arrived at the Pyongyang House. The only customers were a pair of middle-aged men at the serving counter and a younger man, probably a company type, quite drunk, who sat in a corner mumbling to himself.

A woman hunched over a coal-briquette stove saw Hyŏn-t'ae and in a strong P'yŏngan accent welcomed him with obvious delight. "Been a while since I laid eyes on you. Go ahead, go on in," she said, indicating a room behind the kitchen.

Hyŏn-t'ae had discovered the Pyongyang House quite by accident and the first few times he had visited, the woman had made no attempt to conceal her reluctance to serve a man with his appearance. But when she finally realized he was never stingy with his money she was only too happy to usher him to this room.

Having done so, she proceeded to tell him the story of her life. By now he had heard more than once how the woman had lived in Pyongyang before the liberation from the Japanese in 1945, and there had taken in Kye-hyang and raised her with an eye to someday making her a *kisaeng*. And with equal frequency he had heard how in the spring of the following year, having lost everything, she had placed eight-year-old Kye-hyang on her back and suffered the most awful hardships in order to cross south of that horrible thirty-eighth parallel. And when she concluded her lengthy story this woman in her forties whose eyes still retained a trace of beauty never failed to put her mouth to Hyŏn-t'ae's ear and whisper: "And the girl is still an honest-to-goodness virgin—you can tell from how innocent and bashful she is." Hyŏn-t'ae's response was always to nod to the woman and then observe Kye-hyang. Whether the girl was a genuine virgin or not was of no particular interest to him. From the very beginning she had projected no scent of carnality but rather a sort of arrested sexuality. Hyŏn-t'ae, even so, experienced brief moments of repose in the presence of this cold, stony girl. This rare opportunity he wished to enjoy undisturbed, and so he had not told Sŏk-ki about the Pyongyang House.

"Do you have any idea how that girl's been expecting you since last time?" the woman now asked.

The interval in question was less than a week. But one week or even two, it was most unlikely that Kye-hyang had been waiting for him. The woman was exaggerating and Hyŏn-t'ae knew it. With Kye-hyang he was free to come and go as he pleased, and this too he found enticing.

"Something tells me you've found another place. But it won't do you any good."

More than half a year had passed—it hadn't seemed that long—since Hyŏn-t'ae had first set foot in the Pyongyang House. By then he had already fallen into a state of lethargy. After his discharge he had finished college and then joined his father's business, where he had proved a zealous worker. And then one morning a change had come over him, a transformation that baffled those around him. He was taking a taxi to work, and it pulled up at a stop light. Glancing outside, he had noticed a woman in shabby clothes crossing the intersection. Clutched to her bosom was a child of perhaps two. The child might have been sick: the face was sallow, the eyes closed, the mouth half open. As the woman crossed the intersection she clutched the little thing as if it were the most precious object in the world. Suddenly Hyŏn-t'ae felt as if he had seen this mother and child somewhere. A murky room; a young child lying absolutely still, a shriveled arm outside the cover; the mother of the child. *When I went back down there she wasn't the least bit surprised to see me. She wasn't scared like she was in the afternoon. She didn't put up much resistance either. But guess what—when I get up she grabs me by the hand. Well, I knew what that meant. She's scared, and she wants me to stay with her. Can't very well do that, can I? So I got rid of her. Simple as that.*

Hyŏn-t'ae looked down at his hands. They still held the sensation of the woman's quivering hand and the damp of its perspiration. The sensation of the neck, the warmth of dry skin. The little one he hadn't touched. But as he sat in the taxi he experienced a vivid sensation of pressing down on its dry, slender neck. That night he had drunk and drunk. And so too the next night, and the next.

As the Pyongyang House woman was sliding the door shut Hyŏn-t'ae said: "*Ajumŏni,* could you hurry it up with the drinks?"

"And the girl too?"

With a twinkle in her eye the woman disappeared toward the serving counter. A short while later Kye-hyang appeared with a small serving table.

"Hello."

The greeting was polite but bereft of emotion. Kye-hyang took her place at the far side of the table. She sat erect, right knee raised, hands placed atop it. The woman had doubtless instructed her to maintain that posture with a guest, and Kye-hyang had never relaxed it. The only exception was when she served a drink. She would then take the kettle in her right hand and respectfully place her left hand at the cuff of the right sleeve. The motion was mechanical.

Hyŏn-t'ae felt close to exhaustion. His stay in the cold, uncomfortable detention center, though only a day, had left him tired, and now

he felt even more languid. It was almost as if his head were clearing
from the drinks he had consumed with his friends. Almost without
realizing it he tasted repose as he emptied a new drink, and then
another, while observing Kye-hyang's expressionless face, her regular
features neatly made up and so like a plaster mask, the repose that
came from not having to talk or exchange sentiments with her.

The curfew warning siren sounded and the woman returned to sit
beside Hyŏn-t'ae, who realized she must have seen off the two men at
the serving counter. Hyŏn-t'ae passed her his empty glass and filled it.
When she wasn't busy the woman was only too happy to be treated to
drinks. Never, though, did she allow Kye-hyang to be offered a drink.
She was Kye-hyang's teacher, and when she referred to her as a
"genuine virgin" she meant that the girl, despite living in a drinking
house, was so much an innocent that alcohol had never touched her
lips. The woman, her temples flushed from her drinks, lit a cigarette,
drew several times, and then, as she always did, began a litany of
grievances.

"You figure it, *sŏnsaeng-nim*. I leave everything behind, put the
girl on my back, cross the thirty-eighth parallel, and here I am, a low-
class woman who sells booze. I didn't plan it this way. I thought when
that one began to look like a woman maybe I could have myself a nice
little restaurant. Or at least a Pyongyang-style grill. I wanted to be
respectable and it tears me up that I can't."

Hyŏn-t'ae normally let the words pass by, always the same from
one telling to the next, but this time he answered. "What about the
township magistrate?" he said, referring respectfully to this man.
"You could ask him to finance you."

The man in question, now perhaps fifty, vice-magistrate of a township in the Pyongyang area before the liberation, was a regular at the
Pyongyang House. According to the woman, he operated a shop near
Tongdaemun that made socks, and he did a good business. This man
was always received with ample food and drink in the inner quarters
of the Pyongyang House. Once when Hyŏn-t'ae was returning from
the bathroom he had spotted him sitting next to the woman as she

held open the door to the kitchen to order something. Despite the man's age he had a full head of black hair and his face seemed freshly shaved.

Hyŏn-t'ae suspected there was a special relationship between the former magistrate and the Pyongyang House woman—thus his suggestion.

"That tightwad?" the woman said. "Don't be silly." She looked up, snorted, and exhaled a stream of smoke.

Hyŏn-t'ae decided he wanted no more of the woman's story, so he asked that Kye-hyang sing.

"This late at night?" But the woman seemed reluctant to turn down Hyŏn-t'ae's request. To Kye-hyang she said: "Sweetie, how about that song the gentleman likes. Just once."

Kye-hyang's repertoire wasn't exactly a moneymaker but merely a grab bag of popular folksongs. One of them was the Cheju Island folksong she always sang if Hyŏn-t'ae asked for a song. Hyŏn-t'ae tried to remember when it had caught his fancy. Normally he took little pleasure from singing at places like the Pyongyang House. But the woman had once asked Kye-hyang to sing, and the girl's offerings had included the Cheju song. Hyŏn-t'ae had found himself requesting it ever since. Especially that first verse: *Gone, my husband . . .*

Kye-hyang's voice was clear and resonant. As the Pyongyang House woman had said, with a little money for singing lessons the girl might have developed into a first-rate *kisaeng*. Hyŏn-t'ae, who knew little about singing, was in no position to judge. What he did know was that Kye-hyang's clear voice, like everything else about her, held no trace of emotion. Her pale face always held that stony, expressionless look, a look that betrayed no irritation at his numerous requests for the same verse. And her singing reminded him of a scratched record that skipped and constantly repeated. But this did not lessen his enjoyment of his drinks.

It was after curfew when Hyŏn-t'ae left the Pyongyang House. He felt drunker moving about than when seated there. His legs wobbled. The intermittent streetlights stood frosty and alone. The buildings kept a mute silence in the dark. Hyŏn-t'ae's unsteady footfalls on the frozen earth sounded unnaturally loud. Hummed words began to escape with the vapor of his breath:

> Blow, you wind, you raging wind . . .
> Day by day and night by night,
> Our true and steadfast love . . .

He had just passed Chae-dong Elementary School when he heard a voice from an alley to his left.

"Excuse me!"

Hyŏn-t'ae ignored the voice and staggered ahead.

> Gone, my husband, out to sea. . . .

A figure caught up with him—a policeman making his rounds.

"Who do you think you are?"

Hyŏn-t'ae tottered forward without looking around.

"I'm me."

"And who is 'me'?" said the patrolman, blocking Hyŏn-t'ae's path.

"Me is me, that's who. Want to see? Here we go, ID card . . . and my precious discharge notice. I take it with me wherever I go."

"Do you have any idea what time it is?"

"Nope."

"Why you—" The patrolman yanked Hyŏn-t'ae's arm. "Let's go!"

At that moment Hyŏn-t'ae slouched toward the man, embraced his neck, and planted a wet kiss on his face. The patrolman grunted in disgust and gave Hyŏn-t'ae a shove that knocked him to the seat of his pants. Then he retreated a couple of steps and began to spit repeatedly.

Hyŏn-t'ae rose and rushed toward the patrolman, arms out-stretched. To avoid Hyŏn-t'ae's clutches the man retreated, then turned and walked off. When Hyŏn-t'ae proceeded to chase him, he began to run.

Hyŏn-t'ae came to a stop. "Mister Policeman, you can't fool me, no sir!" he shouted. "You figure on going to the station and you think maybe I'll follow—it's not going to work, no sir! You think you can fool me with my mind as clear as a bell? Don't even try. Tell you what—I'll buy you a drink! Come on back! . . . Don't worry, I'm not going to kiss you!"

The patrolman looked back from a distance. He seemed to consider, then returned to Hyŏn-t'ae.

"If you can tell me where you live I'll take you there," the patrolman said, his tone more polite. "Let's go."

"I can find it myself. First let's go somewhere and have a drink. . . . You know, I kind of like you somehow."

The patrolman gently led the insistent Hyŏn-t'ae away.

"Do you have any idea what time it is? The bars all closed a long time ago."

"That case we'll go to my place for a drink."

Presently Hyŏn-t'ae had an arm draped over the patrolman's shoulder and was walking along with his support.

"Mister Policeman, sir, may I sing you a song? *Gone, my husband* —Not so loud, you say? Okay, I'll do it nice and quiet. . . . *Gone, my husband, out to sea, Blow, you wind, you raging wind, Blow three months and ten.* . . . How's that? Mister Policeman, sir, I said 'How's that?' . . . Aren't you going to answer me? . . . Aw, what a policeman you turned out to be. All right, I'll teach you the words. . . . Goes like this: *Day by day and night by night, Our true and steadfast love.* . . . Got it, officer? . . . All right, here's another one for you. . . . Why do people prune fruit trees? . . . Don't know? . . . Well, that's only natural, I suppose. . . . Just one thing you do need to know: you're the only man who doesn't need pruning."

# 10

YUN-GU'S ROUTINE first thing in the morning was to check the
hens and note the weather report in the newspaper. On this particular
day northeasterly winds were forecast, with clear skies in the morning
yielding to clouds in the afternoon. Temperatures would remain cold
for the next few days. Yun-gu frowned when his eyes met this last
part of the forecast. The current cold snap had been sudden and
severe and had suppressed the hens' production for days.

Early the previous spring Yun-gu, with Hyŏn-t'ae's support, had
started a poultry farm on a small plot of land off the Ttŏkchŏn Road
beyond Ch'ŏngnyangni. At one side of the plot he had thrown up a
frame structure consisting of three heated-floor rooms for the chicks
and a fourth room for living quarters. And then, at that time of year
when forsythias still bloom in the shady areas, he had purchased
seven hundred chicks from a hatchery. Yun-gu prepared his own
meals and took on an errand boy to help with chores. Two months
later he built a henhouse and transferred the chicks. After reading
books on the subject and talking with people who had experience in
poultry farming, he decided he should concentrate on keeping the
chickens properly fed and free of disease. But within six months—
the time it took for the chickens to begin to lay—he had had to cull

seventy-odd males from the flock and a hundred of the chickens had died. Still, for a first effort you could consider these results a success.

At the Saturday drinking session Yun-gu told Hyŏn-t'ae that the hens had begun to lay.

"What excitement!" Hyŏn-t'ae joked. "Looking at chickens' hind ends day in and day out!" Friendly drunken banter, to be sure, but this was not to say that the mention of "excitement" was without foundation.

After his discharge Yun-gu had worked his way through college as a live-in tutor to a middle school boy. Subsequently the boy's father had arranged for Yun-gu to find work at a bank in downtown Seoul. Hyŏn-t'ae had demanded to be treated on this occasion and had dragged Yun-gu to a drinking place.

"Didn't I tell you there'd be a bank manager's job waiting when you started losing your hair?" he had jested.

But less than six months later Yun-gu's bank position had come to an abrupt end when his affair with Mi-ran, the middle school boy's older sister, had an unexpected outcome. Upon starting the bank job Yun-gu had found lodging at a boardinghouse. There he was visited frequently by Mi-ran. A fourteen-year-old with peach fuzz on her face when the war broke out, she was now an attractive young woman of twenty-two. Even in his absence she came to visit, tidying the desk and rearranging the various items hanging from the walls. She was by nature a cheerful, dynamic girl, and when Seoul was occupied during the war and Yun-gu had to hide beneath the veranda to avoid detection by enemy troops, she had helped him by keeping watch over movements outside and letting him out for fresh air when it was safe.

Such was the woman who one day arrived at Yun-gu's boardinghouse room, extracted an object from her pocket, and thrust it at him. "*Sŏnsaeng-nim*, would you put this on for me, please?" It was a gold-plated lipstick tube. Yun-gu eyed the tube dubiously, for he had never seen her use lipstick before. He worked the top free and brought the lipstick to her mouth, at which point she closed her eyes and puckered her outthrust lips, head gently swaying. There followed their first kiss ever. Their physical relationship resulted from a similarly incongruous and unprecedented act: Mi-ran appeared at the boarding-house room wearing traditional clothing and asked Yun-gu to adjust the ties, which were already neatly knotted.

Around this time Yun-gu introduced Mi-ran to Hyŏn-t'ae. When Mi-ran and Yun-gu went out—and many were the times that they did so at her suggestion—it was usually to a tearoom, a restaurant, or a movie theater. One Saturday they watched a movie at the Kukche Theater, then stopped at the Kwigŏrae Tearoom, site of the weekly drinking session, where they found Hyŏn-t'ae and Sŏk-ki. As always, Hyŏn-t'ae was in need of a haircut and shave. On their way home Mi-ran said to Yun-gu, "Is he some kind of bum? He looks like a crazy man." Yun-gu had tried to explain: "It's not because he's short of money. And he's not a habitual slob either. You should have seen him after his discharge. Quite the sharp dresser; he wore a different tie every day. But that was then. He says it got to be a nuisance having to change all the time. Well, he *is* different, I'll grant you that. The funny thing is, he was very much involved in his father's company and then for some reason or other he quit, and that's how he's looked ever since." Mi-ran had laughed and said, "Quite a character you're keeping company with."

Several times thereafter they had chanced to meet Hyŏn-t'ae at the Kwigŏrae. On occasion the three had dinner together. And then one day Mi-ran said to Yun-gu: "This man Hyŏn-t'ae is growing on me. I like his style, nothing seems to faze him, there's something masculine about him."

Mi-ran's feelings for Yun-gu cooled and inevitably he felt at a loss. He knew that if Mi-ran found Hyŏn-t'ae to her liking, she would put her words into action. He tried to gauge Hyŏn-t'ae's attitude as well. One thing was for certain: a man as unprincipled in his relationships with women as Hyŏn-t'ae could hardly be expected to reject Mi-ran's advances. For the first time Yun-gu found himself jealous of another man. He felt as if a dark cloud were threatening their friendship, and this was intolerable.

From the beginning Yun-gu had approached Mi-ran somewhat differently from the many young people who act on love alone. To the subject of marriage with her, he attached a condition. Completely alone in the world, Yun-gu was motivated by a desire to use Mi-ran's father, a division head in the Ministry of Finance, as a stepping stone for his own advancement. This was not to say that he sought a marriage of convenience, that he felt not the least affection for Mi-ran. Though he had always thought of Mi-ran as occupying a higher station in life, he believed he loved her with a passion all his own.

After Mi-ran professed her liking for Hyŏn-t'ae, Yun-gu had pressed her on the subject of marriage, and not for the first time. Mi-ran had replied with unaccustomed decisiveness: they shouldn't rush into marriage, but in due course they could mention the subject to her parents. Yun-gu wondered if this apparent moratorium on the discussion of marriage had something to do with Hyŏn-t'ae. It also dawned on him that he was being visited much less frequently by Mi-ran. Something else was different about her as well: a hint of reserve when they were together. Yun-gu refrained from asking Mi-ran if she was seeing someone else. For if she did admit to seeing Hyŏn-t'ae, the situation would become decidedly complicated. Better to be patient and see what developed.

For several days in a row Mi-ran did not appear. When next she visited Yun-gu it was late at night. A dreary autumn rain was falling. No sooner did she enter the boardinghouse room than she asked Yun-gu to embrace her. "Hold me tighter," she whispered breathlessly in his ear. "Tighter—more." Although the urgency of her violent emotion overwhelmed Yun-gu, he felt relieved. Her words and actions left no doubt in his mind that her relationship with Hyŏn-t'ae was over.

The next morning she called Yun-gu at work. Could she see him at lunchtime? They met at the appointed place; her face was pale. She told Yun-gu she had spoken with her father and that he opposed their marriage. "He realizes you're smart and trustworthy, but he says that marriage involves other issues as well."

Yun-gu listened silently, well aware that parents are loath to approve a marriage between unequal partners. After a time he calmly remarked that a lengthy campaign seemed the only alternative.

Meanwhile Mi-ran should bother her parents no more on the subject of marriage.

Thereafter Mi-ran reported that her parents were closely monitoring her outings. Her visits grew scarce. Yun-gu saw her no more than once a week, sometimes once in ten days. And then one day Mi-ran arrived at his room with an animated expression on her face. "I think I'm pregnant," she said. "I haven't had my period for three months. And yesterday I started gagging." Yun-gu's considerable surprise was tempered with the suspicion that Hyŏn-t'ae was the father. Still, he was able to maintain his composure and ask without hesitation if her family knew.

"Not yet."

"We're all set then."

"What do you mean?"

Yun-gu lapsed into thought, considered how Mi-ran's parents might react to the knowledge of their daughter's pregnancy, and decided that an abortion was best. "Tomorrow I'll find a clinic," he announced.

"A clinic?"

"Yes, it's supposed to be a very simple procedure."

After the abortion Yun-gu would figure out what to do next. A delay, unless there was a very good reason for it, could only complicate matters. But Mi-ran surprised Yun-gu by opposing his idea: "I'd rather leave home and find a place where we could live together. I have a few things we can sell if we need money."

Yun-gu tried to reason with her: "I know what you're thinking. But people can't live on impulse. There are other factors to take into account if we're going to live in this society. First we have to consider what others will think. So let's bide our time and see what happens. Tomorrow I'll pick out a suitable clinic. They say it's over very quickly." Mi-ran, her expectations confounded, kept silent. Always cheerful, she now radiated a chill that Yun-gu had never felt before.

On a Saturday afternoon three days later they found their way to a back-alley clinic in Lower Wangshimni. It was set among a stretch of modest tile-roof homes and above its glass door was a handwritten sign consisting of a red cross and the words "Dr. Pak, General Medicine." The words loomed unusually large to the eye. Though it was not an obstetrics and gynecology clinic, Mi-ran said nothing. "The good thing about places like these," Yun-gu volunteered, "is that rumors won't get back to your family."

The arrangements having been made, a wrinkled, fortyish doctor in a stained surgical gown promptly ushered Mi-ran into the examination room, which also served as the surgery. Separating this room from the waiting room was a veneer partition through which Yun-gu could hear the doctor's instructions to the nurse as well as the clink of surgical instruments.

Yun-gu sat on a decrepit couch with the springs poking out and opened a newspaper. The sparse light of autumn slanted through the west-facing window. Yun-gu heard Mi-ran's muffled outcries and the voice of the doctor telling her that she was bearing up very well. Sitting in the sunlight, Yun-gu read the paper halfheartedly, wondering if the bloody mass being removed from Mi-ran had in fact been fathered by Hyŏn-t'ae. But whoever was responsible, the important thing was to extract it now.

Presently the doctor appeared in the waiting room drying his hands on a towel.

"It went without a hitch. Your wife held up remarkably well."

Yun-gu hailed a taxi and they set off for Mi-ran's home. Mi-ran rested her head against a cushion. Her face had lost color.

"You'll be fine in a day or two. Meanwhile, better tell your family you're not feeling well. And stay in bed."

Without a word Mi-ran found Yun-gu's hand and clutched it. Yun-gu noticed the driver observing them in the rearview mirror. Annoyed, he furtively removed his hand from Mi-ran's, produced a cigarette, and placed it in the holder.

Within nine days Mi-ran was dead. The doctor had failed to remove all of the fetus and had torn the peritoneum. Within a week Mi-ran had developed a high fever and vaginal bleeding and was moaning. She was taken to a noted obstetric and gynecology clinic and underwent a second surgery but breathed her last on the operating table.

Yun-gu, of course, was forced to resign from the bank.

"How could you screw up like that?" Hyŏn-t'ae had said to him. "You of all people. With women, what you have to remember is if you're not serious about marrying, then you have your fun and call it quits. If you *are* serious, you fulfill your responsibilities and take her in. Anyway, this one's water over the dam. So what do you figure you'll do next?"

Yun-gu wore a dispirited look. "That's a good question. I'm pretty much at loose ends. Couldn't you come up with something for me at your father's company?"

Hyŏn-t'ae smiled. "I already told you—the Governor has a hard-and-fast rule when it comes to hiring. I could bring him the brightest prospect in the world and it would mean nothing to him."

"What about that time you said you'd find something for me if I was ever hard up?"

"You have an amazing memory," Hyŏn-t'ae said, still smiling. "That was when I still worked at the company. Well, too bad an industrious fellow like you has to go to waste."

For nearly six months Hyŏn-t'ae paid Yun-gu's room rent. He also told Yun-gu that his father had bought up several plots of land in the Hoegi-dong area beyond Ch'ŏngnyangni. He asked Yun-gu to think of a way he could utilize one of those parcels. That was when Yun-gu came up with the idea for the poultry farm.

Yun-gu didn't view this favor as an expression of Hyŏn-t'ae's magnanimity or their friendship based on a shared experience of war. Another motive was involved. Yun-gu suspected that Hyŏn-t'ae, prodigal though he was, felt guilty because of Mi-ran. This prompted another thought: *Mi-ran's dead and gone, and now I have to find a way to support myself. What's the use of quibbling about our relation-ship with her? After all, Hyŏn-t'ae's the one who's helping me out of this fix.*

From now on, Yun-gu told himself, his only option was to be self-sufficient. This had always been a guiding principle in his life. So when Hyŏn-t'ae joked about inspecting the private parts of chickens, Yun-gu did not really care whether this remark was intended as drunken banter or pointed sarcasm. He was quick to acknowledge the six months' boardinghouse rent paid by Hyŏn-t'ae, and he felt obliged to him in addition for the poultry farm's various start-up expenses. But now that the hens were laying, it was fortunate indeed that he was able to repay Hyŏn-t'ae by the month. And naturally he came to regard the eggs, accumulating one by one, as the indispensable cornerstone of an independent life.

And so it was that about ten o'clock, basket in hand, Yun-gu went out to gather eggs. The low temperatures had held constant and the clear skies belied the forecast for afternoon clouds. As he walked toward the henhouse the neighborhood trash heap beyond the fence caught his eye. *What a mess! They'd better get rid of it before spring. The last thing we need is a breeding ground for an epidemic.*

When he first arrived with Hyŏn-t'ae to inspect the site of his future poultry farm, he had heard with crystal clarity the voice of a woman as if she were directly beside him. He had turned to see two women talking about fifty yards distant. The surroundings were that quiet, the air that clear. But all during that first spring, summer, and fall, new public housing followed by residential construction had transformed the area, stiffening Yun-gu's resolve to be vigilant for diseases that affected fowl.

Even on cold days such as this one, the henhouse was pleasantly warm owing to the chickens' body heat and the sunlight passing through the vinyl insulation over the windows. And it was bright. Cloudy though it might be outside, the white of the chickens' feathers never failed to brighten Yun-gu's field of vision. In vivid contrast was the blood red of the combs. Yun-gu scrutinized those feathers and combs for any sign of disease. Then he would pass quietly among the hens, gathering eggs. Leaving the henhouse with a heaping basket, he could feel his chest swell with satisfaction.

Yun-gu made the rounds of the first two coops and entered the third. *Not again!* His heart dropped at the sight of a hen lying on its side, legs wriggling ineffectually, neck elongating in sporadic jerks. A swarm of chickens pecked fiercely at its entrails, which extended far from beneath the tail. The hen's eyes were closed and its bloodred comb had turned purple. Yun-gu rushed over, shooed away the chickens, and took the hen outside. The other chickens followed, pecking at the entrails dragging in the sandy soil.

Another hen had suffered a similar fate in the very same coop two days earlier. Yun-gu's helper, who had been cleaning the henhouse, had emerged holding a bloody mess of a chicken. The bloodstains, vivid red against the snow-white background of feathers, had given the illusion that more blood had been shed than was actually the case.

Few animals are as delicate and fastidious as chickens. Instinctively they peck with a frenzy at anything that suddenly comes into sight. So if some of them happen to stir up grass or feathers, the chickens nearby will instinctively peck at these objects. Yun-gu had seen half-grown chickens pecked in the wing joints or anus till blood was drawn. So frequently did this happen that he felt as if he should keep constant watch over the henhouse.

This pecking tendency had diminished after the hens started laying, which made the two recent incidents all the more worrisome. Another peculiar proclivity had appeared once the laying began: constant fights over where to lay. Generally the hens would lay only where they had nested. No matter how much unclaimed space lay around them, they would stubbornly maintain their own nest rather than move, so that several hens might fight for space in the same nesting area. Yun-gu realized, though, that the bloody hen of two days ago and the hen today with the protruding entrails could not have been the victims of such fighting. Their combs were undamaged.

Yun-gu concluded that the two events were coincidental, yet characteristic of half-grown hens. Probably the first hen had felt an itch, rubbed its wing with its beak, and left a trace of blood at the joint. The wound must have resulted from the other chickens pecking at that spot. The second hen had most likely suffered a similar fate. The nether regions of chickens often swell and shrink, not only at times of evacuation, but on less predictable occasions. The other chickens had probably pecked this hen during one such episode of swelling, drawing blood and ultimately pulling out the entrails.

Yun-gu felt compelled to hold himself responsible for the sad fate
of the second hen because he had failed to take precautions and check
on the hens earlier. Why, though, was it the *third* coop in which these
two incidents had occurred? His thoughts on this question seemed to
narrow down to one answer: a couple of the hens in that coop had
reverted to their old ways. And if that was the case, he should isolate
those chickens at once. But pecking incidents were seldom discovered
at the moment of occurrence; they usually came to light well after the
fact. How was it possible, then, to pinpoint the offending hen? In any
event, Yun-gu told himself, he would have to pay special attention to
this third coop.

Yun-gu's helper returned from delivering eggs and had just
propped his bicycle against the shed when he discovered the carcass
of the chicken outside the kitchen door.

"What happened this time?" he asked in surprise.

Yun-gu directed his gaze to the dead hen. For some reason it
reminded him of Mi-ran's death after the abortion. But soon he
managed to dismiss this thought.

"I want you to check on that third coop more often," he said to
the boy.

"Lousy birds!"

"Might as well boil this one up. Get some water on, will you?"

Less than an hour later Yun-gu was mixing feed in the storage
barn when the single-panel door opened slowly to reveal a woman.
Yun-gu knew immediately who she was. He had been forewarned by
Hyŏn-t'ae. And the previous night, returning from an errand, he had
heard from the helper that a woman had just visited.

The woman came to a stop inside the door and spoke timidly:
"I was hoping to see Mr. Nam."

"Yes, that's me."

The woman approaching Yun-gu was tall and slender and walked
with an upright bearing. She wore pumps, a close-fitting skirt of dark
gray tinged with violet, and a jacket of the same color. Her oval face,
devoid of lipstick and eyeliner, had a natural complexion. Her only
mark of color was her scarf: a pattern of water drops in primary colors

against a milky background. The woman gathered her hands atop her large, black leather handbag.

"Ah, excuse me for asking this. But were you acquainted with Yun Tong-ho?"

"Yes, I was."

The woman responded with a slight bow and introduced herself as Chang Suk.

"Ah, yes."

"I came by yesterday but unfortunately you were out," she said.

"Yes, I was informed of your visit," said Yun-gu.

"I'm afraid I've caught you at a busy time. . . ." She looked in the direction of the henhouse. "Quite a lot of chickens you have here. . . . But if you're not too busy I wonder if you might spare me a moment. There's something I'd like to ask you. Would it be possible for us to go very briefly to a nearby tearoom?"

"Nearby" in this case meant across from the Hoegi-dong police substation. A trip there would take time. But even if that particular tearoom had in fact been nearby, Yun-gu, recalling Hyŏn-t'ae's words of the night before, wished only to give a plausible response to the woman's questions and then send her on her way.

"Might I respectfully suggest we talk here? I would invite you inside if it wasn't so shabby. Would you care to have a seat?"

Yun-gu produced an apple crate from the corner and set it in front of her. Despite the dirty surface, the woman—Sugi, as Tong-ho had called her—perched herself on it with little apparent concern.

"All right. I'd like to ask you something if I might. I believe you and Tong-ho served in the same unit?"

"That's correct."

"And was his death in fact a suicide?"

"Yes."

A faint crimson tinge colored her unadorned cheeks. She fingered the straps of her handbag. "Would you happen to know why he killed himself?"

"I haven't the faintest notion."

"You didn't notice anything unusual beforehand?"

"Hmm. Well, I certainly didn't sense anything."

Sugi dropped her gaze and again fingered the handbag straps. "I'm very sorry to be asking all these questions. Was there any indication that he might have been having a nervous breakdown?"

"No, I don't think there was much likelihood of that."

"Then what do you suppose the reason was?"

Yun-gu remained silent.

Realizing the futility of her attempts to gain information, she sent him a look of obvious disappointment. "Was there by any chance a message for me or anyone else that he—"

Yun-gu's heart dropped. "I have no such message," he interrupted, avoiding her gaze.

"During his time in the army was there anyone besides you and Mr. Shin that he was close to?"

"I'm not exactly sure, but I think probably not."

The morning had passed when Hyŏn-t'ae finally rose. He had a dull headache and his stomach felt queasy. He asked the maid to make coffee.

Presently the maid appeared with a tray bearing a cup of coffee. "There was a call for you."

"Who was it?"

"A lady named Chang Suk. I told her you were sleeping and she said she would call later."

Hyŏn-t'ae wondered if this woman Sugi had failed to locate Yun-gu and was therefore calling him again instead. He drank his coffee, then went to the bathroom and washed. He was returning to his room when his mother summoned him.

"What's gotten into you?" she wheezed. She had recently grown decidedly obese owing to lack of exercise. "Look at your face—really, now! I haven't said anything because you're not a child anymore and I'm sure there's something on your mind. But you're looking worse by the day. For the love of God will you tell me what you're trying to accomplish?"

Hyŏn-t'ae silently toweled his face.

"And will you please explain to me how a man can get put in jail for no good reason when he's carrying proper identification? I don't understand it. Do you realize how much your father and I worried? And why didn't you come home when they released you? Instead you stay out past curfew and a policeman drags you home dead drunk. Did it ever occur to you to call us, just to let us know?"

"Haven't I always asked you not to worry about me?"

"Oh yes, I know that's how you feel. But how do you think that makes *me* feel as a mother? I've spoken with your father about this, I told him I'm not in favor of his hands-off policy toward you, I've asked him to have a talk with you. But you know he has no time for family matters. Every waking moment he's wrapped up in his business."

"As I've said, please don't worry about me. I'll act on my own best judgment. And Mother, you really should take better care of yourself. You could get out and see your friends more, take in some fresh air, that sort of thing."

"You mind your own behavior. Don't be concerned about me. Do you have any idea how much money we spend on you every month? In case you haven't noticed, I'm tired of having to squeeze money out of your father. And what kind of example do you think you're setting for your brother?"

"I don't think we need to worry about him. He'll go his own way regardless of what I do—you'll see."

Hyŏn-t'ae turned to leave but was detained by his mother.

"You don't realize what you're doing, and yet you don't want to hear me scold." Then she produced a square white envelope from her vanity drawer and handed it to him. "Your visa."

In a flurry of activity Hyŏn-t'ae had sat for the Ministry of Education examination, the U.S. Embassy test, and a physical in order to obtain this visa for travel to the United States.

"Mother, would you keep it for me, please? I'm afraid I'll lose it."

"It's high time you collected yourself and got ready to leave."

"This is true."

And in fact Hyŏn-t'ae did feel as if he should leave for some far-away place—if for no other reason than to break out of his ineffectual ennui. In his room he took a meal that served as breakfast and lunch. The steamed rice tasted like sand and after a few spoonfuls he pushed the meal tray away.

That afternoon he met Sŏk-ki at the Yangji Tearoom as they had agreed the previous evening. Sitting across from each other, they finished their hot drinks in silence. Rarely did they take up the thread of the previous night's conversation.

In short order they left the tearoom for the Ch'ŏnbodang eye clinic, near the Hwashin Department Store. There Sŏk-ki's vision was found to have deteriorated.

"Do you have a preference for lenses?" the clerk asked.

"What do you have in stock?" asked Hyŏn-t'ae.

"The full range—German, American, Japanese."

"Aren't German-made the best?"

"Indeed they are. But there's the price to consider."

"Regardless, I'll take the best you have."

Instead of suggesting something less expensive, Sŏk-ki produced the old frames for the clerk while Hyŏn-t'ae selected and purchased the lenses.

Hyŏn-t'ae and Sŏk-ki went next to a second-floor billiard parlor nearby. "Suddenly the world is so clear I can't aim straight," Sŏk-ki said. He kept repeating this as he played, light glinting from his thick lenses, and in fact he scored no better than usual. Hyŏn-t'ae fared little better. A massive weight seemed to press down on his shoulders; his body felt languid. After two games they left.

Clouds had been massing from the time Hyŏn-t'ae left his house and now the heavens were glowering. The weight Hyŏn-t'ae felt seemed to press down deep inside. He had experienced this languid weariness on the battlefield but it had never bothered him as it did now.

"Where to? Shall we have a drink?" asked Sŏk-ki.

"I'd better go home and lie down."

"Then what about tomorrow?"

"I think I ought to take it easy for a few days. Meanwhile, try to get used to those glasses."

On his way home Hyŏn-t'ae dropped by a barbershop. Midway through the haircut he felt drowsy and eased back in the chair. Soon he was fast asleep.

"Would you like to wash?"

Awakened by these words, Hyŏn-t'ae realized he had slept through the shave.

"That lady called again," the maid informed him upon his return.

*What's up with her, anyway? She should have been able to find Yun-gu with that map I drew.* Hyŏn-t'ae was vexed by these thoughts.

"If she calls again tell her I'm sick."

He heated water, bathed, then went to bed. Thus began one of his hibernations, as his mother called them. Once his languid weariness compelled him to lie down, he essentially lived in his bed for days on end. He would sit up to take his meals, then crawl back into bed. It was during these periods that he did most of his reading. He read, fell asleep, awoke to find the book face down on his quilt or beside his pillow, and read more.

## 11

IT SEEMS THAT no two people can establish a relationship without hurting each other. The only variable is the extent of the scarring: its severity, whether it is visible or invisible, conscious or unconscious. Between friends, between man and woman, even between parents and children, such scars are inevitable. We survive them by trying to bury them in oblivion; we try to make ourselves insensible to them.

Hyŏn-t'ae's second encounter with Sugi took place after he had awakened from his latest hibernation and resumed his irregular lifestyle. Milder weather had displaced the recent cold snap and Hyŏn-t'ae was downtown early in the afternoon. He had just walked past the Bando Hotel and was nearing Ŭlchiro when he heard a woman's voice calling him.

He turned to see Sugi rushing toward him, gasping for breath. *She's got me this time.* He chafed as he watched her approach. Her attempts to steady her breathing, the flushed face lacking makeup—indeed everything about her projected an intense determination to seize upon this opportunity. When she asked if he could spare the time to go to a tearoom he saw no alternative but to accompany her.

"I understand you've been ill the last few days," Sugi commented politely after they had found a tearoom nearby and placed their order. "Are you better now?"

The day Hyŏn-t'ae had resumed venturing outside, the maid had informed him that Sugi had called several times during his hibernation. He had then instructed the maid that henceforth she was to tell Sugi that he was out even if he was home. Eventually, he reasoned, she would give up trying to reach him.

"Actually I'm working in the Bando Hotel." Sugi proceeded to explain that a German firm occupying offices in the hotel had hired her as a typist. "I had just finished lunch and was looking out the window when who should I see but you." She still sounded excited about the chance encounter.

Presently she checked her watch. "It's a foreign company and they're strict about time," she said hesitantly with a confidential gesture of hand over mouth. "Forgive me for asking this, but could I possibly see you for a few moments later today? Anytime after five would be fine."

"That might be difficult. I'm meeting someone later on."

In truth Hyŏn-t'ae was to meet Sŏk-ki. The movie they were thinking of seeing would end around three o'clock, but he did not fancy rearranging his schedule to suit Sugi and waiting for her to get off work.

"Then what is your day like tomorrow? It's Saturday, so I'm available after one."

"Tomorrow I have a meeting."

"Oh, you do." Sugi gently bit her lower lip, checked her watch again, and seemed to realize that her only recourse was to take time off from work that afternoon. "Then I wonder if now would be . . ." She looked up at Hyŏn-t'ae, her expression tense with hope.

"Well, I guess I could make some time around one tomorrow," Hyŏn-t'ae said.

Sugi's face brightened. "I'm sorry to be pestering you like this." Before leaving they agreed to meet at the same tearoom.

The following day was cold and blustery. Hyŏn-t'ae arrived at the tearoom some twenty minutes past one. Sugi, sitting in the corner, half rose to signal her presence.

"I appreciate your taking the time to come here," she said in greeting.

The empty cup sitting in front of Sugi and the lack of steam issuing from her barley tea told Hyŏn-t'ae how long she had been waiting. He wondered how Mi-ran would have reacted. He recalled a time he had arranged to see her at a tearoom and arrived slightly late. "Look," she had said to him, indicating with her chin a nearby table where a young woman sat, shoulders slumped and eyes downcast. "How do you think she feels? She arrived just after I did and there she's sat, all alone. Not a pretty picture, is it? You shouldn't make a woman wait in a place like this." As if this lecture were not enough, at their next meeting she had failed to appear at the tearoom, and when he grew tired of waiting he left. Whereupon Mi-ran, scowling, had emerged from the shadows of the alley opposite. "You couldn't wait fifteen minutes," she said. Hyŏn-t'ae had found it absurd. "That's not a very nice thing to do," he said. Mi-ran had laughed. "Yes, not very lady-like, is it? But that's the price you pay for always being late." It was true that Hyŏn-t'ae had eventually lost interest in Mi-ran because she was Yun-gu's lover. But more than that, her cheerful and outgoing demeanor and her self-centeredness, strong to the point of rashness, had become a burden to him.

The woman before him now elicited a very different feeling, something like the flowing of quiet water. She was an annoyance, he told himself, but he would deal with her that day and then she could flow where she would.

As it was Saturday afternoon, the tearoom was so crowded that Hyŏn-t'ae and Sugi had to share a table with others. Even though she felt obliged to initiate the conversation, Sugi was reluctant to do so in such surroundings. She had made up her mind to suggest they go elsewhere as soon as Hyŏn-t'ae finished his drink, but Hyŏn-t'ae spoke first.

"How long have you been with that company?"

"This is my second year." This opening prompted Sugi to describe her workplace: "It's run by West Germans. I had heard rumors, but I was still surprised at how practical they are. They don't go out for lunch except on special occasions. Instead they eat at home. And what's really amazing is that they bring their coffee to work in a thermos. But they're not being stingy, just practical. And they treat the employees all right—no scolding as long as you're at work on time and do what you're supposed to. The main thing is to be punctual." It occurred to Sugi that on the previous day too she had mentioned to Hyŏn-t'ae that foreigners were preoccupied with time. She now wondered if he might misconstrue her remarks as a veiled criticism of his late arrival.

The conversation lagged. When Hyŏn-t'ae had finished his drink Sugi said, "Shall we leave?" With an apologetic expression she rose. Hyŏn-t'ae followed, realizing she had something to say but could not say it at the tearoom. As on the previous day, Sugi paid.

At the intersection where Ŭlchiro begins, Sugi asked: "_Sŏnsaeng-nim_, have you eaten lunch?"

Hyŏn-t'ae had again taken a late meal that morning before leaving to play billiards—the reason for his tardy arrival at the tearoom. The issue now, though, was a quiet place rather than a meal, and on this the would-be speaker and captive listener agreed.

And so across the street to a Chinese restaurant they went. Inside it was chilly in spite of the coal-briquette stove. They merely nibbled at their food.

"_Sŏnsaeng-nim_, you probably think I'm unpleasant," Sugi said, dabbing carefully at her mouth with her handkerchief. "A pest. But I'm facing a serious decision. That's why I'm swallowing my pride and making a nuisance out of myself." She gazed off in the distance, then looked down. "I'm thinking of getting engaged." Whether it was the undertone in which she spoke or an accumulation of thoughts over time, her tone was grave. "At first I kept remembering my time with Tong-ho. I decided to keep him alive in my memory for the rest of my life. My parents and others around me talked of marriage, but I dismissed what they said. There was just no way I could become someone else's wife. That was my only thought."

She closed her eyes, eased her head back, and took a deep breath. "And then . . . little by little I began to question that thought. Here was a person who had killed himself even though I was waiting for him. How could he have done that? And why couldn't I forget such a person? . . . Perhaps the very fact that I could ask these questions was the reason my memories of him began to fade."

"By the way, where do you live now?" asked Hyŏn-t'ae. Not that he really wished to know. Rather, he wanted to redirect her surging emotions, just like still water meeting rapids. But the strategy failed.

"Inch'ŏn. I take the train in every day. Tong-ho and I used to take that train to school. After he went in the army I sometimes had the illusion that he was still on the train with me. And quite a few times I realized I was looking for him among the other passengers after I got off. . . . I've never told this to anybody, not even my closest friends."

"So you knew him a long time."

"Oh yes. Since grade school. But now . . ."

Her voice trailed off and she lowered her gaze in an effort to calm herself. Hyŏn-t'ae could tell by the way her shoulders moved that she was trying to steady her breathing. Those shoulders, encased in her jacket, seemed uncommonly thin. After a time she gently raised her head.

"It's all very laughable, isn't it? In any event, I'm bowing to my parents' wishes and considering marriage."

But now that she had finally confronted the actuality of marriage, she was having trouble coming to terms with Tong-ho's suicide, even though she thought she had resolved her relationship with him. If she could not learn the reason for his death, she thought, it would be impossible to commit herself to a marriage.

"And so I looked through his letters and found out where you were, *Sŏnsaeng-nim*. Because I knew that he was closest to you. But both you and Mr. Nam kept saying you didn't know anything. And that's when I realized you were keeping something from me."

"It's true that we were his closest friends."

"And so you do know about him, don't you?"

"Well, he was quite naive—almost a fool, you might say."

"*Sŏnsaeng-nim*, you're not leveling with me. Maybe I'm going too far, but I think you've been trying to avoid me—even the telephone calls. . . ." As she grew tense and agitated the prominent tip of her nose began to lose color. "Please, tell me what happened. Whatever you say, I can accept it."

"People kill each other for no good reason—why should it be any different when they take their own life? As absurd as it may seem to others."

"But for the person who kills himself there must be a reason worth mentioning."

"How is an outsider to know?"

"But you can guess, can't you? If you were that close to him."

"There's nothing riskier than guesswork and supposition."

"So, you're going to duck the issue till the end."

"I'm not trying to duck the issue or anything else. . . . Let me say just one thing. Talking about the dead is pure self-indulgence, nothing else. When Tong-ho died, I thought 'What a waste.' I thought he was stupid to kill himself, he'd turned weak. But in the end I was simply indulging myself in thoughts about his death. And whether you spend the rest of your life alone thinking about him, or whether you find out why he died so you can marry someone with a clear conscience— ultimately I don't see where it amounts to anything more than self-indulgence on your part."

"I see. So you're telling me not to bother other people just for the sake of self-indulgence."

All color had vanished from her face save the faint yellowish tinge of her complexion. Hyŏn-t'ae found himself thinking that once she was engaged she might have to start wearing makeup.

# 12

HYŎN-T'AE AND SŎK-KI, full of drink and looking for more,
chanced upon the Kwigŏrae Tearoom and stopped for a breather.
The evening crush had eased to the point that business was slack.
Silently they took seats beside the stove and as they were lapsing into
a liquor-induced somnolence the waitress appeared with two cups of
coffee that they hadn't requested. Indeed, as regular customers they
were occasionally allowed to linger without ordering anything. The
waitress gestured with her chin.

"Compliments of the lady over there."

They followed her gaze to a woman off in the corner who nodded
in acknowledgment.

"Who's that?" Sŏk-ki asked as he stirred his coffee.

"Somebody I know."

It had been a week and a half since Hyŏn-t'ae had seen Sugi. He
recalled now that she had asked about his favorite haunt. Bearing
in mind her accusations of evasion, he had answered truthfully,
mentioning the Kwigŏrae. He had attached no significance to her
inquiry, taking it for the kind of small talk with which people say their
good-byes. He had also assumed that the current of strong emotion
displayed by Sugi had returned to a quiet course and flowed past him
forever. What, then, had brought her here tonight? To be sure, he

could simply ignore her presence. But drunk as he was, he felt compelled to approach her. The coffee was left untouched. He felt engulfed, as if by a torrent, and wanted to forge his way through it.

When Hyŏn-t'ae had joined her, Sugi shifted in her seat and said: "Very nice tearoom—a quiet place with comfortable seats."

"I thought the lady was getting engaged."

Taken aback by the bluntness of the remark, Sugi gazed silently at Hyŏn-t'ae: the liquor flush on his face, the hair run riot, the coarse growth of beard.

"I guess it was a mistake to buy you the coffee. Please forgive me, *Sŏnsaeng-nim*. I did it because you looked tired. And you're with someone too."

"I have no problem with the coffee . . ."

"I didn't come here to bother you about Tong-ho. I just—how should I say this?—I wanted to see what kind of life you and Nam *Sŏnsaeng-nim* lived, since you were the ones closest to him."

Hyŏn-t'ae produced a bitter smile. "Tell me, then, what do you see? Someone who looks tired? And drunk? . . . Somebody we wouldn't want seen by those foreigners who live such regular, well-ordered lives? . . . Well, this much you should know: you're mistaken if you think you can see in me your Tong-ho of the past."

"In other words, my coming here is just another useless form of self-indulgence? Fine. Let's say you're right. But where's the harm in it?" A chill, dreary smile played briefly about her lips.

"I can't see where it's any of my concern. But I want you to understand that for someone who's drinking, the worst thing is for someone who is not drinking to be poking her nose in where it doesn't belong."

Hyŏn-t'ae rose, took a couple of steps toward Sŏk-ki, then abruptly turned back and sat down again across from Sugi. He leaned forward, glaring at her with bloodshot eyes. "We can't have you hanging around here until you miss the last train to Inch'ŏn, so I'll say just one more thing. Last time, you said you could accept whatever I told you—correct? Shall I tell you, then? About our pal Tong-ho? He killed a woman. Shot her. A man too. He survived. She died."

Hyŏn-t'ae realized he wouldn't be saying this if he were sober. "The woman was a hostess at a cheap tavern. So now you know the reason our friend Tong-ho killed himself. I'll leave the rest to your imagination. . . . And as a matter of fact he did leave a letter. You want it, you can have it."

Sugi sat stock-still looking in Hyŏn-t'ae's direction. Her eyes, however, seemed to be staring off into space. The blood had drained from her face, revealing her yellowish complexion.

Hyŏn-t'ae was consumed by a cruel pleasure. "How about it? Tomorrow at six? Here? I'll bring the letter."

There was no reaction from Sugi. Her eyes, brimming with moisture that seemed to reflect some distant place, glowed from within.

Hyŏn-t'ae and Sŏk-ki continued their drinking at several other locations. Along the way, Hyŏn-t'ae considered. His words had hurt Sugi, that was for sure. But what of it? For some reason an ill humor had come over him. And strangely he did not feel at all drunk in proportion to the amount of alcohol he had consumed. This realization, though, did little to improve his spirits.

At about eleven o'clock Hyŏn-t'ae and Sŏk-ki parted company for the night. Hyŏn-t'ae set out for home but decided along the way to stop at the Pyongyang House. He found the errand girl nodding off beside the stove. There were no customers in the main drinking area. As he settled himself in the room behind the kitchen he recognized the guttural voice of the former town magistrate. The man was talking with the Pyongyang woman.

Kye-hyang appeared with a modest serving tray, placed it before Hyŏn-t'ae, and poured him a drink. She was the same as always— right knee raised, hands gathered atop it; the mannered ritual of taking the serving kettle in her right hand and deferentially placing her left hand against the right cuff; the fair white face coldly shrouding all emotion. True to his expectations, in the presence of this girl who gave the impression of a frozen rock he felt the repose that comes with the absence of worry.

From the inner quarters came the voice of the Pyongyang woman: "That's all for me—I've had my fill."

"Well, if our Wŏl-sŏn isn't showing her age," said the former magistrate, using the name he reserved for the Pyongyang woman.

_Wŏl-sŏn_—it sounded like a _kisaeng_ name. Hyŏn-t'ae had once asked Kye-hyang if the Pyongyang woman had ever been a _kisaeng_. Instead of replying, Kye-hyang had graced him with a smile that might have meant "Yes," "No," or "I don't know"—a vacant expression produced by a cursory stretching of the lips.

After a period of imperceptible murmuring from the inner quarters the guttural voice of the former magistrate again grew distinct: "What the hell kind of ribs are you serving? Look at this one—where's the meat? If a rib isn't thick like a wooden pillow it doesn't qualify—like this one here. You can hardly feel it go down your throat."

And then with no warning the lights went out. Kye-hyang, moving with unaccustomed haste, rose and left. Hyŏn-t'ae lit a cigarette.

From the inner quarters the Pyongyang woman giggled, then said: "What's gotten into you? Aren't you going to let me clear the table?"

Hyŏn-t'ae always enjoyed listening to her mixture of standard Seoul speech and the dialect of her native P'yŏngan Province. Presently he heard the door to the inner quarters open, and then the Pyongyang woman's voice: "For crying out loud, what's wrong with the lights this time!" She then entered the room where Hyŏn-t'ae sat, located a candle, lit it, and placed it at the edge of the serving table. Only then did Kye-hyang return to her place at the table and resume the familiar posture. The Pyongyang woman had doubtless instructed her never to remain with a customer in the dark.

"Look at her," the Pyongyang woman said to Hyŏn-t'ae. "She's such a simple girl—so innocent she won't be caught with a man in a dark room."

In the flickering candlelight Kye-hyang's face was expressionless as a plaster mask. Hyŏn-t'ae offered the Pyongyang woman his empty glass, intending to pour her a drink.

"I've had too much already," she responded.

It did seem she had drunk more than usual; her eyelids were puffy and swollen as if from an allergic reaction. Finally she accepted the glass.

"All right, then, just a little."

Kye-hyang poured the glass less than half full. The Pyongyang woman slurped the drink and returned the empty glass to Hyŏn-t'ae.

"*Sŏnsaeng-nim*, you look kind of drunk and kind of not drunk. What's the matter? Maybe we'd better pour you a few quick ones." She took the serving kettle from Kye-hyang and said: "Girl, go to the inner quarters and sing a song for our guest."

Hyŏn-t'ae wondered why the woman was ordering Kye-hyang to sing when scarcely half an hour remained until the midnight curfew. As soon as Kye-hyang had disappeared into the inner quarters the Pyongyang woman said: "*Sŏnsaeng-nim,* has something happened? These days we see you about as often as beans grow in a drought. And when you do come it's late at night. Don't tell me you've found another place and you're going to stop coming here."

"But I like it at this hour because there aren't any customers."

"Still, that doesn't leave you any time to have fun here." The Pyongyang woman called out in the direction of the inner quarters: "Kye-hyang, get going with that song!" Presently Kye-hyang began to sing.

"What is it with men? The older they get the less sense they have. Guess what—the magistrate's got his eye on Kye-hyang," the woman whispered.

Hyŏn-t'ae gathered from the confidential tone that her purpose in making Kye-hyang sing was to prevent their conversation from being heard in the inner quarters. They could hear the former magistrate beating his chopsticks against the serving table in time with the song.

"I tell you, these men, when they're young they prefer older women. And when they're older they go crazy for the young ones."

As soon as Kye-hyang had finished, the woman called once more toward the inner quarters: "Girl, now sing the 'Ŏrang' ballad." And then she continued to Hyŏn-t'ae: "You know what he says? He'll give me thirty thousand hwan a month to come here one night a week and sleep with Kye-hyang. And for that miser thirty thousand is splurging. But I'm not having any of it. Think about it. Am I so stupid I'd carry that girl on my back all the way across that wretched thirty-eighth parallel just to get a piddling thirty thousand for her? It doesn't make sense. Oh, it's all right for four visits a month. But we're talking here about Kye-hyang's first night. That needs a down payment of at least this much." And with that the woman spread the five fingers of her left hand, at the same time pouring Hyŏn-t'ae a drink with her right.

Every time Kye-hyang finished a song, the Pyongyang woman gave her the name of another to sing. It was as if someone kept changing disks on a record player. From time to time the former magistrate punctuated his chopstick beating with spirited calls of encouragement to Kye-hyang. As Hyŏn-t'ae listened he asked himself if the Pyongyang woman's incessant requests to Kye-hyang were not so much a means to conceal their conversation after all as a way to monitor the goings-on in the inner quarters. She must have assumed that so long as the singing continued, the man could take no liberties with Kye-hyang. Hyŏn-t'ae decided to have some fun at the Pyongyang woman's expense.

"_Ajumŏni_, listen," he said.

The woman cocked her head.

"Better see what's going on in there—go quickly, now!"

"What do you mean?"

"I bet he's up to no good. You don't want him having his way with that fifty-thousand-hwan virgin for free."

"We don't have to worry about that."

"But there's more to a woman than just her mouth. Who knows what he's up to while she's singing? Better go take a look."

When Hyŏn-t'ae produced money for the drinks, the Pyongyang woman said: "Why not have a few more?" And then, beginning to sound worried about the situation in the inner quarters, she added: "I'll send the girl back here."

Before she could do that Hyŏn-t'ae paid up and left.

# 13

GOING TO BED LATE was not exactly a recent development in Hyŏn-t'ae's life. For someone who drank until late at night and then roamed the streets, you couldn't expect otherwise. And even if he did wake up early he remained in bed. This meant there was little opportunity for him to encounter his father, morning or evening.

Rare too were the occasions when he saw his brother the college student. Apart from his studies, his brother had been fond of hiking since middle school and never missed a chance to go to the mountains on Sundays and holidays and of course school vacation.

His mother, though, was always at home and continued to pressure him to go to the United States. When Hyŏn-t'ae learned that his visa had been issued, he had wanted to leave at once—if only to free himself of the lethargy resulting from his tiresome idleness, a lethargy that shrouded his life and surroundings. And occasionally thereafter he would feel a desire to leave for some distant place. But every time, he would feel it was harder to extricate himself from his lethargy than it had been to penetrate an enemy encirclement during the war.

And so it was that on this particular day Hyŏn-t'ae did not rise till midmorning. The window revealed a cloudy day. He washed up and

had just returned to his room when the maid stuck her head inside
the door. Mealtime, Hyŏn-t'ae assumed. But no, it was the telephone.

"It's the lady who called all those times before. I told her you were
out but she said you were expecting her call."

Hyŏn-t'ae took the call in the living room.

Sugi's voice had a shrill edge to it. "Forgive me, _Sŏnsaeng-nim._
For resorting to a fib in order to see you. I can get out early today
because it's Saturday." She would be grateful if Hyŏn-t'ae could
bring Tong-ho's letter, she added.

It had been nearly a week since Sugi appeared that time at the
Kwigŏrae Tearoom. The following day Hyŏn-t'ae had retrieved the
army knapsack stuck away in his closet, found the letter, and taken it
to the tearoom. But Sugi had not appeared—not that evening nor on
the two or three occasions subsequent when Hyŏn-t'ae had dropped
by. He had to wonder what had come over her to result in this request
nearly a week later.

After his usual meal he left the house. Time remained before the
two o'clock meeting that Sugi had suggested. Hyŏn-t'ae walked aimlessly, crossing the second block of Chongno to reach the second
block of Ŭlchiro, passed the Chungang Theater, and crossed the hill
where Myŏng-dong Cathedral sat. In the middle of the street a beggar
worked the passersby. When Hyŏn-t'ae approached, the beggar stud-
ied his face, then spat through his teeth.

Hyŏn-t'ae turned toward Ch'ungmuro. He was passing the bookshops that lined both sides of the street behind the Central Post Office
when it occurred to him that he had long been keeping his distance
from these shops. After his discharge he had made a point of frequent-
ing these bookshops in central Seoul, but from the time he began
drinking daily this tendency had lapsed.

Hyŏn-t'ae entered one of the bookshops at random. Not with the
intent of buying anything, of course. He scanned the various books.
One titled _Tropical Fish_ caught his eye. It was one of the new pocket-
size editions, a slim volume of less than a hundred pages. The cover
identified it as a picture book rather than a collection of color photos,

leading Hyŏn-t'ae to expect something less than attractive. And sure enough, when he opened the book his first glance revealed pictures with unnatural shapes and colors. Although they were far from realistic, Hyŏn-t'ae assumed, they were peculiar even in outline. And as he examined the features and coloration of the various species, on impulse he decided to show them to Kye-hyang, so he paid for the book and placed it in his pocket.

From the bookshop he walked to the starting point of Ŭlchiro and climbed to the upstairs billiard hall there. No more comfortable way to kill time than this. He occasionally came here with Sŏk-ki, and today there were some faces he recognized. After a single game he left. Outside, a gray sky lowered.

Though it wasn't yet two, Hyŏn-t'ae went to the meeting place Sugi had requested—the tearoom where he had first met her. Sugi was already there. She gave a slight nod of acknowledgment. Her face, devoid of makeup, was more drawn than before.

Hyŏn-t'ae wished to be done quickly with this business. When they finished their tea, he reached for Tong-ho's letter, which had remained in his overcoat pocket for most of the past week.

"Not just yet," said Sugi. "Let's go somewhere else."

Perhaps it was the threatening weather, but the tearoom had few customers at this normally busy hour. And so Hyŏn-t'ae found himself thinking they could have spoken freely in such quiet surroundings. Nonetheless he rose to leave with Sugi. He couldn't very well refuse, so ardent was the expression on her face, a face grown haggard perhaps as a result of what he had told her the previous time. It was a bother, he told himself, but today would be the end of it.

Sugi led him to a Western-style grill in Myŏng-dong, where she ordered fried fish and rice and Hyŏn-t'ae ate salad. While Sugi finished her meal Hyŏn-t'ae drank three whiskeys. Neither said much. Another party entered the restaurant and brushed snow from their heads and shoulders. Hyŏn-t'ae looked out the window. The air was speckled with snow.

"Don't you like snow, _Sŏnsaeng-nim?_"

The question of whether he particularly disliked snow had never occurred to Hyŏn-t'ae. On the battlefield there had been times when bitter cold lasted a week or two, and he had wished then for heavy snowfall. In fact, though, he remembered a snowfall that had blanketed the land, and when on top of this a fierce blizzard was poised to strike, the situation had grown much more difficult.

"I've heard there was an awful lot of snow at the mideastern front."

"It's true. We'd get overnight snowfalls that came up over our boots."

"Then perhaps you don't like it now because you were fed up with it then?"

"Can't really say that. Even people who've lived where there's lots of snow, some of them end up hating it and some enjoy it."

Sugi clasped both hands around her cup. Her face took on a reddish tinge.

"_Sŏnsaeng-nim,_ would it be possible for you to give up some time for me today?"

This was not so much an inquiry as a request. When he thought how bothersome it was to be with this woman, Hyŏn-t'ae was not inclined. But since today would be their very last encounter, he silently yielded.

"Thank you, _Sŏnsaeng-nim._ I was worried you'd say no."

Outside the snowflakes were not that large. The sides of the street, where no foot had trod and tire tracks were absent, were heaped with snow. Hyŏn-t'ae turned up the collar of his topcoat.

In front of the Midop'a Department Store Sugi flagged a taxi and asked the driver if he would take them to the Songdo area of Inch'ŏn. He simply drove off, perhaps loath to drive outside the city in bad weather. Sugi hailed another taxi. This driver seemed open to the possibility of Inch'ŏn but would not go as far as Songdo.

"Tell you what—I'll take you as far as Inch'ŏn and then you catch another taxi to Songdo." Sugi looked at Hyŏn-t'ae as if to say that perhaps this was the best they could do, then climbed into the taxi.

As they rode, Hyŏn-t'ae wondered why they were doing this. When Sugi had asked if he could spare some time for her, he assumed she meant in a tearoom. This taxi ride was completely unexpected. Was it possible that this dreamy woman had thought of taking a drive on this snowy day and come up with the absurd notion of going all the way to Songdo? Hyŏn-t'ae knew nothing of Songdo except that it was a beach resort in Inch'ŏn. He checked his watch—just past three.

Driving through the vehicle-flooded city and watching the snow flutter down gave Hyŏn-t'ae the feeling not so much of a quiet snowfall as of snow being pushed every which way in confusion. The taxi left Yŏngdŭngp'o, entered the Seoul-Inch'ŏn highway, and picked up speed. The windows fogged up and it got difficult to see outside. Snow accumulated at the window well only to be dislodged by the taxi's movement. The windshield became coated except where the wipers left a clear view of the falling snow.

Hyŏn-t'ae reclined his head against the seatback and closed his eyes. Because it was snowing the temperature was a bit milder. Even so he felt chilly now that the whiskey was clearing his system.

"I'm sorry to see you looking so tired," said Sugi. "Could you turn up the heat, please?" she asked the driver.

Hyŏn-t'ae had no idea why Sugi was taking him to Songdo on this nasty winter day. As the taxi rounded a bend Hyŏn-t'ae's body inclined toward the door. He sensed Sugi leaning toward him. But they were far enough apart that their bodies did not touch. Hyŏn-t'ae groped for an answer. This trip clearly had something to do with Tong-ho, but he couldn't think what that might be. The taxi rounded a curve in the opposite direction and this time it was Hyŏn-t'ae leaning toward Sugi. He realized that he probably wouldn't come in contact with her but he tried nevertheless to keep himself from tilting toward her, sitting as erect as if the taxi were traveling a straight, level road. At that point a thought struck him: a night at the Sot'ogomi base after the bombing had started, when Tong-ho was talking in his sleep. Hyŏn-t'ae opened his eyes.

"Driver, isn't there a pass between Seoul and Inch'ŏn?"

The driver eyed Hyŏn-t'ae in the rearview mirror.

"A pass?"

"I'm not sure of the name."

"I'm afraid I don't know . . ." This young driver, it seemed, had little to offer about the geography between the two cities.

Sugi, looking straight ahead, scarf enveloping her head, turned to Hyŏn-t'ae: "Do you mean Wŏnt'aei Pass?"

"Yes, that's the one. Whereabouts is it?"

"It's up ahead. Between Pup'yŏng and Chuan."

"Pretty rugged, is it?"

"Not particularly. But the road is twisty and there are a lot of accidents. In winter if cars don't make a curve they can end up off the road and down the hillside."

Hyŏn-t'ae observed Sugi's face. What could Tong-ho have been dreaming of that night he had cried out in his sleep? Sugi would have no better answer to this than he himself. He closed his eyes again.

Presently Sugi announced that they had reached Lesser Wŏnt'aei Pass.

Hyŏn-t'ae opened his eyes. The taxi was making a broad turn to the right down a mildly steep slope. About a mile ahead the taxi topped a slightly steeper incline and began to descend a series of tight curves.

"This is Greater Wŏnt'aei Pass. This is where all the accidents happen."

Below the curving road there seemed to be a cliff. Hyŏn-t'ae made a point of not looking down.

Snow was falling everywhere in Inch'ŏn as well. In the downtown area they caught another taxi, which proceeded to take them back the way they had come until they were outside the city. Then, turning onto an unpaved countryside road, the taxi began to rattle furiously. Although they couldn't see clearly through the windows, it was possible to make out the sea close by on the right.

They had gone perhaps twenty minutes further when the taxi

made a curving descent around a hillside and came to a stop in an open area that resembled a plaza. A place for tourists who came in the summer for swimming, it now seemed indescribably desolate. Dusk was already falling on this short winter's day.

To the right, toward the sea, was an army base. The quonset huts and tents were shapeless, squatting masses in their covering of snow. Off to their side was a road lined with dwellings interspersed with a hole-in-the-wall shop, a Chinese restaurant, a soup-and-rice eatery, and the like.

Without a word Hyŏn-t'ae followed Sugi along a path that led off from the road. In a hundred yards they arrived at an embankment overlooking the sea.

"Before the war you could swim on that beach. Then it was taken over by the military."

If that was the case, Hyŏn-t'ae wondered, then perhaps the eateries and shops were for the soldiers and not the summertime visitors.

Sugi took the lead, walking along the embankment, her slender build making her look cold and lonely in the falling snow. They had to lean into the strong, moist wind that had been blowing since before they arrived at the seaside.

It looked like the tide was out, the exposed sea bottom spreading out black toward the sea till the snowflakes and dim twilight combined to obscure the sight of it. Snow-draped rocks and clumps of ice looked like white beasts against the black estuarial sediment. At a distance to the left stood a lighthouse. Its lantern began to wink on and off, the light an uncommonly bright yellow.

Hyŏn-t'ae suddenly realized that Yun-gu and Sŏk-ki would be waiting for him about then at the tearoom for the Saturday get-together.

Sugi stood for a time looking out to sea, then began to murmur haltingly: "It was right around here. . . . We didn't talk, just sat. . . . The water was splashing against the bottom of the bank. . . . It was late in the summer."

These words confirmed Hyŏn-t'ae's vague supposition that their trip here had something to do with Tong-ho. Still, as ardent as she

was, why should she have felt compelled to bring him here? He
cleared the snow from his hair.

Sugi stood a while longer facing out to sea before turning away.
It was now completely dark.

They returned to the open area where the taxi had left them.
Hyŏn-t'ae wondered if he should have arranged for the driver to wait.
The snowfall was heavier now. Hyŏn-t'ae checked the time with his
lighter—almost six—then lit a cigarette.

"Don't worry about a ride back to Seoul. You'll be able to share a
taxi. . . . _Sŏnsaeng-nim,_ it's time for me to read Tong-ho's letter now.
First I'd like to find a quiet room. And then I'll spend the night there."

Hyŏn-t'ae resigned himself to escorting her to a hotel. There was
one located atop a nearby hill. After a steep climb they arrived at the
hotel, which was named the Ch'ŏnghyangjang. They were shown to a
second-floor Western-style room facing the ocean. Much of the space
was taken up by a double bed set against the wall. It seemed that,
except for the summer bathing season, the hotel catered to foreigners.
The stove had been lit and the room was toasty.

Hyŏn-t'ae mopped the snowmelt from his hair and face with a
towel given him by the bellboy. Recalling a faroff thumping sound he
had heard as they climbed the hill to the hotel, he asked the young
man, who was at the door awaiting further instructions, "Does this
place have its own power supply?"

"Yes, it does. . . . Would you care for dinner?"

Hyŏn-t'ae turned to Sugi.

"I won't be eating," she said.

"I'll have some whiskey," said Hyŏn-t'ae.

When the whiskey arrived he poured himself a drink and took
several sips. The exhaustion rooted within him began to ease. He
produced Tong-ho's letter from his topcoat, placed it on the nightstand, freshened his drink, and gulped half of it.

Sugi opened a drape and stood at the window, her back to him.
The window had fogged up and outside was black. She must have
wiped the section in the middle, which revealed a clear space larger

than a face. Seen from the rear, she seemed to have forgotten any thought of conversation, even small talk. Without a word Hyŏn-t'ae set the whiskey bottle and glass on the table and rose to leave.

"Could you please wait a minute?"

A short interval passed before she turned to face him. Her hair, freed from the scarf, was uncombed. The hair in front was matted together by drops of water where the snow had melted.

"*Sŏnsaeng-nim,* I can't begin to tell you how sorry I am—all I've done is trouble you. I decided to call you when it looked like it would snow. When I'm at work I can tell when it's going to rain or snow. It's because the train whistles from Seoul Station sound so clear then."

Hyŏn-t'ae realized that he too had a strong hunch it would snow that day. In the billiard hall both of his elbows had been ticklish and then numb. These sensations were always rooted in his wartime injuries and he felt them whenever it was about to snow or rain.

"At first I really did feel I could bear anything I heard about Tong-ho. But when you actually told me, I just couldn't bring myself to go back to the tearoom for his letter. You know, for a while before he died he wasn't answering my letters. Today, though, I decided. To read his letter while the snow falls . . . and then forget about him. . . . The last time I saw him it was snowing like this. . . . So now that I'm going to have to read it, I'm scared again. . . . *Sŏnsaeng-nim,* would you stay with me a little longer?"

After a short pause she continued: "You asked me the last time if I was still engaged. Well, I called it off. Actually, under the circumstances I had my doubts from the beginning."

She fell silent and proceeded to watch Hyŏn-t'ae drink. She would wait for the liquor to take effect. She suspected it was because he was under the influence that he had spoken about Tong-ho at the Kwigŏrae after previously avoiding all mention of him. This time she was determined to hear him out, even if what he had to say was worse. After he had taken several more sips she asked: "Did Tong-ho drink too?"

"Of course he did."

"He didn't before."

"I taught him." A gleam appeared in Hyŏn-t'ae's eyes.

"Was he drinking that day?"

"Some. But I don't believe he did what he did because he was under the influence."

"So he committed suicide because he had killed somebody."

"That's hard to say. He didn't know that at the time. There's only one thing we can know for sure. His suicide wasn't connected to whether the people he shot lived or died."

"In any event, couldn't you have prevented his death, _Sŏnsaeng-nim?_"

Hyŏn-t'ae produced a bitter smile. The wrinkles of a man much older appeared at the corners of his mouth. "Let me get this straight. You're saying I can prevent someone's death? Does a person have that authority?"

Sugi looked Hyŏn-t'ae squarely in the eye: "What kind of woman was she?"

"I told you last time. She worked at a drinking place."

"And?"

"Well, her nose was pointed, kind of a weak chin—"

"That's not what I meant. Well, fine. I understand. She must have been a fine woman. Because he liked her. Someone like me couldn't have matched up with a fine woman like that. . . . All right, I can read the letter now."

With a determined air she perched herself on the edge of the bed and took the letter from the nightstand. The envelope was crumpled and worn from being in Hyŏn-t'ae's topcoat pocket for nearly a week.

Hyŏn-t'ae poured himself another drink. He just wanted to leave.

Sugi extracted the letter and unfolded it. Suddenly her face crinkled up.

"What is this!"

The letter dropped from her quivering hand. Hyŏn-t'ae's eyes darted to the floor where it lay. The sheet was blank.

Hyŏn-t'ae burst into laughter, revealing his white teeth. He was reminded of Corporal Kim's "dirt letter." _Hah—a carbon copy._

"I guess you're supposed to read his mind."

Sugi stared off into space as if she heard nothing, then fell to her side on the bed. "That's not his letter. It's not." Her slender shoulders began to heave.

Hyŏn-t'ae went to her side. "Here, have a little of this. It'll ease your mind."

Sugi's shoulders heaved a bit longer, then abruptly she sat up and struck the hand that held the glass of whiskey. Whiskey spattered the white sheet of paper.

"You're the one who killed him. He wasn't like that before. You made him that way. That's why you were avoiding me. Coward! You can't say anything unless you're drunk." Her face had lost all color except for the bloodshot eyes.

Hyŏn-t'ae felt himself grow indifferent. He poured himself another whiskey and drank. "You say I made him that way? Then I must be a pretty powerful man. But now I'm a coward, just like you said. A coward and a drunk. . . ." Suddenly Hyŏn-t'ae felt a cruel pleasure. "But if I had to name someone else who made our friend the way he was, it would be you. I see now he could never escape that worthless dreamworld of yours—it stifled him till the end, and now he's dead."

"Don't say anything else. And I want you to leave." Sugi covered her ears with her hands.

"That would seem to make us partners in crime," said Hyŏn-t'ae.

Still covering her ears, Sugi fell back on her side.

Hyŏn-t'ae felt a sudden urge to kill her. He plunked the whiskey bottle and glass down on the nightstand, then stood Sugi up and ripped open her coat. The buttons popped out one by one and fell to the floor.

# 14

"HERE YOU GO—it's that time of month again." Yun-gu handed
Hyŏn-t'ae a stack of banknotes wrapped in newspaper. It was the
following Saturday, and they had just seen Sŏk-ki off after the weekly
get-together. For several months now Yun-gu had been repaying his
debt to Hyŏn-t'ae with monthly thirty-thousand-hwan installments.

Yun-gu had told Hyŏn-t'ae he would make monthly payments,
such as they were, once the hens began laying. Hyŏn-t'ae's response
was that instead Yun-gu should give him spending money if he
happened to ask for it. Helping Yun-gu out of his fix was something
Hyŏn-t'ae had done because he had the economic wherewithal, not
because he had expected repayment. But for Yun-gu it was important
to repay the debt as soon as possible so that he could regard the poultry farm as entirely his own. Ambiguous financial arrangements such
as Hyŏn-t'ae's spending-money idea left an unpleasant taste. Would
the indebted party ever know when he had paid in full? And so Yun-gu,
while regarding as over and done with the six months' boardinghouse
rent that Hyŏn-t'ae had paid after Yun-gu was dismissed from the
bank following Mi-ran's death, had calculated the not inconsiderable
sum Hyŏn-t'ae had given him for capital and expenses until the hens
began to produce. And he insisted that he be allowed to repay by the

month. Hyŏn-t'ae had ultimately honored Yun-gu's wishes and agreed to these payments. There was no need for stubbornness on his part, for Yun-gu was only being Yun-gu.

"Seems you're getting along pretty well inspecting the hind ends of hens."

"I wish. Not with all the competition. Which we'll probably see a lot more of come spring."

"You'll stick with it, though. You're too diligent and painstaking to give up."

"I just wish the damn things didn't need so much care. They've got to be the most finicky creatures alive. Turn your back on them for a second and they start pecking away at their rear end or else pull out another one's innards."

"Just like women," Hyŏn-t'ae snorted. "They're harder to handle than you might think. . . . You know, that woman Sugi dragged me out to Inch'ŏn last Saturday."

*So now it's Sugi he's mixed up with*, thought Yun-gu.

"Fathomless creatures, women. They provoke us into doing the most unexpected things. . . . Say, do you ever think about Mi-ran anymore?"

Yun-gu eyed Hyŏn-t'ae and walked on silently, waiting to hear more.

"Remember what I told you after she died? That if you were thinking of marrying her you should have lived together, no matter what. Even if you'd married her, though, it wouldn't have gone smoothly. But then who knows—you're a pretty patient guy. Anyhow, the ones who cling to the past like that woman Sugi are trouble. And I don't like Mi-ran's type either. I know I shouldn't speak of the dead like this, but I was seeing her for a while—that was when I didn't know you were involved with her. To be honest, whatever relationship the two of you had wasn't an issue. If only I'd fallen for her. But I lost interest before too long. Lost interest in any kind of relationship with her. . . . Are you listening? . . . One evening . . . it was raining, I remember, and we were in a tearoom . . . I said to her: 'It's no fun anymore—let's stop seeing each other.' She didn't say anything but it looked like she agreed. . . . So we left. We were walking to the bus stop and as she was going around a mud puddle she stumbled and guess what—she asks me to hold onto her. And so I told her: 'Sure I can— but only when you're actually in danger of falling.' And then we broke up. With women it's easiest if you just pay your money and take your chances. That way you don't feel burdened, see?"

At the third block down Chongno they went their separate ways.

On his way home that night Hyŏn-t'ae stopped in Nagwŏn-dong at the Pyongyang House. All this time he had been carrying around the book on tropical fish he'd bought to show Kye-hyang.

It was still early and there were several groups of drinkers at the bar. The Pyongyang House woman and Kye-hyang were busily making the rounds of the customers. The woman spotted Hyŏn-t'ae, approached, and told him to make use of the room in back of the kitchen. She then added in an undertone: "_Sŏnsaeng-nim_, you're just like one of the family—no need to stand on ceremony." After which she flashed him a smile.

After a time Kye-hyang appeared with a serving table she had prepared and poured him a drink. Then she left. As the woman had said, they were on friendly enough terms that he could be left to drink by himself until the customers at the bar had thinned out.

After another interval Kye-hyang returned with apologies for her absence. But her expression was not in the least apologetic. The Pyongyang woman had no doubt asked her to look in on Hyŏn-t'ae after some of the customers at the bar had left.

After Kye-hyang had served him a few more drinks Hyŏn-t'ae produced the book on tropical fish: "Kye-hyang, wait till you see these." He opened the book at random and showed Kye-hyang a picture. Her only reaction was to crane her white neck so she could see.

"What do you think? They live in the tropics—the areas that have a hot summer all year long."

Her expression betrayed little sign of wonder. "Goldfish," she murmured.

"No, they're not goldfish." Hyŏn-t'ae indicated one of the fish in the picture. "It's called a butterfly fish. The tail's strange, isn't it? Like the fold of a skirt. Now take a look at that fin coming out of its chest. See how it's shaped like a butterfly wing? And that fin on its stomach looks like a mustache. Interesting, eh?"

Kye-hyang's stonelike countenance showed no reaction.

Hyŏn-t'ae turned the pages to another picture. "This one's even better. . . . It says they kiss."

Kye-hyang's expression remained unchanged except for a smile that partially revealed her white, closely set teeth: an emotionless smile that showed neither skepticism about Hyŏn-t'ae's explanations of the fish nor admiration of these creatures she had never seen or heard of. Something told Hyŏn-t'ae that the subject of tropical fish was not going to bring them closer together. This confounding of his expectations, though, had the effect of putting his mind at ease.

As Hyŏn-t'ae was about to leave, the Pyongyang woman entered. Outside the room it was quiet. The customers at the bar had probably left.

"Turned out to be a pretty good night," the woman said to herself. Then to Hyŏn-t'ae: "You're not going already? Are you upset about something? Let's have a drink. I'm happy when I get a lot of customers."

They served each other several drinks. The woman was indeed in good spirits and she wasted no time finishing her drinks. Before long she was pleasantly drunk.

"*Sŏnsaeng-nim*," she began, then turned to Kye-hyang: "Girl, go to our room, wipe the floor, and set out the bedding so it'll have time to warm up."

After Kye-hyang had departed the woman lit a cigarette, nestled it in the corner of her mouth, and took a couple of puffs. "*Sŏnsaeng-nim*, let's have a heart-to-heart talk. Tell me, what do you think is lacking in that girl? Is something wrong with her nose? Is she missing something a woman should have? She's a genuine virgin, you know—the real thing! And do you realize how much she likes you?"

"Is that a fact? . . . Well, shall we make a deal?" From his topcoat Hyŏn-t'ae produced the money from Yun-gu and set it in front of the woman. He couldn't have explained why he was doing this. It just seemed the natural thing to do.

For her part the woman spread out the money and then looked askance at Hyŏn-t'ae with bleary eyes, contemplating this immediate response to her words. "You can do better than that," she said. She was recalling their previous discussion of fifty thousand hwan as the price for Kye-hyang's "first night." "Give me another ten thousand."

"That's all I got on me," Hyŏn-t'ae responded, lapsing into the woman's P'yŏngan dialect without realizing it.

"I didn't know you were such a tightwad." At the same time, she gathered the bills and stacked them on the table and then left the room. You didn't often find a man who would part so readily with such a sum of money, she thought, congratulating herself on her insight: she had _known_ that hidden beneath Hyŏn-t'ae's seedy looks there was a man with money.

Shortly the woman returned with an armful of bedding. Behind her stood Kye-hyang, wearing a blank expression, pillow in the crook of her arm. After the woman had laid out the bedding she reminded Hyŏn-t'ae that he must undo Kye-hyang's jacket and skirt. This would put him in the bridal-chamber mood. And then she disappeared.

Cold and smooth: her flesh gave him no other sensation. Hyŏn-t'ae recalled the Chosŏn-period celadon bowl in the living room of his home. Whenever he stroked its surface the limpid white color and gentle curves reminded him of a woman's body. But with Kye-hyang's body it was the reverse: merely the cold, sleek sensation of a white porcelain pot; nothing feminine there. Nor any feminine reaction. Although the act itself was disappointing, the impression she normally gave him was intact, producing in him a kind of relief. The combination of alcohol and exhaustion quickly put him to sleep.

The next thing he knew, the Pyongyang woman was calling someone. He opened his eyes. The window was bright with day.

"Such a sleepyhead! Time to rise, child," came the woman's voice, amiable and affectionate, almost a whisper.

Immediately Kye-hyang rose, dressed, and left, without so much as a glance in Hyŏn-t'ae's direction. Her face was cold as ever, cold as a white porcelain bowl could be. Hyŏn-t'ae had always felt out of sorts when he woke up next to a streetwalker. It was the change in the woman's looks: the tangled, bushy hair, the smudged makeup, the messy face, the dead-fish eyes. There was no escaping the loathing he felt when he realized this was the woman he had fondled the previous night. To be sure, with Kye-hyang the act had held no excitement for him. But that face, altogether chill and hard after their night together, left him feeling unencumbered. You didn't have to be obligated to a person like that. While mulling this over he fell back to sleep.

# 15

THE WOMAN was staring at the billboard of the Cinema Korea when Hyŏn-t'ae saw her. He was on his way home from meeting a former homeroom teacher from middle school who had contacted Hyŏn-t'ae about a job. Emerging from an alley he had glanced indifferently at the woman, at which point she set off toward the main street. There she hesitated, trying to choose, so it seemed, between City Hall on the one hand and Kwanghwamun on the other. Hyŏn-t'ae stopped to light a cigarette and that brief pause set the two of them on a peculiar course of action. Hyŏn-t'ae looked up from his cigarette to see the woman steal a glance in his direction. It was obvious she was aware of him. He realized that he had stopped at the same time the woman had. This coincidence had no doubt led her to think he was shadowing her. Before he realized it a grim smile had formed on his haggard face. Might as well take advantage of the situation and follow wherever she leads me, he told himself.

The woman opted for Kwanghwamun. Hyŏn-t'ae followed, keeping a distance of half a dozen strides. At the Kwanghwamun intersection the woman crossed toward Chongno and the offices of the *Tonga Daily*. She didn't look back, but something about the stiffness of her gait told Hyŏn-t'ae that she was aware of him.

Where the Hwashin Department Store became visible in the distance, the woman abruptly turned down an alley to the right. Hyŏn-t'ae followed. A glance told him the alley appeared to be a cul-de-sac. Sure enough, the woman reversed her direction. Her face was thickly made up and she looked straight ahead as she passed Hyŏn-t'ae and exited the alley. Hyŏn-t'ae followed her out the alley, again keeping his distance. He wondered if the woman had known all along that the alley was a dead end and had entered to see if Hyŏn-t'ae was in fact shadowing her.

The woman crossed Chongno toward the Shinshin Department Store and then the cross street to the Hwashin store, which she entered. Hyŏn-t'ae did likewise. He followed her to the third floor, where she made a cursory round of the fashion displays. Every now and then she would pretend to inspect one of the items of clothing, but at the same time she seemed to be checking on Hyŏn-t'ae. Presently she went up to the sixth floor and proceeded to peer one by one at the stills displayed at the movie theater there. Hyŏn-t'ae too looked over the unremarkable scenes.

A short time later the woman left the store, crossed Chongno to a bus stop, and boarded the waiting bus by the rear door. Hyŏn-t'ae boarded by the front door. The next stop was the second intersection of Chongno, and there, just as the bus was about to depart, the woman quickly exited. By the time Hyŏn-t'ae, several straphangers distant from the woman, made his way to the door, the bus had already picked up speed and the bus girl shook her head, refusing to let him off.

Hyŏn-t'ae was let off at the third intersection of Chongno. He found himself in front of the Tansŏngsa movie theater. The film must have started, for only a couple of people were at the box office. Hyŏn-t'ae gazed up at the large billboard on the front of the theater. Even when he went to movies there, the billboard never drew his attention. This particular billboard portrayed, larger than life, a half-naked woman stretched out on her side, and close behind her, also facing the viewer, a man. The movie was *The Prodigal,* starring Lana Turner.

Hyŏn-t'ae gazed vacantly at the painted scene from this movie, then peered at a pair of stills in the plate-glass display beside the box office. One photo showed a nearly nude woman dancing, the other showed two men fighting. The old-fashioned dance and the out-of-date clothing styles suggested that the movie was set in the past. The next pair of stills, from a coming attraction, showed a couple on a terrace kissing with such force that their faces were distorted and, shot from above, the figure of a reclining woman beneath a beach parasol at the ocean—scenes both familiar and yet remote from the viewer's experience.

Hyŏn-t'ae entertained the fleeting thought that once he made up his mind and boarded the plane he could jump right into the lifestyle of those people. He recalled his homeroom teacher's concern when he asked if Hyŏn-t'ae were interested in a social studies position that had opened up at his old middle school. There was such a rush of candidates for the position, the teacher had said, that he had obtained prior approval for Hyŏn-t'ae from the principal. Hyŏn-t'ae was deeply indebted to this teacher, who surprisingly cared for him despite his unremarkable grades. He wanted to follow the suggestion of this teacher who was so devoted to him. But without really thinking about it he had told the teacher he was about to leave for the United States. This unhesitating reply was occasioned not so much by the possibility of freedom from the inertia of his lethargy as by the clear, shining eyes of the children he had seen as he entered the school.

He was about to turn away from the stills when he sensed someone behind him. He turned to see the woman. In spite of himself he smiled. After the woman had observed the stills for a time, she crossed the streetcar tracks and turned in the direction of Ŭlchiro. Hyŏn-t'ae followed, keeping a certain distance as before, even as he asked himself why he was playing this game. At the third intersection of Ŭlchiro she seemed about to choose between going toward the Kukto Theater or the Sudo. But to Hyŏn-t'ae's astonishment she turned right, crossed Ŭlchiro, and walked straight into the police station there. Hyŏn-t'ae came to an abrupt stop, certain the woman was reporting him. But it would be awkward if he were to turn and walk away. And so he too crossed to the police station, keeping the same pace, and looked inside as he passed, to see the woman dialing a phone number. Past the station he stopped and waited as if for a companion who had business inside.

The woman emerged and headed toward the second intersection of Ŭlchiro. Hyŏn-t'ae followed at the same distance as before. This time it seemed her destination was the Chungang Theater, but she walked past it and turned up the hill toward the cathedral. That was the location of the Myŏng-dong Theater, Hyŏn-t'ae realized. When the woman had almost reached the cathedral a piece of paper got stuck to one of her heels, a scrap of newspaper no larger than the palm of your hand. The woman pretended to ignore it and walked on, but it appeared she was constantly aware of its presence and her pace became unbalanced, for with every step the scrap fluttered briefly into view. When she had passed the high point of the hill a beggar boy ran to the woman, removed the scrap by stepping on it, and extended his palm for a reward. The woman ignored him and walked on by. The boy picked up the dirty, punctured scrap and threw it at her back. The headline "Government Rice Released" was visible.

Before the woman reached the Myŏng-dong Theater she entered a tearoom. Hyŏn-t'ae followed her inside. The woman sat down across from a young man. She checked her watch. It all became clear to Hyŏn-t'ae. The woman had a date with the man, and for her the chase was merely a means to pass the time beforehand. It was the same with Hyŏn-t'ae except that no imminent appointment awaited him. He had time on his hands and had used part of it to play this trivial game with her. No harm done. Hyŏn-t'ae ordered coffee, drank it slowly, and left.

Again that day Hyŏn-t'ae met Sŏk-ki and they began drinking early in the evening. At Sŏk-ki's suggestion they went to a place in Taok-dong that specialized in grilled sparrow. In the summer you could sample domestic whiskey there; in winter sparrow and *chŏngjong* were offered.

Sŏk-ki accepted a third drink from Hyŏn-t'ae. He seemed to be pondering something, eyes blinking behind the thick glasses.

"I saw Chong-su this afternoon. The little kid who sat in the front row in middle school, remember? . . . He's been living in Taejŏn, he said. . . . Told me Chae-min and Yŏng-un were killed in the war."

Hyŏn-t'ae had heard of the deaths of other classmates from middle school, but not these two.

"They were always very close. Chae-min was in the north when the war broke out. He came south and joined up right away—made first lieutenant, so they say. But Yŏng-un enlisted before the cease-fire and when they stationed his unit at the front line Chae-min had him pulled back to battalion HQ. He was thinking it might be a little safer there. I guess he took a lot of flak for that. And then the night Yŏng-un arrived, their camp took a direct hit from an enemy shell."

A battlefield where danger and safety lived side by side and every young man was subject to the unpredictable nature of war: some had to die, some were wounded, and others survived—but all with invisible hurts. Hyŏn-t'ae mulled over what Tong-ho had said just before his suicide: *Are we the victims or the victimizers? As far as I can see, every young man who comes out of this war is a victim.*

"You think so? I can see myself as a victimizer," Hyon-t'ae muttered as if he were answering Tong-ho.

Sŏk-ki regarded Hyŏn-t'ae. "Hammered already?" he smirked. Then he gestured with his eyes off to the side. "What kind of enjoyment do you figure he gets coming here by himself? Always a smile on his face, though."

It seemed that every time Hyŏn-t'ae and his friends came to this drinking place, this Australian named Harry was here. Companion or no companion, he always wore a broad, toothy smile. In the course of an evening he would nurse two or three drinks, never with snacks. And when the serving woman poured him a drink he never failed to say thank you, in the accent of Westerners speaking Korean. And if the woman attempted a joke he was able to respond in Korean. The woman must have been bored that day, for she began a routine with the Westerner that Hyŏn-t'ae had heard several times before.

"Mister Harry, how old are you?"

As he always did Harry displayed three fingers of one hand and one finger of the other and said in his accented Korean, "Thirty-one." And then, pointing the one finger toward his forehead, "I'm an old bachelor." That forehead was the only part of his ruddy, glistening face with wrinkles, several of them etched across.

"Mister Harry, you're a grandfather."

This was met with an instant retort: "And you, my little porker, you've had five children."

At first it seemed the Westerner disliked hearing that he was old and meant that the woman was getting on in years, too, but by now his words could be passed off as just a joke.

Sŏk-ki looked on for a time, then raised his drink to his lips. "Bet you won't find another Westerner as good-natured as our pal there."

"Oh, I don't know."

"What's that supposed to mean? How could he act like that if he's not good-hearted?"

"He's lonely."

To Hyŏn-t'ae Harry looked particularly incongruous sitting there that day. Hyŏn-t'ae knew intuitively that the broader-than-usual smile and the bantering tone with the serving woman were an attempt to fit in with the mood of the drinking place, but all he found in those foreign blue eyes was a tinge of cheerlessness. Hyŏn-t'ae imagined himself, once abroad, like Harry was now. Earlier that day he had thought he could plunge into the lifestyle of those people simply by boarding an airplane and maybe divest himself of the idle life he'd been leading. Now he was not so sure.

He and Sŏk-ki left. Next on their itinerary was a drinking place that featured skewered snacks. They ordered. Hyŏn-t'ae drank, not touching the skewers. "You ever felt like you had too much freedom?" he suddenly blurted. And then as if he hadn't expected a response in the first place: "I don't mean an excess of freedom in and of itself. I mean the excess you feel when you can't deal with that freedom. . . . You know what it's like once you've fallen into that situation? At first you move your foot a little and you think you can get out of it. But it doesn't work. You can move your whole body, but the more you move the deeper you go. . . . And there's something else. When you fall into that swamp, you have no idea the situation you're getting into. You find you're in up to your knees, then up to your waist, then your chest, then your neck, see? . . . While it's happening, you figure you can call out for someone to save you. But it doesn't work that way. Once you fall into an excess of freedom it's all over. Once you realize where you are, you're already in over your neck."

He turned his drink-red eyes toward Sŏk-ki and continued: "What the hell is it makes you fall into that state? . . . What makes a man so incapable that he can't handle freedom when it's given to him? . . . When does it happen? Where? And who the hell is it that makes a man incompetent? Hmm?"

But he didn't seem to expect an answer here either. Meeting Sŏk-ki's eyes, he picked up his drink and muttered: "I wish I was back on the battlefield. I wish I could face death and get my confidence back. I was absolutely sure of myself then."

Sŏk-ki looked intently at Hyŏn-t'ae: "You've turned into a pussy of a drinker, pal."

Silently they sipped their drinks. This was the usual pattern: to chatter about this and that once they'd reached a certain level of intoxication, then drink more, and then fall silent while continuing to drink.

Two young men entered, visibly intoxicated, and took the adjoining table. "You're too timid, that's why," said one of them. He wore a navy blue topcoat. Sŏk-ki and Hyŏn-t'ae had occasionally seen this man there.

"I did it the only way I knew—you know a better way?" said the other, who wore an ash-gray overcoat. He stole a glance at Hyŏn-t'ae and Sŏk-ki as he spoke. Hyŏn-t'ae and Sŏk-ki had never seen the second man.

"Well, as long as you're going to scam your way out," said the man with the navy-blue topcoat. "You've seen this, haven't you?" So saying, he spread out the fingers of his right hand on the table. The index finger was severed at the second knuckle. The young man flashed a smile. "It was over in a second. Close your eyes tight, *whack!* and it's gone. I cut it off during the war and it's been a good-luck charm ever since."

The man in the ash-gray overcoat observed the hand in silence. His face was pale and there was a gleam in his eye.

The man in the navy blue topcoat proudly flourished the hand, emptied his drink, and erupted in laughter. "What's the matter? So what if I didn't cut it off to avoid the northerners' army? Who cares when I did it? The important thing is, I decided to do it. And once I did, everything was okay. 'Cause I didn't need any papers to show. Didn't have to starve myself like you every time you had a physical and pretend to have TB. Fact is, it's better than a discharge notice. You can lose the notice, but here I've got the proof as long as I live. And you never know, if there's another war—"

"Shut the fuck up, you weasels!" bellowed Sŏk-ki. Until then he had been silently drinking, leaning slightly forward.

The conversation between the two young men came to an abrupt halt.

"You little weasels—I hope your children are born without a finger and catch TB," Sŏk-ki spat in his low-pitched voice.

Presently the two young men rose and paid their bill. As they were leaving, the one in the navy blue topcoat turned back toward Sŏk-ki.

"Why don't you step outside, asshole?"

Sŏk-ki slowly rose and turned in the young man's direction. The man picked up an earthenware cup and heaved it toward Sŏk-ki. Drunk though he was, Sŏk-ki managed to avoid it. The cup skimmed just beneath Sŏk-ki's ear and shattered against the wall. Before Sŏk-ki could give chase the young man shot outside the door, which his companion was holding open.

"Come on," said Hyŏn-t'ae. "Sit down and drink. I don't like all this commotion."

"Who does? But you heard those assholes." Sŏk-ki removed his glasses and cleaned off the liquid from the flying cup. "What are you supposed to do with guys like that?"

Hyŏn-t'ae and Sŏk-ki drank a while longer before deciding to move on to a drinking place with hostesses. Sŏk-ki left first while Hyŏn-t'ae went to the bathroom. By the time Hyŏn-t'ae went outside, Sŏk-ki was in a boxing stance and a man lay sprawled in front of him. Behind the man, casting shadows in the dim light of a streetlamp, stood half a dozen men poised to attack, the two young men in topcoats among them.

Hyŏn-t'ae's head cleared in a flash. He dashed back into the drinking place, flung down his jacket, and grabbed an empty bottle. He hurried outside and broke the bottle over the skull of the first man he saw. The man cried out and slumped to the ground. Hyŏn-t'ae now thrust out with the jagged neck of the bottle at the throat of the young man in the navy blue topcoat. But before the bottle could reach its target a foot caught Hyŏn-t'ae in the pit of the stomach and sent him sprawling. He tried to collect himself and rise, but was kicked in the chin. The world started spinning and he blacked out.

The next thing he knew, someone seemed to be calling him. His mouth was filled with a sticky liquid; he spat. And then he realized the voice was not calling him. "Stick him! Stick him!" It was the young man in the ash-gray coat. His eyes had their distinctive glint and his face looked a shade paler in the faint light cast by the streetlamp. The man he was addressing had a knife and was slowly advancing toward Sŏk-ki, who was still in his boxing stance. Sŏk-ki's glasses were gone and in the light of the streetlamp Hyŏn-t'ae saw him squint at his opponent, a smile flickering at the corners of his mouth. _You have to get up_, Hyŏn-t'ae told himself. _Have to get up and tackle the guy with the knife. Figure the distance and it's easy enough._ But all he did was look in Sŏk-ki's direction. Sŏk-ki kept his stance, and the wisp of a smile, waiting, solitary and implacable. "Stick him! Stick him!" The man with the knife moved with measured steps, then in one motion reached Sŏk-ki and stabbed him in the side. Sŏk-ki's fist shot out but only connected with air. The man stabbed Sŏk-ki several times in quick succession. Sŏk-ki threw more punches at the air before collapsing with a moan that seemed to issue from deep inside.

By the time Hyŏn-t'ae picked himself up and went to Sŏk-ki's side the thugs had disappeared and just as quickly a crowd had formed.

"Drive him to the hospital!" someone shouted.

"Back off, all of you! Don't touch him!" Hyŏn-t'ae barked as several onlookers prepared to lift Sŏk-ki. He hefted Sŏk-ki onto his back and threaded his way through the crowd.

Two weeks after the Songdo hotel incident Hyŏn-t'ae received a call from Sugi. They arranged to meet and Hyŏn-t'ae hung up. *It was only a matter of time.* He realized that while he had tried not to think about their last encounter, it had been oppressing him all along.

The first thing Hyŏn-t'ae noticed in the gaunt figure that confronted him at the Kwigŏrae Tearoom was a glimpse of hatred. He resigned himself to that hatred, whatever its manifestation.

Sugi fixed Hyŏn-t'ae with a sullen gaze he had never seen from her, a look that made her eyes seem larger. While he waited for her to speak he looked out the window behind her. The wind was coming up. The bare branches of the trees lining the street swayed back and forth above the hunched forms of people pressing forward with their flapping coats gathered about them. The door to the tearoom kept up an endless clatter. Hyŏn-t'ae was reminded of what Sŏk-ki had muttered a short time before as Hyŏn-t'ae gazed at the gusty scene outside the hospital room window. "Darn it—wish I didn't have to lie on the same side all the time. Can't wait to be out in that wind, walking around. And find those weasels and beat the crap out of them." Fortunately the stab wounds to his right side had missed the heart and lungs. Sŏk-ki had been led to believe he would be fine once those wounds healed. What he didn't know was that the wound to his left wrist had severed the radial nerve and he would never be able to use the hand. It would take time for Sŏk-ki's side to heal, and Hyŏn-t'ae understood that the reason for not telling him the full extent of his injuries was to spare him the bad news. He wondered how Sŏk-ki would take it when the bandage was finally removed to reveal his useless wrist. Hyŏn-t'ae had asked the doctor to tell Sŏk-ki the truth even if the shock of it resulted in a longer recovery. *When would be the best time to tell him?*

"I just couldn't leave things as they stand. I had to see you once more. And in the light of day. . . . Though there's really nothing I have to say." She bit down firmly on her lower lip, her face cold and pale. "You told me I could interpret Tong-ho's unwritten letter anyway I wanted. But to me it was just a blank sheet of paper. In the end, he had nothing to say and I had nothing to hear."

Hyŏn-t'ae shifted his gaze from the window to Sugi. "Am I responsible for that?"

"Is that all you can say?" Sugi responded with a brief, cold smile. "How in heaven's name can you talk of responsibility when you and your friends don't care about it at all? You try to avoid everything, even yourselves. . . . " She turned away, unable to control her violent emotions. A milky halo of perspiration formed at the tip of her nose and the sides.

Hyŏn-t'ae looked back out the window. The wind continued to shake the trees. The branches shook, the window shuddered, voices buzzed about them, and directly across from him Sugi was full of anger. Hyŏn-t'ae found himself descending a quiet and lonely mountain slope in uninhabited territory. The rays of the summer sun beat down relentlessly. Visibility infinite. Dwellings crouched below, half a dozen or more, thatched roofs looking impossibly heavy. Rifle close to his side, muzzle forward, Hyŏn-t'ae took one careful step after another. But why was this quiet and lonely space, free of impediment, such a stifling obstacle? He looked to the side. Keeping a six-foot interval, Tong-ho advanced cautiously, eyes intent on what lay ahead, rifle close to his side. Hyŏn-t'ae wanted to say: *Hey, Poet, how would you describe your feelings at a time like this? Wouldn't you rather have an enemy in sight?* The trees still shook outside, the window still shuddered, voices hummed inside the tearoom, Sugi full of hatred, face averted, was directly across from him, and he heard himself saying to Tong-ho: *Look, Poet, what are you giving me that disgusted look for? When I went down there that woman didn't put up much resistance. But guess what—when I get up to go she grabs me by the hand. Well, I knew what that meant. So I got rid of her. Simple as that. But you know. . . .*

Sugi's gaze turned back to Hyŏn-t'ae. Her eyes burned with an inner fire. "The lot of you . . . Tong-ho, yourself, you're beyond salvation." Her lower lip quivered. She rose from her seat. "There's no reason for us to see each other anymore."

# 16

SŎK-KI HAD LOST the use of three fingers on his left hand in addition to the wrist. He could bend his ring finger about halfway; the little finger alone moved freely as before. Normally so cheerful, for several days after he learned of his disability he lay listlessly on his side, his face dismal, making little attempt to talk when Hyŏn-t'ae visited.

One day, when his side had healed enough for him to move about, he squinted at Hyŏn-t'ae and said: "They say I can't use my wrist now. I just wish I could move my thumb and forefinger so I could shoot billiards—this ceiling's starting to look like a billiard table. But I ought to be thankful—I can still hold a shot glass." He managed a smile as he displayed his good hand.

To Hyŏn-t'ae this seemingly resigned smile was more painful to witness. That smile coupled with Sŏk-ki's acknowledgment of his misfortune appeared even more forlorn to Hyŏn-t'ae than when his friend had lain in silence, his face dark in reaction to the awareness of his infirmity. But then the way Sŏk-ki had forbidden intervention that night of the fight outside the drinking place: Hyŏn-t'ae could have prevented his friend's infirmity, but for some reason he didn't reproach himself for his failure to do so.

Using the prescription from the eye clinic where he had taken Sŏk-ki, he bought his friend a new pair of glasses. Sŏk-ki tried them on, observed Hyŏn-t'ae momentarily, and said: "No good—everything's too bright." Removing the glasses, he added: "I don't want to be looking through these when I see my mother."

Hyŏn-t'ae had seen Sŏk-ki's mother at the hospital. She was small in frame and stature, unlike her son, and had silently approached his bedside where she sat motionless, hands clenching the bedsheet. Her face was lined with wrinkles thick and fine. Before anyone knew it her eyes, almost a part of those wrinkles, began to spill tears. In Sŏk-ki's mother Hyŏn-t'ae saw a woman caught between husband and son and suffering silently on that account.

According to Sŏk-ki, his father had worked as a legal aide for over thirty years and his one dream was to launch his son in a career as a judge. He wanted to see, realized in his son, the majesty of a presiding judge in judicial robes, seated high at the bench, wielding his gavel, and after freezing the courtroom into silence, solemnly pronouncing sentence. Astonishingly, though, Sŏk-ki had developed a craze for boxing. Angered, his father had taken every opportunity thereafter to harangue his wife, saying that she had made their son the way he was owing to her inability to raise him properly. Not once, though, did his mother ever scold Sŏk-ki. For one thing, he was their only son. But more important, his mother was by nature tenderhearted—one who could not bring herself to look directly at her son after he returned from the war with his eye injury.

"It would be easier for me if Mother nagged me like Father does," Sŏk-ki had added. "But all she does is read my face like she's afraid of what I might say. It drives me crazy."

Such was the woman who had located her son's room, sat at his bedside clutching the sheet, and wept soundlessly before saying in her small voice that Sŏk-ki's father was too busy to visit. It had sounded like an excuse. Sŏk-ki, lying on his side and not looking at his mother, had bluntly responded: "Go on home now." And yet his tone was tinged with a child's pristine sentiment for his mother. This was not the first time Hyŏn-t'ae had seen this side of rough-and-tumble Sŏk-ki. He could understand Sŏk-ki's reluctance to see his mother's wrinkled face close up.

Sŏk-ki fumbled the glasses into their case with his right hand and said suggestively: "I don't have to see in order to bring a drink to my mouth."

Outside the hospital Hyŏn-t'ae was walking aimlessly in the direction of Ŭlchiro when someone hailed him from behind. He turned to see a man who had just walked past him in the opposite direction.

A gentle smile appeared on the man's face. "Excuse me, but weren't you stationed at Sot'ogomi during the war?"

Hyŏn-t'ae couldn't place the man.

"You may not know me, but I think you might remember Sergeant First Class Sŏnu. At the canteen? The one who was drunk and acted strange?" He went on to explain that he was Sergeant An, who had followed Sŏnu around trying to persuade him not to drink.

A recollection surfaced from the far reaches of Hyŏn-t'ae's memory, but he had trouble relating the man he saw before him with the Sergeant An of that time.

An asked Hyŏn-t'ae to join him for a short while and they went to a nearby bakeshop.

"I think I've seen you on the street," An said. "But you looked so different I was afraid to just walk up to you."

"You have a good memory for faces. So what are you doing these days?"

"I'm in divinity school."

Hyŏn-t'ae searched his mind for the man possessing the remarkably gentle tone and manner An now displayed.

"I was really upset when I heard that quiet-looking man killed himself. But then I don't think any of us were in our right mind back then." An skewered a section of doughnut on his fork. "And there was another one. He had a dark-complected face."

Hyŏn-t'ae told An about Yun-gu's poultry farm.

"Well, good for him. I prayed for that man once. Remember at the canteen when Sergeant Sŏnu fell down drunk and that man said: 'Quite a performance'? That remark really saddened me. To say such a thing when someone's in distress. . . . " This was uttered in a tone even gentler—characteristic of those who follow the religious life. "So, a poultry farm," An continued. "There's a kind of truth to be discovered there. Take a mustard seed, plant it in the ground, then look at the shoot that comes out, and there you can find the mysteries of the universe. It's the same with an egg. You can analyze it scientifically—a certain percentage is water, a certain percentage fat, part of it's the white, part is inert. But isn't there another part that can't be explained that way? What I mean is the mystery of life. I hope that gentleman's heart can extend to that point."

Such puerile but commonsensical remarks coming from a divinity student struck Hyŏn-t'ae as ridiculous. But they were so artless and sincere he could not really scorn them.

"Is Sergeant Sŏnu in Seoul now?" Hyŏn-t'ae felt compelled to ask.

"Yes, but he's in the hospital—it's been quite a story."

Hyŏn-t'ae wondered if Sŏnu had been drinking too much. "He always seemed to have a tremendous appetite for booze."

"Actually he quit drinking. . . . The problem was, he was never able to find peace of mind and so he had himself admitted. But he's all better now and it won't be long before they let him go home. I'm going there now and I expect I'll find out exactly when." An produced a beatific smile. "I was wondering . . . if you're not too busy would you like to come along? He'd like that very much. You should have seen how happy he was the other day when I showed up with our minister and our lay preacher."

An's motive for hailing him on the street, Hyŏn-t'ae now suspected, was to take him along to the hospital to help cheer up Sŏnu. But Hyŏn-t'ae could not remember Sŏnu any more than he had remembered An. Sŏnu was merely someone Hyŏn-t'ae had happened to meet while drinking one evening during his army days. And to Sŏnu, Hyŏn-t'ae was likely the same.

No matter how he considered it, visiting Sŏnu seemed nothing short of awkward. He doubted the man would recognize him, let alone take delight from his visit. But then from the recesses of Hyŏn-t'ae's mind there surfaced the image of a man in fatigues staggering to a hesitant halt, turning slowly, ever so slowly, in Hyŏn-t'ae's direction, and fixing him with a grin. Hyŏn-t'ae suddenly felt a desire to see Sergeant First Class Sŏnu. He wanted to see what a man looked like who had recovered from a nervous breakdown.

Hyŏn-t'ae followed An through Anguk-dong to Sudo Military Hospital. Along the way An related the circumstances resulting in Sŏnu's hospitalization. Two years previous An had been discharged and entered divinity school. Sŏnu, however, made a firm decision to remain in the military, and was transferred to a base in Seoul. Around that time Sŏnu finally gave in to An: he quit drinking and began to attend church regularly. One Sunday the two of them were on their way home after the service when Sŏnu fixed a penetrating gaze on a middle school student and followed him off the bus. An got off as well, asking Sŏnu if he knew the student. But Sŏnu remained silent, his expression serious as he followed the boy. When the student turned down an alley, Sŏnu followed and to An's surprise ran up to the boy and ripped the back pocket off his pants. Then, his hand trembling, he handed the astonished student the scrap of cloth.

"He said that when he saw the opening of the pocket he felt an irresistible urge to tear it off. I didn't think too much of it at the time—I thought maybe his nerves were a bit strained."

A month later An and Sŏnu were at the Sunday service. Sŏnu was fidgeting constantly and didn't seem interested in the sermon. The veins stood out in his temples as if he were straining to suppress something. Finally he reached out to the back of someone sitting in front of him. A small piece of thread was stuck there. Carefully he removed the thread, then hastened to insert it between the pages of his Bible. Instantly a peaceful glow lit up his face, along with a relieved smile. Outside after the service Sŏnu asked An if he had a match. When An said no Sŏnu produced the thread from his Bible, rolled it into a ball between his fingers, buried it in the corner of the churchyard, and tamped down the soil with his foot.

"After that he didn't leave the base for a week. When I didn't see him at church I got to wondering and went looking for him. Guess what—apparently he'd been acting peculiar and they'd recently admitted him to the hospital."

An had rushed to the hospital. When the medical officer assigned to Sŏnu learned that he was a childhood friend of the patient he plied An with questions about Sŏnu's past. When the doctor told An that Sŏnu needed treatment, An proceeded to relate in detail the massacre of Sŏnu's parents in the North during the war, Sŏnu's exaction of blood revenge by shooting an enemy sympathizer, and the image of that incident, which haunted him when he was drunk.

Sŏnu was in a ward with three other patients. When he saw An, he greeted him in normal fashion. But when An asked about his condition, Sŏnu responded equivocally: he seemed about to say something but then looked away and began repeatedly and needlessly to reposition his Bible and wipe its cover. An wondered if, as the medical officer speculated, this behavior reflected Sŏnu's desire to erase the anxieties and obsessions resulting from a dormant but deep-seated guilt complex and skepticism about God.

With every subsequent visit An found Sŏnu worse. Sŏnu seemed to recognize An but kept his face averted and spoke not a word. During this time his psychological affliction degenerated into schizophrenia.

"It was awful. When the doctor asked if he had eaten he'd say yes, he had gone for a walk. Or if the doctor pointed to a light and asked what it was, he'd say it was God. Always with an empty smile on his face. And he ripped up the Bible he used to cherish so much. It got to be too painful for me to watch."

An lapsed into a thoughtful silence before continuing: "And then, miraculously, he began to take a slow turn for the better not so long ago—thanks mostly to his doctor. I've never seen a doctor so committed whether he was trying shock treatment or psychotherapy. He kept up with him for a year. I did what I could, praying for him morning and evening. In any event, we can think of it as God's grace. These days he takes his Bible reading very seriously. Do you remember when he said, 'You can't prove God exists, and you can't prove he doesn't. To the ones who believe in him, he exists; to those who don't, he doesn't.' And then he said he didn't believe, and so he could put his mind to rest. Well, it turns out he realized that God did exist. . . . Anyhow, it seems we've come to the end of that chapter in his life."

The psychiatric ward was at the end of the left corridor of the hospital's front wing. At the head of a short flight of steps they entered the ward to find a broad hallway lined on both sides with sickrooms. Although it was midday, the interior was gloomy enough to make you feel that lights were needed.

An, a frequent visitor who would likely be recognized by everyone on duty, gave a simple greeting to the soldier at the reception desk and proceeded past him.

"One moment, please."

An turned back.

"You're here to see Sergeant Sŏnu, room 103?"

"That's right."

"Would you check in first with Captain Pak, please?"

"The director of the ward?"

"Yes."

An turned to Hyŏn-t'ae. "I think he wants to talk about the discharge formalities. Could you wait here for a minute, please?" An proceeded to the second door on the left and knocked. The occupant responded with a grunt. An entered.

A short time later An emerged with a shortish, round-faced medical officer. Even in the dimly lit hallway An's face was noticeably pale.

"How could this have happened?"

"That's what I'd like to know."

"So there's no chance of seeing him?"

"There's no point. He doesn't recognize anyone. Though he's calmed down a little this morning."

"What do you think it was?"

"Well, there's nothing we've been able to isolate. Just the previous day he told me that his mind had never seemed clearer or his mood better. And then yesterday afternoon, as I told you, he wanted to sharpen his pencil and the nursing officer brought him a fruit knife. You see, when he reads his Bible he underlines with the pencil. So she didn't think anything about the knife. But when she turned to leave, he jumped her and stabbed her in the back. She's all right—the point was blunt—but it was a close call. But when he stabbed her he shouted the strangest thing: 'Let's see if you fall backward when you die!' And he kept shouting it till late at night." The tone of the medical officer's methodical account showed his disappointment at the failure of his painstaking efforts over such a long period.

"I'd like to see him if he's calmed down." An's face revealed a mix of suffering and uneasiness.

"Hard to say when that might be. He's still mumbling about something or other. . . . What if we take a listen at the door to his room?"

So saying, the officer set off ahead of them. Hyŏn-t'ae followed An, who had been avoiding eye contact with him.

The officer came to a stop in front of a small room at the end of the hall. After testing the doorknob to see that the door was locked he stepped aside to reveal number 108 on the door. Probably a private room where Sŏnu had been transferred, Hyŏn-t'ae told himself. From within they heard muttering; the voice was hoarse. By straining to listen they could make out the words:

> Yet I planted you a choice vine,
> > wholly of pure seed.
> How then have you turned degenerate
> > and become a wild vine?

An put his ear to the door and closed his eyes, concentrating on the words:

> The whole land shall be a desolation;
> > yet I will not make a full end.
> For this the earth shall mourn,
> > and the heavens above be black . . .

An opened his eyes. His expression had brightened slightly. "It's Jeremiah," he explained to the medical officer in an undertone. "One of his favorite books. Do you think he's reading from the Bible or quoting from memory?"

"It has to be from memory. After what happened yesterday he ripped his Bible up just like he did that other time."

"What's the outlook? Can we hope for another recovery?"

"That's difficult to say. We'll just have to see how it plays out." Hyŏn-t'ae heard despair in the officer's voice.

The hoarse voice continued from within:

Woe is me because of my hurt!
My wound is grievous.
But I said, "Truly this is an affliction,
and I must bear it."

Hyŏn-t'ae left the hospital. An stayed behind to learn more about Sŏnu's condition. An inexplicable anger surged through Hyŏn-t'ae. He wandered aimlessly before deciding that this sudden fit of rage was ridiculous: what did Sŏnu's relapse have to do with him? Hyŏn-t'ae felt utterly exhausted. He wanted to lie down. After returning home he began another period of hibernation.

# 17

"I BOUGHT THE TICKET. Your flight leaves Tuesday. Remember that."

Hyŏn-t'ae was about to venture out for the first time in days when his mother summoned him into her room with these words. During his hibernation following the visit with An to the military hospital, she had visited him in his room again and again to lecture him. It had been two months since the visa was issued—why was he frittering away the time like this? Three times she'd extended the departure date for him—did he realize how embarrassing it was for her to have to explain this to others? This time she would tolerate no more excuses. She had notified relatives and friends already living in the States, she said, and then proceeded to enumerate them. To every such lecture Hyŏn-t'ae would readily respond, "Yes, I'd better go."

Perhaps his mother felt that if she didn't act promptly her son wouldn't leave of his own accord. And so she had made a point of purchasing his plane ticket herself. "Allow yourself enough time to get your shots and pack. Otherwise the last few days will be frantic. Everything else is arranged. And you'll want to get a haircut. . . ." She seemed to ponder this last request, then added: "Best save the haircut for the day before you leave."

Who else but a mother would treat her children as youngsters even after they're grown, Hyŏn-t'ae silently observed. But sometimes motherly affection backfired and got annoying. On this particular day, though, Hyŏn-t'ae silently heard out his mother's scolding and was about to leave her room when on impulse he said: "Mother, please don't go to the airport on Tuesday."

"What is that supposed to mean?" She eyed Hyŏn-t'ae dubiously.

"Oh, nothing special."

Hyŏn-t'ae knew that when the day came, she would accompany him to the airport. And she would cry. And for a brief time reproach herself, as any mother would do, for hurrying her son off to a distant place. Hyŏn-t'ae, though, would allow no trace of sorrow to appear on his face. On the contrary, at the time of departure he would turn a smiling face to his family: to his father, preoccupied with planning his new business, hands folded behind his back, a distant look in his eyes as he regarded Hyŏn-t'ae; to his younger brother, perhaps outlining in his mind the hike he would take the following Sunday, the slight excitement he felt at his brother's departure giving way to the delight of anticipation; and to his mother, perhaps steeped in sorrow at assuming that her son's stoic exterior masked the sadness he wished to suppress for her benefit. But Hyŏn-t'ae, to the very end, would display no sign of regret. He would briefly consider the state of his mother's health. Yet even this was of scant concern, given the increasing efficacy of her medication these days. He would feel no cause for concern for any of them. With unencumbered mind he would board the plane. Without a backward look. And that would be it.

With such thoughts Hyŏn-t'ae left his mother's room.

It had been quite a few days since he had been outside, and the street seemed unusually bright. It was rather warm for the beginning of March. His overcoat hung heavily from his shoulders.

Hyŏn-t'ae headed for the hospital in Taok-dong where Sŏk-ki was being treated. It was a route he had often taken. Still, he carefully observed the streetside shops—their interiors and surroundings—

wondering if this place and that had been there the previous time. But he could recall nothing about what kind of shops they were.

He'd been absorbed in a recurring thought: he had come up against an impasse and must now reach a decision. It took effort to deflect this thought, but he did so by telling himself that everything would work out once he boarded that plane. *Good old Sŏk-ki ought to be a lot better by now. But he's such an impetuous guy—he's going to have a devil of a time getting used to doing things with one hand. Says he won't wear his glasses because he can't bear to see his mother's wrinkled face up close. Imagine a big, strapping guy like that telling his mother to go home! Listen, pal, it's no good being so tenderhearted.*

Hyŏn-t'ae found Sŏk-ki sitting up in bed and looking outside. At Hyŏn-t'ae's approach he squinted at his friend and said in a tone of great delight: "Well, look here. I thought you'd dropped dead. Good timing on your part."

"Why's that?"

"I'm getting out tomorrow."

"Is that what your doctor said?"

"He said the day after tomorrow, but what difference does an extra day make? So he agreed on tomorrow. And you know what day it is tomorrow?"

"What?"

"It's Saturday. Hey, don't tell me you forgot the weekly get-together."

Hyŏn-t'ae, amazed at Sŏk-ki's concern with the Saturday gathering, could only observe his friend's face.

"I'll bet one drink sets my head spinning," Sŏk-ki said, stroking his chin with his right hand. His beard had grown out unevenly, giving his face a shabby appearance.

"Hey, use a little common sense. You need to plant your butt at home for the time being."

"Not me. I've been going crazy here—felt like running away. I've got to get moving—bad if I don't. Doctor told me he's never seen a patient whose muscles regenerated as fast as mine. There's no restriction on what I can do now. Anyhow, tomorrow's a fresh start. I'll be all right."

Hyŏn-t'ae changed the subject: "I'm all set to leave the country." He proceeded to tell Sŏk-ki that a plane ticket for the following Tuesday had been purchased.

Sŏk-ki momentarily regarded Hyŏn-t'ae with his slit eyes, then said weakly: "Well, it really has been a while since your visa was issued." His face clouded. "Asshole!" he suddenly spat to no one in particular. Then he resumed in his guttural voice: "This means we'll have to combine the Saturday get-together with a last-minute sendoff for you. You've told Yun-gu you're leaving, right? So I need to scheme my way out of here. Oh, could you pass this on to my father? I was going to have my mother do it, but now that I've got you here. . . . If my mother gives it to him he'll raise hell with her again on account of me. Seems they had a similar go-around about the bill when I was admitted." So saying, Sŏk-ki produced an envelope from the bed-stand and handed it to Hyŏn-t'ae.

"You're writing to tell them you're getting out? Then how come it's so thick?"

Sŏk-ki burst into laughter. "No choice. I have to make sure he pays up without a fuss—there's sixty-five thousand wŏn left on my hospital bill."

"Oh, I get it. A literary gem."

"Of course," Sŏk-ki laughed. "The gist is simple. I'm asking him to hire me as his assistant. So this letter is a kind of employment exam essay question."

Hyŏn-t'ae laughed as well. "Swell. So the honorable judge ends up the assistant of a legal aide."

"Still, the outcome is in doubt. Father's been doing the same work for thirty-odd years now, and it won't be easy to suit his fancy. He can listen once to the client and then write out a bill of complaint without having to correct a single word."

"I bet you could ask to be his apprentice if he won't take you on as assistant."

Both laughed, though the matter was not especially laughable. Hyŏn-t'ae rose from his chair.

"Going?" said Sŏk-ki. "All right, then. Don't forget the letter. And next Tuesday—you said Tuesday, right? When's your flight?"

"Eleven," Hyŏn-t'ae said, though he was unsure of the exact time.

"Okay, I'll catch up with you on everything when we get together tomorrow."

Hyŏn-t'ae left the hospital and walked as far as the Ministry of Home Affairs, near where Ŭlchiro began. There he found a taxi with a passenger headed for Hoegi-dong and climbed in. The taxi passed through Ch'ŏngnyangni and let Hyŏn-t'ae off at the end of Hoegi-dong.

Along the road to Yun-gu's poultry farm Hyŏn-t'ae noticed many new homes and public housing. A few small sundries shops had appeared as well. Hyŏn-t'ae recalled the sketch map to the farm that he had prepared for Sugi. As if to push thoughts of her from his mind, he looked around wide-eyed and located the tobacco shop he had drawn as a landmark. It was buried among the other shops.

He entered the plank gate to the poultry farm to see Yun-gu and a carpenter hanging the door to a new henhouse. Even from a distance he could see that Yun-gu's movements were energetic. Instead of calling out to Yun-gu he remained in the yard and turned his gaze to the original henhouse. Many of the chickens were pecking away at their feed. In another henhouse Yun-gu's helper was feeding the chickens, who had formed a solid mass around the feed bucket. Finally Yun-gu noticed Hyŏn-t'ae.

"Hey, when did you get here?"

"Just now."

Yun-gu stopped what he was doing and approached. His tanned face, characteristic of someone who worked in the open air, had a firmness and luster to it. The sawdust and bits of grass in his kinky black hair seemed to hint at his tenacious temperament.

"This is getting to be a pretty big operation."

"Has to be. No use raising chickens on a small scale. Sink or swim,

I'm going to try big." Despite the connotation of "sink or swim," Yun-gu said this with the assurance of someone who had done his calculations.

An elderly man with a bamboo basket emerged from a henhouse and walked past Hyŏn-t'ae and Yun-gu toward the storage shed. He had been hired at the time Yun-gu decided to expand by buying new chicks.

"Care for an egg?" asked Yun-gu.

"No thanks."

"You might think someone who raises hens can eat eggs any old time he pleases, but it doesn't work that way." _Said like a business-man,_ Hyŏn-t'ae told himself. "Let's see—we ought to go inside and sit. But I've been keeping the new chicks in the living quarters. The three of us share that room across the way and it's a mess."

"Actually I need to run."

"Let's talk first—it's been a while since you were here." Yun-gu addressed the elderly man as he appeared from the shed: "Could you bring me that bench?"

The man went to the new henhouse and returned with the bench. It was obvious that it had been built along with the new henhouse, for the grain of the rough-planed lumber retained its original hue. Yun-gu blew dust from the bench, then perched on its edge along with Hyŏn-t'ae. After explaining various aspects of his predicament in managing a poulty farm he turned to the subject of Sŏk-ki.

"How is our friend coming along? I keep telling myself I should visit. . . . Close to a month he's been in the hospital, isn't it?"

"He'll be out in two or three days." Hyŏn-t'ae did not mention Sŏk-ki's decision to have himself discharged the following day, or his desire for a Saturday get-together. Nor did he tell Yun-gu about the ticket for the Tuesday flight.

"I think he drinks too much too. And—"

"Why don't you get back to work? I've got to go. But first I need to borrow some money."

Yun-gu had suspected that Hyŏn-t'ae had a motive for visiting. He wouldn't have come all the way to the farm just for fresh air or to say hello. But hadn't his helper sent Hyŏn-t'ae this month's installment just three days ago?

"You did get the money from the boy, right?"

"Yeah."

"Then how much more do you need?"

"Whatever you have. Sixty, seventy thousand."

*So he's got a new woman,* Yun-gu told himself. Thank heaven he hadn't agreed to Hyŏn-t'ae's proposal for spending-money loans. Here he was approaching him out of the blue for money even after the monthly payments had begun. If Yun-gu had consented to Hyŏn-t'ae's idea wouldn't their financial dealings have got even messier?

"That's going to be a problem. All the money I've managed to scrape together went into that henhouse there."

"Not much you can do then," Hyŏn-t'ae said, raising himself from the bench.

"Hang on," said Yun-gu, reluctant to send Hyŏn-t'ae home with the situation unresolved. "The boy has some money he's been saving up. Wait here." Yun-gu called the boy and together they went inside. A short time later Yun-gu emerged with a stack of crisp banknotes. "It's not quite fifty thousand—forty-five to be exact. Will that work?. And instead of a loan think of it as a month-and-a-half installment in advance."

Hyŏn-t'ae shared a taxi back to the city. He was left off in front of the Ministry of Home Affairs and from there he returned to Sŏk-ki's hospital. Just to the right of the main entrance was an examination room. Hyŏn-t'ae entered. A doctor was reading the evening paper. At Hyŏn-t'ae's approach he looked up. The doctor confirmed what Sŏk-ki had said—yes, it was possible for him to be discharged. Hyŏn-t'ae left the examination room, combined his own money with the funds Yun-gu had given him, and got to work on the discharge papers.

After paying Sŏk-ki's hospital bill Hyŏn-t'ae produced from his overcoat the letter Sŏk-ki had asked him to forward to his father. On one side of the envelope he wrote: "Passed employment exam; letter unnecessary. Sole remaining condition: interview with Father." He was about to hand the letter to the nurse when he remembered to add: "Have to skip tomorrow's get-together."

Twilight was falling. Hyŏn-t'ae entered a streetside tearoom, ordered coffee, drank.

Back outside, he followed his footsteps, arriving at the Cinema Korea. He bought a ticket without looking at the billboard to see what was playing. The screen was a mass of moving color. The movie was set in a circus but the story was not compelling. The only well-known player was an actress whose mouth always arched up at the side; the actors Hyŏn-t'ae did not recognize. The colors were unnaturally harsh and thick. Even so, Hyŏn-t'ae tried to follow the story line and made himself concentrate on the screen. _What is her name?_ He just couldn't think of it. The movie ended, but he elected not to stay and see the part he had missed. As he walked down the steps of the theater he lit a cigarette. And finally it came to him. Her name was Anne Baxter.

He went to the Kwigŏrae Tearoom. "Well, this is a surprise," said the waitress. Early in the evening, alone, sober: this was a first for Hyŏn-t'ae.

He ordered tea with a shot of whiskey. After removing some of the undissolved sugar at the bottom of the teacup and then half the tea, he added the whiskey. He stirred, then drank a sip at a time. This was the first time he had finished a shot of whiskey so deliberately.

He lit another cigarette. He felt his body demanding more liquor. He ordered coffee, no cream, and drank it as slowly as possible. Over and over he told himself he had reached an impasse that absolutely demanded a decision.

A record was playing. He strained to listen. Jazz. The cheerful rhythm waged a constant battle with his powers of concentration. Still he made an effort to listen. He smoked continuously. His tongue began to feel sandy and thick like a layer of extra skin. He continued to smoke nevertheless. It numbed him and at the same time cleared his head.

He went to the counter and paid, then turned to go. The telephone caught his eye. He picked up the receiver and dialed. He heard the ring. It sounded unusually resonant, perhaps because of the large, empty interior at night. Hyŏn-t'ae felt he was listening to the call of a living creature. A click sounded, and then "Hello?" It was the lucid voice of the maid. Someone at home must have heard the ring. "Hello? . . . Hello?" came the maid's lucid voice. Hyŏn-t'ae replaced the receiver.

He walked from main thoroughfare to alley and back again, completely at the whim of his feet. At the corner of a cramped alley, from an unlit house, he heard a child cough. The coughing continued, the sound carrying around the corner of the alley. *What am I looking for here?*

A street stall with an array of hardware came into sight. He was about to pass by when he seemed to hear a scream: *Stick him! Stick him!* His mouth formed a smile. Unfinished business. He purchased a knife at the stall and placed it in his overcoat.

The prospect of killing seemed easier now than it had during hand-to-hand combat in the war. He returned to the drinking place that served skewered snacks, the place where the fight had taken place. He found several groups of customers drinking boisterously. He examined the faces one by one, then asked the owner if the young men in the gray and navy blue overcoats had ever returned. No sight of them was the answer. Hyŏn-t'ae then canvassed all the other drinking places in the vicinity, moving with the same agility he had shown on the battlefield and with the same gleam in his eye.

Next he covered the area leading to Myŏng-dong. His compulsion to find the two men and knife them gradually yielded to a simple desire to confront them. The siren heralding the imminent curfew sounded. As he watched the closing of the drinking places and the headlights of scurrying cars he was oppressed by feelings of utter loneliness. And the more lonely he felt the more he wanted to take some matter, any matter, into his own hands. What could he do?

He had no desire to return home in this frame of mind.

At the Pyongyang House the errand girl was laying out her bedding on a bench near the stove.

Hyŏn-t'ae stopped inside the door. From the inner quarters he heard a woman sobbing. Dull thumps like the sound of a fist on a back punctuated the sobs. And then the snarl of the Pyongyang House woman: "Who do you think you are, saying you don't like the honorable magistrate? So what if you don't like him? You miserable bitch!"

"Ma'am, we have a customer!" the errand girl called out, perhaps bothered by the unseemliness.

The door to the inner quarters opened. "_Sŏnsaeng-nim,_ is that you?" the woman said in her P'yŏngan accent. After a moment of confusion she broke into a smile and emerged from the room, slippers scuffing along the floor. "It's been so long I almost didn't recognize you," she said, leading him to the room behind the kitchen.

Before removing his overcoat he produced his remaining money —some six or seven thousand hwan in hundred-hwan notes—and handed it to her.

The woman moistened a finger with saliva and counted. "What a miser. Why not pay for a month at a time?" She scowled at Hyŏn-t'ae. This was never an expression of dislike but rather a coquettish display.

Hyŏn-t'ae said, "Don't bother with drinks."

"No _yakchu?_ Nothing? What's got into you tonight? Acting the proper bridegroom for once, eh?" The woman left and returned presently with bedding. Behind her was Kye-hyang, pillow tucked beneath her arm as before. Her cold face betrayed no hint of the sobbing a short time before.

"Will you _please_ make sure this girl gets up early tomorrow morning?" With a lewd grin the woman left.

"Was the magistrate here?" Hyŏn-t'ae ventured.

Kye-hyang made no reply.

"Does she beat you like this very often?"

The girl kept a stony silence.

As before the sensation was cold and sleek, like a porcelain vessel. But unlike before, his manhood failed to respond. Kye-hyang lay there, not stirring. The more vexed Hyŏn-t'ae became, the more his manhood shriveled. Nothing to do but back off. He began to explore her body. This would give his manhood time for arousal. The body he touched was a perfect porcelain vessel. His hand came to rest on a breast. Its rough protuberance clung to his palm and he could feel the beanlike mass beneath the nipple. He took it in his mouth and bit. She produced a short moan but remained unmoving. In the end he felt tranquillity at the thought that it was no use performing the act with this woman. He withdrew from her.

His mind was clearing. He had arrived once again at the impasse, and his thoughts began to crystallize. *Get on the airplane.* But if he did so as matters stood presently, what difference would it make? Wouldn't he just be prolonging his present situation? Continuing a meaningless lifestyle? And wouldn't that be like committing a crime against himself? So be it. The question was, did he have strength enough to maintain even that meaningless life?

Though his mind was clear, physically he felt exhausted. He'd been roaming the streets for hours, after all. But hadn't he also been hibernating the last several days? This was nothing compared with the fatigue he had felt on the battlefield. Clear of mind but weary of body, he fell into a sleeplike state only to be awakened. Kye-hyang was sobbing.

"What's the matter?"

She didn't answer immediately. And then, speaking as if to herself: "I want to die."

It was the first time Hyŏn-t'ae had heard emotion in her voice. He had never expected such words from this impassive woman. He looked in her direction. She was lying there just as before. He realized he could no longer find repose here. He remembered the knife. He rose, produced the knife, and offered it to her.

Still recumbent, she directed her gaze to the knife.

"Here. . . . No, you don't hold the blade—take it by the handle." So saying, he turned his back to her and lay down. She ceased sobbing and all was quiet. There was nothing for Hyŏn-t'ae to do but wait.

He was standing beneath a gigantic tree. Branches and leaves screened out the sky. Without warning a flight of jet fighters appeared

and started strafing. He faced the oncoming jets, making no attempt
to hide behind the tree. The bursts of the fighters' guns filled the air.
Branches and leaves were hit, fell to the ground. The formation circled,
silver wings glinting, and nosed in his direction. Again he faced them
squarely. The bursts of the guns filled the air. More branches and
leaves fell. He met the formation head on, and each pass brought
down more branches and leaves. Finally none were left on the tree.
He pondered. _Now it will bear lots of fruit, like a fruit tree that's been
pruned._ Nonchalantly he faced the oncoming jets. Finally, just as he
was expecting a blazing burst of gunfire, the jets froze in midair.
_Damn it!_ Hyŏn-t'ae opened his eyes.

He heard moaning. He turned to see Kye-hyang's pale face outlined against the gloom. She was moaning in pain. The quilt and mat
were mottled with blood. He considered leaving her. But then he
thought he heard mumbling among the moans. He could only think
she was trying to tell him something. He drew near and placed his ear
near her mouth, but she turned away from him. Suddenly Hyŏn-t'ae
was oppressed by the thought that once again he was utterly alone in
this world. His mind cleared. Once again he was lucidly, vividly aware
he had reached an impasse. _There must be something I can do with
my own hands._ He took the knife that lay beside Kye-hyang's right
hand. This time he could do it. Just push down with his hand. But
the next instant he was overcome by the utter senselessness of it all.
Kye-hyang, that imbecile, had beaten him to it. As he held the knife,
his mouth formed a smile of self-contempt that spread through
the gloom.

Yun-gu was culling stunted hens with mediocre production to sell to a
dealer. It was a morning in early June when several days of nasty rain
had given way to clear skies.

A year's experience raising hens had taught him how to care for
chicks more scrupulously. And the results were remarkable. Last year
some fifteen percent of his chicks had died; this year that figure had
been reduced by half. And he was much better able to keep the mid-
size hens from pecking at random. Whenever a new shipment of

chicks arrived, Yun-gu was particularly attentive to the lighting in the henhouse. The best thing was to provide light only when he fed the hens, keeping them in the dark the rest of the time.

After loading the hens in a cage on his bicycle, the dealer said to Yun-gu: "I heard there were quite a few males mixed in with the females you bought."

"Yes," said Yun-gu. "A good ten percent of the total."

It was easy to make mistakes when you had to examine the private parts of each and every chick at the hatchery in order to distinguish male from female. Even so, Yun-gu couldn't help suspecting that a certain number of males had deliberately been added to the females before delivery. He also knew that females were never added to males sold for future consumption.

"Is it true you can tell males from females by the shape of the egg? They say the long ones are males and the round ones are females."

To Yun-gu it was a frivolous question. When he made no reply, the dealer added, as if answering his own question: "If you have that kind of talent, you can get by without getting your hands dirty." The red tip of the man's nose made Yun-gu wonder if he was an alcoholic.

As Yun-gu handed the dealer one by one the chickens he had culled, he told himself that if he could realize his breeding plan next year, then he could cut down on the number of hens who were not laying at present. The chicks he bought at the hatchery always included a certain number of rejects, and these he wished to replace with good-quality fowl. To this end he decided to mate only those brood hens and roosters with large, thick combs and glossy, golden legs and beaks.

"Now this one's sticking out too—that's really a bad case," said the dealer in a by now familiar refrain as he held up a hen that Yun-gu had given him. The hen's nether regions were red and protruding. "I wouldn't give it long to live, for goodness' sake."

"It's all right," said Yun-gu. "It keeps laying two at a time, that's why. But they're so small they're only worth about one good-sized egg."

"A man I know, his wife had twins three times in a row, and the last time did her in."

The dealer began prattling, and it was hard to tell if this was the truth or if he was just telling stories. Yun-gu decided he didn't care and went inside the henhouse to cull two more hens and round off the total. It was then that the dealer, looking toward the main gate, announced the arrival of a visitor.

Yun-gu emerged from the henhouse. It was Sugi, but he did not immediately recognize her. She wore a sky-blue traditional skirt and jacket and white flats. She did not resemble the woman who had visited Yun-gu the previous winter. And not merely because her clothing was different.

"How have you been?"

She folded her hands on top of her handbag and produced a weak smile. Her face, unrecognizably rough without makeup, gave an impression completely different from that first time.

Yun-gu failed to respond to her greeting, wondering what business she had with him.

"It seems like you're always busy," she said politely. "Please don't let me keep you from your work."

Yun-gu went into the storage shed and returned with the bench. "Would you like to sit for a moment?"

"That's all right. I think I'll take a look at the chickens."

After setting her bag on the bench, she walked to one of the henhouses. Suddenly her field of vision felt wide open and bright—the effect of the glossy white feathers, the direct sunlight playing on them, in sharp contrast with the bloodred combs. Sugi opened her eyes wide to take in these colors.

How long had she been standing there—a minute? It felt much longer than that. Catching a shared taxi at Seoul Station and walking the rest of the way here seemed to have taken place in the distant past. The next instant the red and white gradually began to blend and flow together, then changed completely to black. _I can't let myself collapse here._ She clutched the mesh of the coop and closed her eyes.

She returned to the bench and perched there listlessly. She gathered her hands over her forehead. The buzz of the conversation between Yun-gu and the other man gradually sounded clearer, then stopped, and the surroundings grew quiet.

"Are you feeling all right?" she heard Yun-gu say. She looked up, realized her forehead was sticky with sweat.

"You don't look well," Yun-gu said politely.

"No, I'm all right. . . . Could I have some water?"

Yun-gu went in the kitchen and returned with a bowl of water. He was the only one at home that day. The errand boy and the elderly man had left to gather acacia leaves for the hens.

Sugi drank.

"The white feathers dazzled me. . . . My, how you've expanded since the last time." So saying, she produced a handkerchief from her bag and dabbed the perspiration on her mouth and forehead.

Again Yun-gu tried to decide what might have brought this woman here. With Hyŏn-t'ae in prison for three months now following the death of that girl at the drinking house, he could think of no reason why she should be visiting him. Was she wanting news of Hyŏn-t'ae? Seen from the gallery during his trial, Hyŏn-t'ae was clean-shaven and in general appeared healthier than he had before his imprisonment. He had pleaded guilty to each and every one of the charges lodged by the prosecutor. Later the prosecutor had argued that to judge by the defendant's mental state, his actions were more serious than simply abetting and assisting in a suicide. In fact they constituted manslaughter. He concluded by saying that such antisocial behavior, already common among teenagers, must be stamped out and in this case the punishment must be heavy. He had demanded an indefinite sentence.

"It's so quiet around here," Sugi said.

"Not really. A lot of new homes are going up."

They exchanged small talk for some time.

Sugi had decided, less than wholeheartedly, to come to Yun-gu only after the long accumulation of various thoughts. Granted she had set out to see him only when she could no longer remain at home or keep her job. But now that she was here, the words she had made up her mind to say just would not come. Finally, after patting the handkerchief against her perspiring face once again, she spoke resolutely.

"The fact is, I have a favor to ask, _Sŏnsaeng-nim._" She dropped her gaze. "Would it be possible for me to stay here a while?"

Yun-gu had no idea what this meant.

The tinge of color in Sugi's downcast face vanished, and she gripped her handbag.

"I'm pregnant."

Suddenly everything became clear to Yun-gu. Instinctively he surveyed Sugi's body and noticed that her seated posture seemed somehow uncomfortable.

Sensing Yun-gu's gaze, Sugi shielded herself by embracing her handbag and spoke in a clear undertone: "I don't know how many times I decided to do away with it."

Yun-gu directed his gaze to the bag Sugi held. "Now I understand. But I'm afraid it would be uncomfortable for you here."

"I know it's an unreasonable request. But if I can stay here just through the delivery, then I'll bother you no more. I'll do anything I can to help while I'm here . . . cooking and such. And if there's no spare room, couldn't I stay in the shed or build something? I have some money I could use."

Yun-gu took a cigarette from his pocket and placed it in the holder.

"Why haven't you told him?" Yun-gu asked politely.

"He can be damned for all I care. I'm not going to compromise on that."

"I see." Yun-gu pondered. "As long as you've taken this step, what would you think of contacting his family? Making some sort of arrangement?"

"No." Sugi shook her head. "I wouldn't dream of it. I'll see this through myself."

"I understand. But wouldn't it be better to let them know? If you explain the circumstances, they can't very well ignore you."

"Please don't say any more on the subject. I've made up my mind."

Yun-gu lit his cigarette.

"Well, now, I *am* aware of your state of mind. . . . But if his family finds out later that you've stayed here, wouldn't that make it uncomfortable for both of us? To be frank with you, I've had a very painful experience that no one else knows about. I have no desire to cause more trouble on account of someone else." Even now he was unable to think of Mi-ran without relating her to Hyŏn-t'ae. "So at this point I think it's better to go straight to his family and—"

"All right, I understand."

Sugi steadied her breathing, then rose silently. And for the first time she gazed directly at Yun-gu:

"I don't know about the painful experience you mentioned, *Sŏnsaeng-nim.* But in a larger sense is there any young person who hasn't been hurt by this war? Hyŏn-t'ae appears to be no exception. And perhaps I'm not, either."

"I see. . . . So you're planning to have his baby and raise it yourself?" Yun-gu asked politely.

She looked away.

"I don't know. . . . But in any event I have to see it through. . . . I'm sorry to have bothered you."

Sugi turned silently toward the gate.

# Afterword

## The War Stories of Hwang Sun-wŏn

Wars, both domestic and foreign, have affected modern Korea as much as any nation. Japanese and Chinese troops skirmished on Korean soil during the Sino-Japanese War (1894-1895).[1] The Japanese established a formidable military presence in Korea from the outset of the Russo-Japanese War (1904-1905).[2] Soviet and American troops occupied the Korean peninsula to accept the surrender of Japanese forces at the conclusion of the Pacific War in August 1945. Subsequently South Korean soldiers fought in the Vietnam War as allies of the United States. Most traumatic of all, of course, was the Korean War (1950-1953).[3] But whereas the war in Vietnam has figured prominently in several Korean novels,[4] the Korean War has received scant treatment. Indeed the late Kim Chong-un (a veteran of the war) observed in the introduction to his book of translations of post–Korean War short fiction:

> Relatively speaking, the Korean War produced no great, not even fair, war novels commensurate with the import of the tragic event itself. Even those sparse exceptions that managed to come into being strangely shunned the frontline activities.

. . . No portrayals of heroism or military valor adorned the
fiction of the war-torn country.

Why? Was the abruptness and immediacy of impact and the
proximity and involvement of milieu too great to give Korean
writers necessary perspective and detachment? Perhaps so. But
. . . the real reason must be sought perhaps in the tragic nature
of the war itself: it was a civil war in which no real or worldly
gain or glory was at stake except that elusive thing called ideol-
ogy. An instinctive abhorrence of portraying tragic fratricidal
battles probably lay at the root of this.[5]

Hwang Sun-wŏn (1915–2000) is a rare exception. He wrote several
fictional works that portray soldiers in wartime, among them the
novel translated here and the stories "Moksum" (April 1951; trans.
"Life," 1972), "San" (June 1956; trans. "Mountains," 1993), and
"Nŏ wa na man ŭi shigan" (July 1958; trans. "Time for You and Me
Alone," 1983).[6] Hwang himself was never a soldier, but like all
accomplished storytellers he made use of the firsthand accounts of
others to create tales that bear witness to the experience not only of
an individual but of a people. As he noted in regard to "Life": "I was
compelled to put pen to paper by a feeling that the protagonist's final
outcry was not that of one person alone."[7]

The war that Hwang Sun-wŏn writes of is not so much the conflict
that takes place between opposing armies on the battlefield as it is the
conflicts taking place within and between individual soldiers. War, in
other words, offers Hwang a backdrop for his ongoing fascination
with the duality and ambivalence that pervade human experience.
The concepts of duality and ambivalence offer a useful approach to
dealing with the variety of Hwang's hundred-odd published stories.
By *duality* I mean a dual state or quality, a doubleness, and not the
philosophical distinction between the ideal (immaterial) and the
corporeal (material). I understand *ambivalence* both in its general
sense of uncertainty or fluctuation—especially when caused by an
inability to make a choice or a simultaneous desire to say or do two
opposite things—and in its psychological meaning of the coexistence

within an individual of positive and negative feelings toward the
same person, object, or action, drawing the individual in opposite
directions.

Why do ambivalence and duality offer a useful approach to
Hwang's fiction? One reason is that they expand the critical arena for
scholars inclined to view Hwang narrowly as a romanticist, a lyricist,[8]
or a local-colorist. These two concepts—duality in particular—may
also serve as an antidote to those who see Hwang as a "Western"
writer. For dualities have abounded in the Korean literary tradition
since early times, especially between the more conceptual Chinese
influence on premodern Korean literature and the exuberance and
emotive expression in the native Korean tradition.

How do "Life," "Mountains," "Time for You and Me Alone," and
*Trees on a Slope* fit into Hwang's oeuvre? At the time they were written, Hwang was approaching the midpoint of his career and the
height of his creative powers, as evidenced by such masterful stories
as "Hak" (January 1953; Cranes), which deals elliptically with the war.
Like other of Hwang's works, these four may be seen as variations on
a theme. Hwang composed other sets of variation both before and
during the war stories. His first story collection, *Nŭp* (1940; The
pond), contains several modernist stories populated by young people
such as Hwang himself (who was a student at Waseda University in
Tokyo at the time he wrote them). Shortly before he began writing
the war stories Hwang treated various social problems in his collection *Mongnŏmi maŭl ŭi kae* (1948; The dog of crossover village).
And in the 1950s he became interested in the theme of the outcast,
as evidenced in *Irŏbŏrin saram tŭl* (1958; Lost souls), a collection
that includes the war story "Mountains."

The theme-and-variations nature of the war stories is immediately
evident: "Life" consists of two characters; "Time for You and Me
Alone" has three characters; "Mountains" includes more than half a
dozen. "Life" takes place in summer, "Mountains" in autumn, and
"Time for You and Me Alone" in winter. All three are stories of survival: physical survival (against heat and thirst) in "Life," psychological survival in "Time for You and Me Alone," and survival in a primi-

tive power struggle in "Mountains." Structurally "Life" and "Time for You and Me Alone" are linear in that both stories end with the prospect of physical survival at hand. "Mountains," however, is cyclical: exemplifying the parallelism that Hwang delights in when structuring his stories, this one ends with Pa-u vanquishing his captors and packing a young woman home on his back—just as his father many years earlier had overcome the social restraints imposed on him because of his *paekchŏng* (outcast) status and eloped with Pa-u's mother to the mountains.

*Trees on a Slope,* first published in book form in 1960,[9] concerns three young men who are thrown together in the South Korean army during the latter stages of the Korean War: Hyŏn-t'ae, a squad leader confident to the point of arrogance; Yun-gu, stolid and dependable; and Tong-ho, sensitive and inexperienced. War affects the three men in different ways. Tong-ho, after shooting a man and a prostitute in a fit of jealousy, commits suicide. Hyŏn-t'ae, by turns homicidal and jocular as a soldier, becomes feckless and hesitant upon his discharge, perhaps brutalized by his murder of a woman villager during the war. Returning to civilian life, he begins drinking heavily, abandons intellectual pursuits, vacillates over a trip to the United States for graduate study, rapes the deceased Tong-ho's fiancée, and finally deflowers a young bar hostess before inducing her to kill herself. The practical Yun-gu is the only one to make a successful transition to postwar life. As such he is perhaps emblematic of Korea over the centuries: surviving encroachments by more powerful neighbors, exploiting limited resources, and capitalizing on the lessons of harsh experience.

*Trees on a Slope* is one of the few Korean novels to describe in detail the physical and psychological horrors of the Korean War, which left virtually no Korean untouched. Hwang, though not a veteran himself, draws on firsthand accounts of life at the front lines in order to capture the psychology of those who have faced death. Like many soldiers, alpinists, and other adventurers, Hyŏn-t'ae finds his abilities most fully realized in situations of mortal danger. Removed from this environment, he withdraws into liquor, bonding only with a few drinking companions, until at the end of the novel, as he sleeps with the young hostess, he finds himself impotent. Spiritually alienated in civilian life, ultimately he becomes physically disengaged as well.

How are this novel and the three stories that precede it significant from the point of view of duality and ambivalence? One obvious answer is that an extreme form of ambivalence—civil war—forms the background of the works. Consider also the situation of soldiers in action: they are trained to kill so that they and others may live. Life and death, then, constitute a basic duality of the battlefield experience. Finally, ambivalence and duality are for Hwang an epistemological response to a world that often seems to make no sense—and never less so than in wartime. It is human nature to try to comprehend the apparent contradictions we see all around us. For the curious, this impulse is irresistible. And it is evident from the occasional detailed asides in Hwang's work—his accounts of Cheju Island dialect and plant life in his September 1956 story "Pibari" (The diving woman), for example, and his descriptions of plant grafting and falconry in his 1972 novel *Umjiginŭn song* (The moving castle)—that his curiosity is wide-ranging. Duality is also in keeping with Hwang's Christian beliefs, which militate against a deterministic worldview and lend themselves rather to an open-ended outlook on life while at the same time positing an eternal spiritual battle between the forces of good and evil.

Some war stories are built around accounts of combat itself. Others, such as Stephen Crane's *The Red Badge of Courage,* focus on the individual's psychological reaction to combat. Hwang's war stories are of both types. They are naturalistic studies: survival is the focus of all three stories and one chapter of *Trees on a Slope.* In each work individuals are isolated from society, allowing us to see the conflict that arises within and between them. "Life" and "Time for You and Me Alone" are devoid of social structure apart from the relationship between the two soldiers in the former story and the three soldiers in the latter. The social structure in "Mountains," such as it is, is based on naked power. Korea's highly stratified society, present as subtext in many Korean stories, is not a strong presence in these works. Ambivalences and dualities, then, are seen within the individual instead of within the society (as is more common in the issue-driven branch of the contemporary Korean literary establishment). In sum, the key to understanding Hwang Sun-wŏn's war stories might very well be found in William Faulkner's sentiment, expressed in his Nobel Prize address, that the only subject worth the labor of the artist is "the human heart in conflict with itself."

## Notes

1. See, for example, C. I. Eugene Kim and Han-kyo Kim, *Korea and the Politics of Imperialism 1876-1910* (Berkeley: University of California Press, 1967), 80.
2. Ibid., 117, 121.
3. After decades of relative neglect the Korean War began to receive increased scholarly attention with the publication of Bruce Cumings's *Origins of the Korean War: Liberation and the Emergence of Separate Regimes* (Princeton: Princeton University Press, 1981). Steven Hugh Lee's *The Korean War* (London: Longman, 2001) is a good survey.
4. See, for example, Hwang Sŏg-yŏng, *The Shadow of Arms*, trans. Chun Kyung-ja (Ithaca: Cornell University East Asia Program, 1994), and Ahn Junghyo, *White Badge* (New York: Soho Press, 1989), both involving the participation of South Korean soldiers in the Vietnam War.
5. Kim Chong-un, trans. and ed., *Postwar Korean Short Stories*, 2nd ed. (Seoul: Seoul National University Press, 1983), xi.
6. "Moksum," in *Hwang Sun-wŏn chŏnjip* (Complete works of Hwang Sun-wŏn) (Seoul: Munhak kwa chisŏng sa, 1980-1983), 2:217-229, trans. Kim Se-yong, "Life," *Korea Journal* 12(8) (1972):13-17; "San," *Hyŏndae munhak*, July 1956, trans. Bruce Fulton and Ju-Chan Fulton, "Mountains," in *Land of Exile: Contemporary Korean Fiction*, trans. and ed. Marshall R. Pihl, Bruce Fulton, and Ju-Chan Fulton (Armonk, N.Y.: M. E. Sharpe, 1993), 34-57; "Nŏ wa na man ŭi shigan," *Hyŏndae munhak*, October 1958, trans. Kim Chong-un, "Time for You and Me Alone," in *Postwar Korean Short Stories*, 99-108. Month/year citations in the Afterword are dates of

composition as they appear in *Hwang Sun-wŏn chŏnjip*. For dates of first publication see Kwŏn Yŏng-min, ed., *Hanguk kŭndae munin taesajŏn* (Encyclopedia of early-modern Korean writers) (Seoul: Asea munhwasa, 1990), 1357–1360.

7. Hwang Sun-wŏn, afterword to *Kogyesa* (Clowns) in *Hwang Sun-wŏn chŏnjip*, 2:317. About "Life" Hwang also noted that "various incidents are drawn from my own experience of the chaos of the civil war and from accounts of those who had returned from the front." It may not be coincidental that the *Kogyesa* collection was first published on June 25, 1952—two years to the day after the outbreak of the war.

8. See, for example, Cho Tong-il, *Hanguk munhak t'ongsa* (Comprehensive history of Korean literature), 3rd ed. (Seoul: Chishik sanŏp sa, 1994), 5:490; and Kim Ch'i-su, "Sosŏl ŭi sahoesŏng kwa sŏjŏngsŏng" (The societal and the lyrical in fiction), in *Mal kwa sam kwa chayu* (Language, life, and liberty), ed. Kim Pyŏng-ik et al. (Seoul: Munhak kwa chisŏng sa, 1985), 53–65.

9. Hwang Sun-wŏn, *Namu tŭl pit'al e sŏda* (Seoul: Sasanggye sa, 1960).

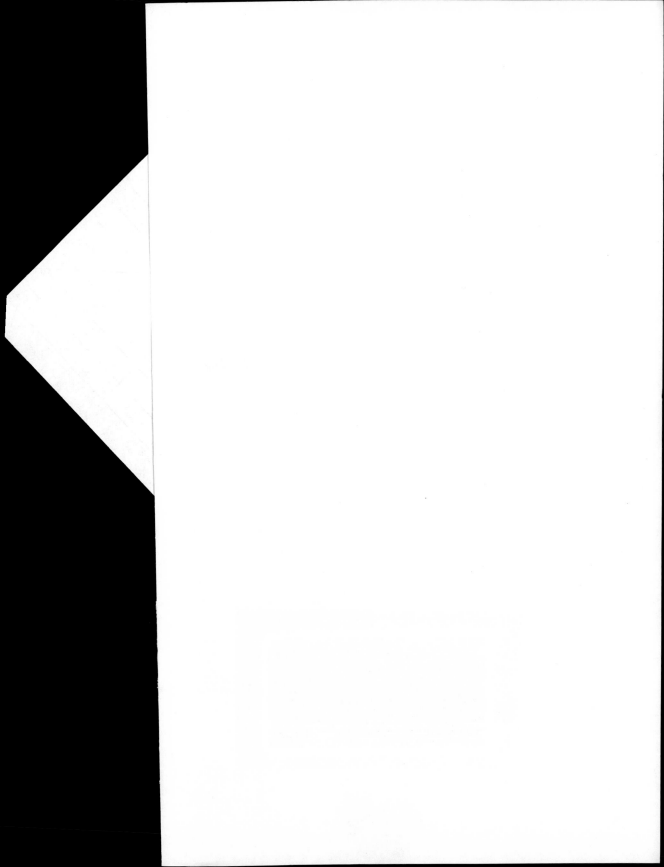

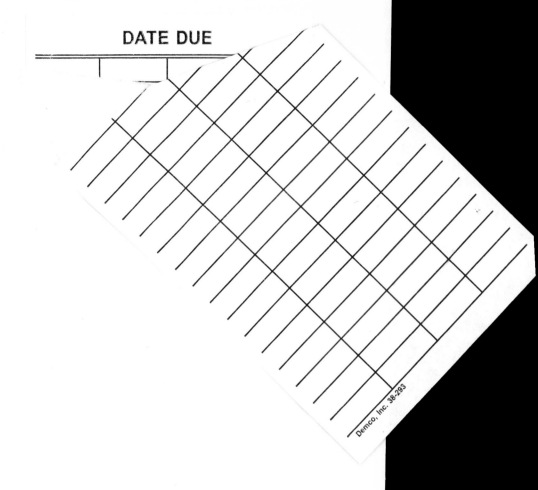

Lightning Source UK Ltd.
Milton Keynes UK
07 April 2011

170517UK00002B/74/A

9 780824 828875